RASHURE
CODEX

J.R. Phillips

ISBN 978-1-64114-586-2 (paperback)
ISBN 978-1-64114-588-6 (hardcover)
ISBN 978-1-64114-587-9 (digital)

Copyright © 2018 by J.R. Phillips

All rights reserved. No part of this publication may be reproduced, distributed, or transmitted in any form or by any means, including photocopying, recording, or other electronic or mechanical methods without the prior written permission of the publisher. For permission requests, solicit the publisher via the address below.

Christian Faith Publishing, Inc.
832 Park Avenue
Meadville, PA 16335
www.christianfaithpublishing.com

Printed in the United States of America

This book is dedicated to my Church family at the
Cowboy Church of Ennis, Texas
and
especially my dear wife Laurell, for her
continued love and support, and
my daughter Sierra, that inspires me every day to be
a loving and nurturing father.

Contents

The Fishermen 7

The Archaeologist 25

The Astrophysicists 50

The Union 63

The Revel 74

Sharing the News 93

The Chaos Begins 131

Beginning Rashure 166

Departure of the Earth 236

Beginning the Trip to a New Earth 256

Chapter 1

The Fishermen

It was an early morning in a garden near Golgotha, April 6, 33 AD. Three women walked slowly through the garden with spices and oils to anoint the body of Jesus. As they arrived at the tomb, they were astonished to discover that the tomb was open.

A beautiful day surrounded them on all sides. There was a slight breeze, which had taken away the worst of the heat that was already beating down on the garden. The women had chosen this early time for two reasons: firstly, they wanted to avoid detection. Followers of Jesus were being targeted by the authorities. Their faith was strong, but their desire to stay safe and spread the Word of Jesus Christ was strong too. Secondly, they knew that the day would bring unbearable heat. The tomb itself would be sheltered from the worst of the baking sun, but the walk to the tomb was long, and the oils and spices they carried were heavy. The beauty of the day was not in the minds of the three women as they trudged along the walk to the garden and the tomb that lay within. They were there to perform a duty.

The three women approached the tomb frantically. They had followed Jesus for as long as they had known and feared that he had been delivered further punishment than his crucifixion. They were worried sick that they would find his body mutilated or beheaded. The Romans that he had defied were known for their brutal treatment of people they thought were a threat to their dominance. None was a greater threat than Jesus Christ.

The tomb was a plain burial chamber with a stone rolled over the entrance. It was deliberately chosen as something that would attract no attention. Jesus had suffered enough in his life. His followers were being hunted by the Romans, and they wanted somewhere that seemed insignificant to visit Him. It was situated in a garden in Golgotha, close to the hillside. The flowers that grew around the area of the tomb were in bloom, and the air was filled with the sounds of insects and birds working their way around the countryside. It was peaceful setting for anyone to behold. It was seldom visited by anyone because of its remote and unremarkable location. It was far from the roads that joined Jerusalem to Golgotha and other local towns, so people had no reason to be there. It was solitude personified, but the quiet sounds of life going on around were interrupted by the low cries of the three women.

Once the tomb was entered, the fear turned into confusion. Jesus was nowhere to be seen. Even the Roman army would not take a man away from his final burial place, would they? The three women began to cry uncontrollably. They looked at each other for consolation, but their glances at each other were not filled with comfort but of anguish. The thought that the man they held dear as their savior was gone filled them with dread. At least, in death, they knew he could be tortured no more. But now they had no idea what had happened to the man they followed and held dear.

Moments later in the streets of old Jerusalem, a man was seen to be serenely walking through the town. He was instantly recognizable as one of the prisoners that were crucified the day before.

Jesus walked through the streets as the three women who were at the garden to anoint him sat in a dazed confusion, wondering what they should do and who they should tell. Their grief was strong, but it was punctured by a desire to do something practical. They had to find Jesus.

The walls seemed closer to the streets than ever. I have walked these streets a thousand times, but this is the last. I have passed through the walls of the city on to the streets where I can be with the people. I know that the cruelty that was delivered to me yesterday was the will of the Romans rather than the will of the people of Jerusalem. I must protect them. I must be strong for them. I pass the inns that house the weary travelers, the houses of people that live and work here and on upwards towards the heart of the city. My work here is done for now. I am sure that I will return one day.'

Jesus walked through the streets with slow intent. He was there to complete his task. There was unfinished business that he had to attend to. The purpose of his time on earth had yet to be fulfilled. Jesus knew that his very presence would cause a stir among those who recognized him. He was seen to be killed just three days before, so anyone that witnessed his slow walk through the city on that morning was bound to be alarmed. It was still early in the morning, and the streets had yet to fill as they inevitably would later in the day for the market that dominated the city. People would visit from as far as they could walk to trade goods or buy the essential items that they had grown accustomed to under Roman rule. If Jesus was seen during the busiest time of the day, then he was sure to be seen by his enemies. But at this early hour, he saw almost nobody. His next step was to find his apostles and talk to them. He had a longing to spend time with them and reassure them everything would be all right.

The streets remained silent as Jesus completed his walk to the destination of his choosing. Jesus stopped at a home. He alerted the occupier to his presence by gently knocking at the door. On any other morning, this would be no time of the day to wake someone. Today was different. The occupant was expecting the guest and opened the door. Jesus looked around and silently entered.

I have reached this point to speak to those closest to me. I don't want anyone who follows me to doubt the significance of this morning. I will break bread with my brothers and then explain that my time is short. I only have forty days before I will leave them again, and they must remain strong. As I look around this room and await my followers, I know that this will not be easy for them. They have been exposed to great danger, and this will continue over the coming hours, days, and weeks. I have no desire to put my people in the line of danger, but their faith will carry them through. This is the place that we will meet again.'

The room was small, and Jesus sat alone. The walls were painted white on the inside and outside of the building. This reflected away the harsh rays of the sun that were present just about every day of the year in Jerusalem. People could not escape the constant glare of the sun when they were outside, but they did everything they could to remain cool when they were in the comfort of their own homes. The room had been especially prepared for the meeting. The followers of Jesus were sufficient in number that they were still able to find a safe meeting place and network out to connect with all the apostles, so they were able to meet with Jesus in security and comfort. It had been freshly swept, and the house had been put in order. Nothing was to be out of place for this important meeting. There were flowers on the table, along with a basket of bread that smelled as though it had just come out of the oven, and jugs of water and wine. This was to be a meeting that was only attended by Jesus and his apostles, so there was nobody to pour wine and bring fresh supplies. Everything had to be set out before any of the guests arrived.

Jesus waited.

At around ten o'clock, all the apostles had been gathered to a secret meeting place inside the city walls. Jesus knew the dangers of meeting in the city of Jerusalem, but he had to meet with his closest followers and let them know his plans. His time on the planet was growing short.

The apostles did not believe that this was Jesus sitting in front of them. They had seen him die and be taken down from the cross. None could believe that the same man they saw crucified the day before was sitting with them right now. Their disbelief caused Jesus some distress; He wanted them to know that he loved them, but their disbelief bordered on distrust. He rebuked them for their unbelief and hardness of heart. Then Paul spoke. "Lord, please forgive us. It is hard for our head to comprehend what we can see with our eyes.

Only yesterday did we see you leave us. We have spent the night grieving your loss and worrying about our own fate. Now today you sit among us. This is not the world that we know."

Paul was afraid to speak up, but he felt he had to explain how he felt and how he assumed the other apostles felt too. They had been prepared for the departure of their leader when they had all gathered together for supper four days earlier. The Last Supper is an event that has been passed down from generation to generation and lives on today. The events of that night have been the source of recent speculation, thanks to the writings of Dan Brown, but what had really happened is consistent with the story we are all told in church. Jesus gave each of his apostles a piece of bread and told them that it represented his body; He prepared them for his death. However, nothing could quite prepare them to see him again a day later.

"I could not prepare you for my return. You would not have believed me at that time. You scarcely believe it now, and I am sitting here right in front of you," Jesus replied.

There was a murmur of noise from the room as each of the apostles considered what Jesus had said. None of the apostles wanted to speak. They loved Jesus and were happy to see him return, but they did not understand. Also, there was a feeling that this return was not permanent. None of the apostles could quite put their finger on it, but each felt as though Jesus had brought them together to deliver bad news. None had discussed this with any of the others, so they could not know that they all felt the same way. That feeling was right.

"My friends, I have news for you. I have departed once, but I will depart again soon. I am here now among you, but in forty days, I will leave you again," explained Jesus.

There was an audible gasp around the room. The apostles all looked up either at the ceiling or down to the floor. None could look at each other, and certainly none of them felt the strength to look at Jesus. They wanted Jesus to stay.

But they knew that they would respect the wishes of their leader.

The forty days passed quickly. The apostles spent a lot of time with Jesus as they prepared for his second departure. None wanted him to leave, but he had prepared them for life without him. The

Last Supper had arrived quickly, and the revelation that he was about to leave them didn't sink in that night. The apostles had been shaken to their core by the news that Jesus was going to give his body for them. The evening had come and gone in a flash. It seemed as though one second Jesus told them he was to leave and the next he was gone. The second time around, they had forty days to listen to Jesus and say their farewells.

On the fortieth day, the apostles and Jesus walked together to a point outside the city of Jerusalem. Although they had felt relatively safe over the forty days since the resurrection, the city was still not a completely safe place for the followers of Jesus to be. Jesus had to stay inside for much of the time and was looking pale as a result. The lack of sunlight made him feel weaker every day since the ordeal of his crucifixion. He knew that he just had to survive these forty days, and he would be able to recover fully after that. His worry was not for himself but for the others. The Roman army had been harassing people known to be followers of Jesus. Although they had not discovered the opened tomb where Jesus had been buried, they were more suspicious of the followers of Jesus than ever before. The three women that had arrived to anoint Jesus in the morning after the crucifixion had made sure that the tomb would never be discovered. On their return to the city of Jerusalem, they were told by fellow followers that Jesus has risen from the dead and was among them. They had quickly gotten their husbands to join them at the secret location, close the tomb, and cover it with as much vegetation as they could find. Even if a traitor told the Romans that Jesus was buried outside of Golgotha, there was no sign of the tomb to those that didn't know the exact location, and even then, it was difficult to find. In fact, it wasn't found again until 1867. The garden tomb of Jesus was so well hidden that it was not uncovered for nearly another two thousand years when a man with a biblical-sounding name, Gabriel Barkay, discovered it.

The Romans worshipped gods that were immortal, and they could not understand why the Christians were still worshipping a man that had now been slain. To the Romans, it was complete proof that Jesus was mortal and could not be worthy of such devotion. If only they knew.

I look towards my followers and see that they are strong. The time I have been able to spend with them over the past forty days has readied them for today. They know that they will be able to continue my good work and spread the Word of God to the people. They are no longer afraid of the terrors that the Romans can bring to them. I am also ready for the next part of my life. There will be tough times ahead for my people, but one day all will be put right again.

"Lord, we are ready, but where will you go?" asked Mark.

"You are ready for your journey, and I am ready for mine. From here, we take separate paths, but we are all working towards the same goal. Stay strong, and we will see a better world—one day," replied Jesus. He seemed to be already thinking about his next step on the path. He was saying the words, but it was as though they were coming out of his mouth automatically. He was present in body, but his mind was already taking large steps towards his next destination.

It was a cloudy day on the outskirts of Jerusalem. Jesus had gathered his people with him late on this day to say good-bye. As they walked to the chosen spot, Matthew had felt a few spots of rain. The clouds were churning, and it appeared that a storm may be on the way. Wherever Jesus was going from here, he was bound to be rained upon, thought Matthew. He was glad that he was close to home.

Each of the apostles said good-bye to Jesus in turn. He spent a couple of minutes with each, and they shared a little story from their past before some instruction and positivity about the future. Jesus inspired each of them in turn. As each one had said good-bye, they stood a little way down the hillside so that the next could take their turn to speak with Jesus. After all of the apostles had spoken to Jesus, they all stood together. The positivity that each had felt when speaking alone to their leader was multiplied when they all stood as one.

Just as the group fell silent, Jesus began to rise from the ground. It was as though he had become completely weightless. He rose a few feet at first and then stopped. The apostles did not know if this was something Jesus had control over. They looked up towards Jesus and saw after a minute or so he had started to rise again. This time, he moved a lot more quickly. As his rise started again, Jesus turned to his apostles and smiled. They were sure he was going to a better place.

As Jesus reached a height taller than the highest tree any of the apostles had ever seen, their gaze moved upwards to the edge of the cloud. They saw the edge of something appear through the churning cloud. It was something that none of them had ever seen before. They were sure that it moved through the sky, but all they could see was the very edge of it. It was nothing of their world. They had no reference point for this thing that they saw. None of them ever spoke about it in case they had been the only one to see the apparition. All saw it, but none ever spoke of it again.

Jesus moved out of sight. The apostles were alone again, split from their leader, but they felt more able to cope with it than when he had been wrestled from them in the past.

The apostles made their way to John's house to eat together. They wanted to spend time in each other's company. Something happened that day that none could explain. They ate and drank together as they had done on The Last Supper. They told stories of how they met Jesus and the great deeds they had witnessed Him carry out. But there was something unsaid that nagged away at them while they spoke. All of the apostles were there in body, but their spirit still stood on the hillside where Jesus had left them.

They stood together at the edge of the city after they had eaten. John's house was near the western edge of Jerusalem, and from where they stood, they had a view of the place where Jesus had risen into the sky. They stood together and watched the sun set over the hill. It was a fitting end to that day. The last thing they all saw together was the sun setting over that hill.

There was a fog hanging over the sky that day. The rain that Matthew had forecast had only fallen as drizzle. It was a hazy view of the place where they had said good-bye to Jesus, but it was a view that the apostles treasured.

Present Day

It was an early morning on Lake Palestine in Texas with the fog hanging low on the water. There were three people in a boat getting ready to "wet the hook" as they would say.

"Preacher, I got your fishing rod over here," Daniel said as he walked across the large boat deck. Daniel was the owner of the boat and a member of the preacher's church. It was Daniel's forty-foot pontoon boat that they were going out on. He liked to take the preacher fishing as often as possible.

Daniel had known Simon the preacher for ten years. They met through the church. Simon was in his late forties and loved the company of his friend. Simon was Native American and was raised by two loving parents. His father was also Native American from Oklahoma. His mother was from England. Simon's father was also a Christian preacher in Oklahoma. They raised Simon to respect the land, which led him to become a landscape architect in his early years before he felt the pull to preach God's Word. And as a landscape architect, he was trained as a steward of the land as well. This land, its beauty, and the wide-open spaces are important to Simon.

To relax and find occasions to do some deep spiritual thinking, fishing had always given Simon's opportunity. Additionally, Simon and Daniel's other pastime was searching for meteorites. In fact, between the two of them, they had found over nine hundred small-to-medium size meteorites. Simon usually explained why finding a meteorite fascinated him so much by quoting scripture from Revelations 9:1: "The fifth angel sounded his trumpet, and I saw a star that had fallen from the sky to the earth." Daniel just explains, "I give thanks each time I find a meteorite that this one did not hit my hard head."

In fact, Simon had been to a recent meteorite show where collectors and scientists gathered to show their findings, sell a few of the findings, and get scientists to review and comment on their findings. At this event in a town near Simon's church, he had a conversation with a scientist from Texas A&M University when he was drawn to one of Simon's larger meteorites.

What made this meteorite interesting to the scientist was the appearance of a small gold speck on the surface. He told Simon that he had a very rare and probably valuable finding. He invited Simon to bring it to his university lab to conduct a few studies. Simon did two weeks later.

At the university lab, many tests were made to authenticate the meteorite. One test with an electron microprobe and a mass spectrometer showed the mineral makeup of the special meteorite. But the small gold spec appeared to be a larger embedded piece of gold. Simon left the meteorite with the professor to be further analyzed and to expose the gold piece by removing carefully the stone around it.

Daniel was also a minister and, by this stage, was in his sixties. They were both from Texas and wore cowboy hats all the time as was the fashion among Texan men. There was a third person with them on the boat that morning. It was a very sleepy ten-year-old girl. She was lying asleep across one of the long-cushioned benches under no fewer than three old blankets. She loved to go out on the lake, but experience had taught her to protect herself from the cold. Sierra could feel herself starting to stir.

"Dad, it's awful early, where's breakfast?" said Sierra in a soft voice from under the blankets.

Daniel spoke up. "Sierra, I got eggs and bacon on the grill in the cabin."

That was when Simon spoke up. "Oh, sign me up for some of that morning grub!"

Daniel was always a very accommodating individual that made you wonder if this was what Santa Claus might look like on his days off. He was a jolly old man with a big belly and a big red nose with a smile permanently etched on his face. You could also hear that smile in his voice. Daniel sounded just like an auctioneer or a radio announcer. His voice drew your attention in a warm way when you were good and a voice that demands respect when you were not. It was just an amazing voice to spend your time listening to. As a minister, Daniel assisted Simon at his church doing weekly readings of Psalms and Proverbs on Sundays before Simon's sermon. Daniel's

Hispanic heritage helped him and the church relate to part of the community that their church served. But Daniel had a handicap; he was wounded in the Korean War. He lost his left leg when a hand grenade was thrown into the foxhole he was in with three other soldiers. He threw his backpack on the grenade to protect his fellow soldiers. It worked, but some of the blast came out and took his leg below the knee. He got a Purple Heart for that act of bravery but wore his fake leg with the same amount of pride.

Sierra pulled the blankets from over her head to let the morning light from the reflections off the lake wash across her face.

"Daniel, those eggs and bacon sure can get a person out of bed," announced Sierra. That put a big smile on the faces of the other two in the boat. Sierra rolled off the big bench. As the three blankets tangled her legs, she fell onto the boat deck. Sierra looked up at her dad. Without a word between them, they both smiled. Sierra stood up and walked into the cabin to get some breakfast.

Now Simon and Daniel had the opportunity to start planning the day's fishing activities. Daniel glanced at his watch: 6:11 a.m. Daniel was already sitting in his big leather swivel chair at the bow of the boat. Simon walked up to the other big leather swivel chair and sat down next to Daniel. In front of them both were two fishing rods secured in their holders. As a light breeze skimmed the boat, the two of them scanned out over the calm waters of Lake Palestine. The fog was blowing across the bow of the boat.

Lake Palestine felt as though it had been there forever. With the name Palestine, you could be forgiven for thinking that it had been on the planet since biblical times. But it had not. It was created in 1962 when a dam was built across the Neches River. Now it was forty square miles of tranquility that Daniel, Simon, and Sierra were about to head out on. They would be the first of many to spend time on Lake Palestine that day. It was an area used for fishing, camping, canoeing, biking, and walking. The three had used the lake many times before and loved the fact that it was part of their community.

Simon spoke up. "Daniel, it is always amazing to me what the Lord has created here on earth for us to all enjoy."

"Amen," exclaimed Daniel. "Do you think the good Lord has created any fish for us to enjoy this morning?" Simon grinned.

Daniel answered in his low commanding voice, "Well, let's find out."

As he threw in his fishing lure, at that moment, the two of them felt as though they were in the most peaceful place. They had each other for company and had their own solitude as well.

Simon and Daniel fished all morning and caught as many fish as they needed. When they arrived back at the dock, they tied the boat up and took their fish from the live well on the boat.

"Daniel, we've got some work to do now, cleaning these fish for tonight's fish fry at the church." Daniel agreed as they loaded his truck and headed off away from the lake, along the road and on to the church. It was a journey that they had traveled together many times before. They regularly used their catch to feed people at the church. It felt to them that they were helping their community come together.

The events that night at church included a fellowship dinner. Dinner was mainly a fish fry; the event was going to be held outdoors in their courtyard. The smoke from the fish fry and the barbecue grill were drifting across that courtyard. Simon called for everyone's attention. "Can we have a prayer before we enjoy the fellowship and this wonderful catch of fish from today? Lord, thank you for this bounty that has been provided for us to partake on this beautiful world. You have given us this place that can provide us all the things for our survival, including your Word from the Bible. Bless this food and bless this family tonight. Amen."

The hundreds of people began to line up for fish or barbecue. There were kids and their parents and older church members all talking and laughing together as they waited for their food. Pastor Simon was there, along with half a dozen other folks, to perform. They were singing and playing guitars, piano, and electric violins. Simon sang the open song by John Denver that has become church standard, "Back Home Again," but Simon changed up the lyrics a little for the church welcome song.

After finishing the welcome song, Simon motioned for Sierra to come onto the stage. Then he welcomed his daughter, Sierra, on the stage to sing a new song that she had been preparing for that night. Simon said, "Please welcome my daughter, Sierra, tonight to sing a new song for everyone."

Sierra had been performing with her dad and other relatives at church since she was about four years old. She had become a very good singer and guitar player just like her father.

Sierra had a cute summer dress on as she walked up to the microphone stand with a big smile on her face. Simon began to play on his guitar, and the others joined in playing the song, "How Great Thou Art." Sierra had been listening to various female performers chant that song as she prepared for tonight. Carrie Underwood's rendition was one she really liked. So, Sierra began to sing. Her rendition sounded a lot like Carrie Underwood's. Halfway through the song, you could hear Sierra's voice quiver as she was getting a little choked up. Her thoughts wandered to her mother and father and how blessed she was to have such loving parents. But she got her composure and continued to belt out the rest of the song. By that time, most folks at the fish fry were tearing up too. Sierra finished and made a small curtsy to the applause from the crowd. Simon smiled with so much pride in his little girl. He felt truly blessed to have a loving and caring daughter.

As Sierra started to walk off the stage towards her mom, Simon said, "Wow, that was a great opening song. Good job, sweetheart." Then he adjusted the microphone stand a little higher for him to use. "Now I am going to sing a new song as well. This song was a request by a few of the folks in the church going through some tough times." The stage lights dimmed, and a spotlight focused on Simon, who was sitting on a stool with his twelve-stringed guitar. Simon began to sing a Chris Young song, "The Man I Want to Be."

Sierra was standing in front of her mom, who had her arms around Sierra as they both watched Simon sing.

God, I'm down here on my knees,
'cause it's the last place left to fall,
Begging for another chance,
If there's any chance at all,
That you might still be listening,

Lovin' and forgivin' guys like me . . .
I've spent my whole life getting it all wrong,
And I sure could use your help just from now on,
I wanna be a good man, a do like I should man,
I wanna be the kind of man the mirror likes to see,
I wanna be a strong man,
And admit that I was wrong man,
God, I'm askin' you to come change me,
Into the man I wanna be,
If there's any way for her and me to make another start,
Could you see what you could do to put some love back in her heart,
'Cause it gonna to take a miracle, after all
I've done to really make her see,
That I wanna be a stay man,
I wanna be a brave man,
I wanna be the kind of man she sees in her dreams,
God, I wanna be your man,
And I wanna be her man,
God, I only hope she still believes in the man I wanna be,
Well, I know this late at night that talk is cheap,
But, Lord, don't give up on me, yeah.

Then the music plays without singing, and Simon sat with his head down. Then he raised his head to finish singing the song.

I wanna be a givin' man
I wanna really start livin' man,
God, I'm askin you to come change me,
Into the man I wanna be.

The music played to an end. The last few bars of the song brought an intense hush to the rest of the room. Those that had sung along earlier stopped singing. It was as though the whole church was lost in the same thought. All the lights on stage went out as everyone stood and applauded, and there were also a few whistles in approval.

The music went on for about one hour while everyone was eating. The full moon was rising in a clear black sky full of stars. Since the church was in the countryside, away from the city's light pollution, it was easy to see the bright stars against the black sky. You could even pick out the constellations if you knew what you were looking for.

Simon was walking from one table of folks eating to the next with his guitar on one shoulder as he visited and spent time with everyone. He came to one table of young people, and there was one older kid with them. Simon could sense the older kid, about thirty, was upset about something. Simon, as he always did, stuck his hand out for everyone to shake it and said, "Hi, I'm Simon Howard." He would do this even if you had known him for years. He was just that way. When he came to this gentleman, Simon offered his hand to shake his, and the man reluctantly raised his hand.

Simon said, "Welcome, I'm glad you were able to come and enjoy the fish fry." The man just nodded his head. Simon asked for his name, and he said, "John." That just opened the door for Simon to witness to this troubled young man. By the end of the night, the man was laughing and seemed to be at ease with everyone. That is just how everyone reacted to being around Simon.

At another table across the courtyard, a group of teenagers were standing and sitting at one of the round tables. Sierra was standing in that group. When one of the fourteen-year-old girls said, "I wonder sometimes if Jesus and God are real or just imaginary like my dad says."

Well, Sierra's face got all serious and started telling the group of kids that "God is real and that Jesus really did live two thousand years ago. And He was crucified by the Romans."

One of the other teenage girl responded, "Well, you are just a preacher's kid."

Sierra said, "Yes, I am, and I am lucky. I have learned all the history around Jesus and all that the Bible says about these things."

Now Sierra's mom overheard the conversation from across the courtyard. She started to walk slowly towards the group of kids. She did this just in case Sierra needed any support.

Sierra continued, "After Jesus rose from the dead as he said he would do, he was seen by many people, both Christians and non-Christians, as written in the Bible. He stayed with the apostles for forty days before leaving the earth to be with God. And before he left, he told the apostles that he would return someday." By now, Sierra's mom was standing behind her, but Sierra had not seen her yet. When Sierra was finished, her mom softly put her hands on Sierra's shoulders and said, "From the mouths of babes comes the truth. Kids, it is late, and we all need to get home now. We will see you tomorrow in church. Good night."

Sierra's mom could see that Sierra needed no support when talking about her faith. She was a good kid that had listened to her father when he was preaching. She would grow up to be a great person someday, and perhaps even become a preacher herself, thought her mom.

The hour was getting late, and many of the church members had already left. It had been a good night, and all the people that had been there had enjoyed the food, music, and company. Daniel was leading a group of volunteers cleaning the floors, bagging trash, and stacking chairs and tables. Daniel was walking bags of trash out to the dumpster when Simon grabbed a bag and walked with Daniel out to the dumpster across the parking lot. "This was a success. Everyone enjoyed themselves," proclaimed Daniel.

"Amen to that," said Simon.

As they both approached the outer edge of the parking lot, Daniel noticed all the cows in the pasture next to the parking lot were gathered in a tight circle and not making a noise. "That's odd. Look at those cows. And listen to the silence," commented Daniel.

They both looked around. Then Simon glanced up. "Where are the stars?" he whispered to Daniel.

Daniel took his eyes off the cows and slowly raised his eyes upward. "O Lord . . . something has happened to our stars," Daniel whispered back.

Sierra came running towards her dad and Daniel across the parking lot. "Daddy everyone is ready to leave," she shouted. Simon turned quickly towards Sierra and motioned with his hand to go away . . . but Sierra could not see his hand in the dark. She continued to run up to him, jumped up, and hugged him. At that moment, a bright, warm light washed over the three of them as they were standing in the parking lot. They became buoyant. Simon held onto Sierra, expecting her to be frightened. If either of them were scared, then they didn't allow it to show to each other. But Daniel was swinging his arms and legs around out of fright. Then as quickly at the light came on, it went off, and the three of them were gone. And standing back at the church building was Simon, and Daniel was speechless. They had witnessed everything that had just happened, and they could not believe what they had seen. They were in shock.

J.R. PHILLIPS

Chapter 2

The Archaeologist

That same morning in the Bolivian Titicaca Basin, waking up in a tent smelling breakfast being grilled outside was the husband and wife team of archaeologists. Doctors John-Paul and Michelle Moreau from Paris-Sorbonne University were on a summer sabbatical to study the Puma Punku ancient ruins. The Sorbonne is a world-renowned university that is known for its support of their teaching staff. They actively encourage their doctors and professors to go out into the big wide world and gain experience that will help their students. The Sorbonne has such a high reputation that people believe it is as old as the rest of Paris. As a university that sits at the highest table of world research, it is thought to have been around as long as the luminary universities of England such as Oxford and Cambridge by most people in the world. In fact, the teaching university was only set up in 1970. Their passion for excellence sits well in the city of Paris surrounded by architecture, culture, and art that is known as some of the best in the world. Paris is the most visited city on the planet, and you mix with locals and tourists on every street corner. John-Paul and Michelle were a long way from the comforts of their home in the Latin Quarter.

"I'm so tired after the journey to get here, can't we just order room service?" Michelle spoke from under the covers.

John-Paul smiled as he sat on the edge of his cot. "Michelle, the breakfast . . . smell the breakfast," he said as he waved his hands in the air. "Pull the covers off your head and see where we are! We have been talking about being here at Puma Punku for over a year. Now we are here. Get up!" he exclaimed as he slapped her on the butt. He glanced at the watch, it displayed: 7:11.

John-Paul walked out of the tent and turned his head to a brilliantly bright landscape lit by the rising sun. The morning air was cool with a little extra humidity that reminded him of Paris in October.

His thoughts flashed back to the Sunday before they started their journey to Bolivia.

He was walking out of Notre-Dame de Paris with his wife, and elderly mother and father.

His mother asked, "John-Paul, do you have to take this trip this time? I had a dream last night that something happened, and it changed you."

"Mama," John-Paul said as he reached out to touch her face, "stop worrying. I am right with Jesus, and I know if something bad happens, Jesus watches over me." They all smiled as they walked to the nearest café for lunch.

John-Paul felt lucky that he had grown up in this area, that he had been raised in the faith of his parents, and especially that his church was one of the most beautiful in the world. He never missed a Sunday in church when he was in Paris. It would have felt strange to most that they were worshipping in church while surrounded by tourists taking photographs and lining up for tours, but this was the worship that John-Paul, Michelle, and their families had known since they were young. Even in the days of John-Paul's parents' youth, the church was subject of much attention. The 1833 book, The Hunchback of Notre Dame, *by Victor Hugo and the subsequent movie that was released in 1939 brought this finest example of French Gothic architecture to the attention of the rest of* the world. For the family of John-Paul, it was something they saw on the Ile de la Cite out of the window of their home every day and their mother church. For those that live outside of the city of Paris, it was a tourist attraction and an opportunity to listen to a guide or take a plethora of photographs.

There are no bad cafés in Paris. The French in general and the Parisians in particular dislike one thing more than bad food, and that is bad coffee. The Moreaus could have chosen any one of a hundred cafés within walking distance of the church, but they settled on an old favorite. The Café Panis was owned by an old friend of the family, Gerard Picardie. It was a traditional Parisian with dark walls that were still stained from the cigarette smoke of a time when people were allowed to smoke in restaurants. There was a typical French heavy use of wood, and there were enough chairs and tables to spill out onto the street if the weather was good enough.

On that Sunday, the weather was fine, so the family sat outside, ordered a coffee and a croquet monsieur each, and sat to watch the world go by. Parisians are masters of conversation, and they never let something as mundane as food and drink get in the way of that. Food that would have been gulped down in a matter of minutes by most of the world was savored over for an hour by the Moreaus as they said their good-byes before the trip to Bolivia. John-Paul couldn't think of a better way to spend a morning.

If he closed his eyes, he could picture Paris again, but in reality, he was in South America in the month of June. The Bolivian stewards had a very nice table set for six between the four tents. The smoke from the grill was slowly drifting over the table where six place settings were arranged.

John-Paul was the first scientist to sit at the table. Once he sat, the main steward walked over and asked if he would like some coffee, espresso, fruit juice, or cappuccino. John-Paul cupped his hands around his empty cup and smiled at the steward. "We have cappuccino?"

"*Oui, monsieur,*" snapped the steward. John-Paul lifted up his cup with a bigger smile. "*Service incroyable ce matin, monsieur!*"

He waited to see if the coffee would live up to his expectations. In some ways, anything that was hot would probably have sufficed, but the Parisian was always in John-Paul, and as such, he was a coffee expert. He had no desire to be critical, but he really wanted the coffee to live up to the high standards that the service had already set. And he knew that his wife Michelle was even more demanding of her coffee than he was.

The other scientists started coming out of their tents. These individuals were from all around the world. From Cambridge, Massachusetts, were two esteemed scientists. Bill Fleishmann was a professor of Central and South American cultures, and Dr. Bob Phillips went by the title of professor of paleogeology and of geomorphology. Bill was a typical Indiana Jones type, infamous for finding unusual artifices where no one else could on a dig site. He didn't have any particular technique that helped him find things. He looked around and got a feel of the site before having the uncanny knack of being able to find the right pieces. It just seemed to happen to him. And he was also quite the ladies' man with his good looks and short black beard, and he always seemed to be smiling. That came naturally for Bill too.

Bob, on the other hand, was all business. He always appeared to be carrying a camera of some type around his neck and on his shoulder. At every turn, there he was clicking away with one camera or another. He never asked permission from people. Sometimes they would turn around, and he would be there with a camera taking photo after photo after photo. This had started in the days of digital cameras, but if his habit had been around when you needed film, then it would probably have cost him hundreds of dollars a month and could have given him a place on the board of Kodak because he would have kept the company afloat on his own! Even this morning, he was polishing a camera lens as he walked over to the breakfast table to meet John-Paul for the first time.

"Good morning," Bob said as he set down two cameras on the table and reached his hand out to John-Paul. "I'm Dr. Bob Phillips from Cambridge."

"*Bonjour, monsieur.* I'm John-Paul Moreau from Paris, and this is my wife, Michelle." Michelle just came walking from the tent, already dressed for the day's exploration but still with that just-woke-up look. John-Paul knew that coffee would solve that, and he looked around for the steward to bring over the coffee that he had promised. She searched deep within herself and was able to find a small smile as she walked to the seat next to John-Paul.

"*Bonjour a tous,*" Michelle said as be bent down to grab her cup, "*le cafe s'il vous plait.*" John-Paul knew that this was the moment of truth when it came to the coffee. Not that Michelle would have been rude to the steward, but her mood would have been lousy all day. John-Paul watched patiently as the steward brought the coffee over from the stove. It was as though it was happening in slow motion as the coffee was poured and Michelle took a sip. The silence that followed was all the confirmation that John-Paul needed that the coffee had passed muster. He breathed a sigh of relief that was noticed by all others around the table except his darling wife. She was in coffee heaven.

The other scientists joined the group at the breakfast table. From Beijing University, there was Dr. Wang Lee, professor at the school of archaeology and museology and noted expert in Paleolithic archaeology of human evolution. The university was another that was known for its research, although it was not quite as widely acknowledged as the Sorbonne. The university was heavily funded by the Chinese state as well as receiving donations from the big companies that were starting to emerge into the global economy from China. It was ranked the forty-first university in the world by this stage, and this was after many years of investments and progress. Dr. Wang Lee was one of the most respected professors from Beijing University, and his trip to Bolivia had received a lot of attention in the media in China.

From the University of South Africa, Dr. Zaadee Khan, a paleo-ethnobotanist, had been to many sites like Puma Punku where the ruins of a vast population do not correlate to the known vegetation of the region for ancient hunter/gatherers or agriculture-based cultures. To those that knew anything about research, Dr. Khan was a leading light in the study of ancient peoples and had written many academic books on the findings of her research. The University of South Africa is the biggest university on the whole continent and as such receives a lot of attention from researchers from one end of Africa to the other. Dr. Zaadee Khan was the foremost authority that the university had. In a time when there was a brain drain of top talent leaving the entire continent of Africa to study and work in Europe or America, Dr. Khan was an example that you did not have to leave to achieve success. She had been at the university all her working life, and it had never held her back. She used her position to lecture others in Africa that they should stay and help to build the continent up again rather than emigrate and add to the woes by leaving. The work that Dr. Khan had done attracted new funds, professors, and researchers to the university. The University of South Africa was so pleased that they allowed her to travel on all these new expeditions because the coverage meant that they were able to add to their teaching roster. The more high-profile work that Dr. Zaadee Khan did, the easier it became for the university to recruit.

This was how scientists at universities operated. The better the work they did, the more attention they got. The more attention they got, the better funding there was. The better funding there was, then the better work they did. And the cycle would start again. There were many awards and grants for scientists, but deep down they were all in it for one thing—their legacy. To be able to discover a new element and have it named after you, to find a new dinosaur and give it your name, or to find a cure for a disease were the end goal of all the scientists whether they admitted it or not. To be able to look back on a life and a career and see that something wonderful came from their work was all the reward that any scientist needed. But in the meantime, they needed funding to make this happen.

All of the doctors and researchers gathered together around the table. Those that had been on these expeditions before knew that the morning and evening meals situated around the fire in the camp were the most important parts of the day. It was where all the preparation and all the debriefings took place. The interaction between scientists of a high level was always a meeting of the minds. The results were new ways of tackling the problems they faced and new solutions to the puzzles they uncovered during the day.

"*Bonjour*," John-Paul said to Dr. Lee and Dr. Khan. "Welcome to the Tiwanaku Team and Puma Punku." Dr. Lee and Dr. Khan bowed to the group and took the remaining seats at the end of the table. John-Paul stood up and thanked everyone for arriving last night on schedule. "As the leaders of this summer's exploration of Puma Punku, Michelle and I are excited about finally being here. I had a dream last night that the next few weeks will be amazing and earth-shattering." Everyone had a slight smile and a puzzled look on their faces from his nonscientific proclamation. "Please enjoy this beautiful Bolivian breakfast, and we will be driving a short distance to the first site within the hour."

A tableful of empanadas frites, buñuelos with melted hot honey, and api morado or blanco were arranged in a buffet style with fresh, hot bread rolls and plates of local homemade cheese. The scientists started eating heartily. They knew that it would be a long day and that they might not eat again for some time. The day of discovery often led to time being forgotten. People became so engrossed in what they were doing that the normal daily rituals of coffee breaks and lunch were just forgotten. One could start on a piece of research on a site like Puma Punku and then only realize what the time was when it became dark.

John-Paul was a perfectionist when it came to time. At exactly fifty-five minutes after he had announced it would be time to leave, four relatively new Range Rovers arrived at the camp. They were packed with provisions and tools for the exploration of Puma Punku and Templo de Kalasasaya. This took five minutes, so on the hour, they all left for the first day on the site. It would be a day of setting up and preparing the site for the future of the exploration. Not that they had time to waste, but everything needed to be set out, so anything they found would be recorded properly. The part of the site that they would be working on would be set out into zones, so if something was found, it could easily be attached to a specific area of the dig. As more things were found, the picture grew. A mass of data would be uncovered during a normal dig, and it would be easy to lose sight of exactly what was going on. Being organized was another behavior that John-Paul had in abundance. Linked to his desire for everything to run on time, he believed that this was what made him a great researcher. As he was at one of the top universities in the world and leading this team, there was little reason to think he was wrong.

John-Paul glanced at the small clock built into the Range Rover's dashboard. It was showing 9:11 a.m. As the caravan of vehicles approached the first site, Dr. Lee and Dr. Khan had their windows down in their Rover, enjoying the crisp morning air. Softly coming through their windows were the sounds from the song "Kashmir" as performed by Led Zeppelin. They both looked at each other with an amused but surprised look.

"Where is that coming from?" asked Dr. Khan. Dr. Lee just shrugged his shoulders. In the lead Range Rover was John-Paul with his window down as well. John-Paul leaned over and whispered to Michelle, "I hear that the porters apparently received my message to have some welcome music playing when we arrived at the site." John-Paul just smiled. "But I did not expect Zeppelin." (The song was being played, "I'm a traveler of both time and space")

The first site was Templo de Kalasasaya. The group of scientists walked to approach the gate of the temple with the same song still playing from just beyond the gate. *John-Paul is such a romantic*, Michelle thought with a smile on her face as they all walked up to the stone gate structure with that song still just audible in the background. Dr. Fleischman and Dr. Phillips arrived at the stone gate last. They both had the look of kids in a candy store, which all scientists get when they encounter something new. Fleishmann commented, "The stonework is more amazing in person than any photo could express." But the stones seemed like they didn't fit with everything else they found in this part of Bolivia. The type of stone, the color of the stone certainly, did not fit within the local geology. The scientists spent the entire day measuring, photographing, taking small samples of the stone and taking samples of the soil so that all of this could be taken back to their labs at their respective universities.

Puma Punku was an important archaeological site. The ancient people here centered their lives around Puma Punku. It was the place that they believed the world was created, so it was constructed with great care and attention. The mystery of how the stones arrived up in the Bolivian part of the Andes still troubled researchers today. The heaviest blocks were over one hundred tons in weight. It was truly the most fascinating ancient site uncovered on the planet to that date. The amount of information that could be put together by a team of highly skilled researchers at a site like this is staggering. Puma Punku is the key to unlocking our understanding of the ancient civilization that built these temples. And the Templo de Kalasasaya was the jewel in its crown. The idea was to locate, register, and remove as many artifacts of significance that they could find on this expedition and dig.

However, on this trip, Dr. Phillips brought a field lab to do some immediate analysis of the stones and surrounding soils. He could not wait until he arrived back in Cambridge to study all the results from the field. John-Paul walked over to Dr. Phillips and Dr. Fleischman as they were busy collecting samples of the stones that had been cut so finely. The large blocks were set around the site as if they were laid out to be reconstructed, but nobody knew how. It was like a large jigsaw puzzle that somebody had set centuries ago but with the lid of the box missing. There were no instructions to use, no picture to follow.

"Dr. Phillips," John-Paul asked, "what are your thoughts so far this morning? I know this is your first visit to the site."

"Amazing! These are remarkable works of stone shaping for the age of the stones. I have done a lot of reading prior to making the trip, on the research to date. From the initial chemical tests this morning and my visual analysis, these stones are not from this region of Bolivia," commented Dr. Phillips. "And honestly," he added with a smirk, "there are some trace elements of iridium and others that make me think these blocks of stone are not from this planet!"

As the words came from the mouth of Dr. Phillips, he tried to swallow them back up again. He was a scientist who based every piece of his life's work on evidence and understanding the place of everything. Yet the site of Puma Punku had him thinking unworldly thoughts. His mind had wandered the night before when looking up at the sky. It reminded him somehow of the stories of H.G. Wells when he was younger. All the thoughts of worlds other than his own had come flashing back into his mind. The area had a mystique about it and air of the alien that Dr. Phillips just could not wrap his head around. He was there to gather evidence and take part in a serious scientific research expedition, but all he could think about was time travel and spaceships. It wasn't like him. He was, at least, a little embarrassed that he had spoken of science fiction in front of the group when they were there to deal with science fact.

This seemed to turn Dr. Phillips's focus on his work for the rest of the day. As he worked harder to try to prove himself to the others as their equal and not some schoolboy who was transfixed on works of fiction, the rest of the team buckled down too. Soon there was a hush over the entire site of Templo de Kalasasaya as the team got to work on their own areas of expertise. It was only when someone made a discovery or wanted some clarification that the industrious silence was broken, and some conversation took place. This was the way with research expeditions. People looked for their own thing. Every scientist on the team had their own idea of what it was they were looking for and what they expected to find. The research that they had put in before the trip gave them a specific area that they wanted to explore, so it was easy for John-Paul to assign tasks because people were already gravitating towards the area that interested them the most.

It was a typical scene in every way. It was typical of the Bolivian plain to hit you with heat immediately. The day was hot to begin with and would only get hotter. Dry heat saps energy immediately, and the people that visit are aware straightaway that they are being baked. People worked hard with their head down and only really noticed the intense heat when they stopped for a few moments and felt light-headed or weary. In archaeological exploration where there was a flurry of activity in sudden bursts and then periods of no movement at all, scientists would spend a lot of time very still, concentrating on one particular area in minute detail. Then they would find something and get very excited indeed. They would call for help from the assistants, get a colleague to double-check what they were doing, and then record and preserve their finding. Then it would go back to almost silence and stillness again until someone else found something that got them excited, and the movement would explode again. It was typical of a dig led by John-Paul because every member of the team knew what they were doing. He was the ultimate organizer and had this ability to give everyone the free reign to look into what particularly interested them but with enough structure that everyone worked in separate areas and work in an efficient way.

The fact that everything felt as though it was another ordinary day on the Bolivian plain, another typical day on an excavation, and another typical day working with her husband was not lost on Michelle Moreau. She drew her eyes across the scene in front of her. She loved her work and couldn't think of anything else she wanted to do more in the world. She was one of those lucky people that loved what she did for a living. She looked forward to many more days of this with her darling husband. She wanted to do this until she died.

The day moved on quickly. All the things that would normally take over on a day like this were put to the back of the researchers' minds as they worked on. The heat of the sun would usually have people running for shade, but the team worked on without really noticing it. They would take on water but stay in the same spot so they did not lose track of exactly where they were with their work. The flies were all around but apart from the occasional sound of a slapped hand on exposed skin, it was as though they were not there. This was not a large team by any means, so they needed all members present and fit to have any chance of completing the foreboding task that they had set themselves. The fact was that the site was so sensitive that they did not want to flood it with thousands of people. They could have hired scores of local people at very low cost and cleared the site in no time, but that wasn't the way to keep the local people or the scientific community on side. Puma Punku is still treasured by the Bolivian people, and they want the site preserved as much as possible. It took some intense and delicate negotiations to be able to research here at all, and John-Paul and Michelle Moreau, as the leaders of the expedition, were charged with making sure that the hundreds of restrictions and covenants in the agreement were adhered to.

One false move, and there would be financial penalties incurred and political ramifications that would probably keep the site closed off to further research for decades to come.

    The pressure of this had taken its toll on John-Paul in the run up to the trip, although he had tried to hide this from his wife, Michelle. He had lost a lot of sleep while lying in bed next to her, thinking about what might happen to their career if there was an international incident arising from the dig. He had been on sensitive expeditions before, but this was the first one he had led. Their teaching and research posts at the Sorbonne were due for renewal in two years' time, and he feared that casting some poor light on the institution would jeopardize their chances of what had always looked like an automatic renewal. He had to make sure that the site was preserved and the politicians were happy. He didn't get into science to play politics, but sometimes it had to be done. John-Paul hated politicians. He thought that they were only in it for themselves. He would have been devastated to be thought of in the same light. He wanted to walk away from the expedition with it being heralded a success by all. He wanted the scientists that worked with him to congratulate him on the organization that he had delivered. He wanted the local people to declare that their sacred site had been preserved and left intact. He wanted his own university to be happy with the research he did and the artifacts he brought back with him. He wanted his wife to be proud of all they had achieved together. He also wanted the scientific community to learn from all the research that was being done at Puma Punku. If everything went right, then he would be a happy man. This was the first day, but John-Paul was already looking to the future. He couldn't help it. He had always been a planner. The weight of responsibility sat heavily on his shoulders, but it was a weight that nobody in the world was better equipped to handle.

    Night was beginning to fall, but the teams were slow to leave the temple. If there had been light twenty-four hours a day, then they probably would have stayed around the clock. Tiredness doesn't really kick in until you stop working and realize how long you have been concentrating. But the team knew the fading light would do them no favors. It was time to pack up, get something to eat and drink, debrief, and then get some rest to do everything again tomorrow. John-Paul called everyone in. It was time to put the temple out of their minds for a while. The journey back to the camp would be in near-darkness. The team would need to have their wits about them, even though they would be driven by people that knew the area. Even when not driving, you want to have your full concentration on the road when the conditions are treacherous. It is the same when being driven through snow or along a narrow pass. All eyes are on the road, not just those of the driver.

In the distance, the headlights of the Range Rovers were ready to take the scientists back to their camp. In fact, a low ground fog was starting to drift in from the wide-open prairies in the distance. As John-Paul was walking with Michelle towards the Range Rover lights, the midst of the fog shimmered as it drifted in front of the light beams. All the noises that are associated with a plain in the middle of the night were just starting to turn up their volume. Howls from pumas were heard during the daytime, but at night they took on a creepier note. The wind rustled in the tall grass. Even the slightest breeze generated a rustling sound through the leaves of the few trees that surrounded the site. The whole atmosphere was electric as the scientists stood waiting for the Range Rovers to arrive with the hairs on the back of their necks also standing on end. John-Paul was lost in his thoughts.

This is the life. I get to see the most wonderful places. It is like having a backstage pass to nature and the ancient civilizations that we study. And to top it all, I get to do this with the most beautiful woman in the world. Although I have still yet to see somewhere to rival the elegance of Paris, I have been truly privileged to see some magnificent places on this planet. The work is one thing, but to stand here taking in this view, these sounds, and this atmosphere is something else. I wish my parents could see this.'

Beep. Beeeeeep.

John-Paul was so lost in his thoughts that he had failed to notice the Range Rivers arriving, and the others started to load up the equipment that they would not leave in the temple. He ran across to where they were parked, engines still running, and helped to lead the last of the equipment aboard.

Now that the Range Rovers were loaded with all the scientists and equipment, they headed back to the camp. As they all arrived weary, it was a pleasant surprise that the porters had a very nice campfire started with very nice comfortable chairs circling the campfire. There is something very elemental about a campfire. It harks back to older times when people spent a lot of their time outside with the stars for company. It was a feature of expeditions that a campfire was the focal area where everybody gathered. It provided a safe place where all could see each other and look after each other against whatever dangerous animals might be out there. But it also provided somewhere to unload all of the findings and theories from the day's work. Each scientist will have formulated a theory or two while they were working during a day. Having other brains around as large as their own gave them someone to bounce ideas and develop thoughts. It was a meeting of the minds on a very high level.

Each one of the scientists left their tools and instruments in the Range Rovers to be used in tomorrow morning's continued studies. Everyone went into their own tents to refresh themselves before having dinner as a group. It was an integral part of working together to be able to spend time discussing their work and learning from each other. Dr. Fleischman, however, went straight to the easy chairs around the campfire and lit up his pipe. One of the porters came right over to him and asked if he would like to have a cocktail. Dr. Fleischman said, "But of course, my good man."

All the scientists began to come out of their tents and assemble in the easy chairs around the campfire. They started talking about what they encountered and the amazing experiences that they had that day at the temple. Each one had already grabbed something from the dinner table and brought it to their chair around the campfire. The conversation continued, and of course, Dr. Phillips and John-Paul competed with their terrible jokes.

Dr. Wang Lee approached Dr. Phillips to discuss his results of the day and compare notes. Dr. Lee said, "I was told briefly that your initial thoughts supported that these stone blocks may not be of this earth."

"That is correct," Dr. Phillips said.

Dr. Lee sipped his tea and knotted his head in support. Then Dr. Lee stated, "What I saw today also made me puzzled."

"Please share, Dr. Lee, you are among friends." Dr. Fleischman urged as they all sat around the campfire.

Dr. Lee smiled. "I need to confirm, but the carvings I found on a few remote stone blocks reminded me of African symbols from the Dogon."

"Interesting," muttered Dr. Phillips.

As the hour continued to grow later, the conversation got quieter. The porters were still standing back away from the circle of chairs, waiting to serve the scientists. When Michelle commented how quiet it had become. Dr. Lee agreed and whispered, "It is so quiet it's deafening."

The stars were so brilliant in the sky after the sun had set. But as Michelle was looking around in the sky and had lost interest in the conversation, she thought she saw some of the stars disappear in the black sky before reappearing again. Michelle was quiet as she visually tracked this dark area in the sky move in front of the stars. The dark area positioned itself over the temple, which was slightly down the hill from the campsite. Now Michelle was getting frightened.

She thought she had seen something in the distance that was not obvious to the rest of the group. As she looked around at the rest of the team by the campfire, it was obvious to her that she was the only one that had seen the movement near the temple. She was very concerned about what might be going on. Sitting in a clearing in the middle of the Bolivian plain was an experience that Michelle dreaded at the best of times. For a scientist, she was quite scared of animals. The sounds of pumas, and even the breeze through the trees, had made the hairs on the back of her neck stand up in the same way as all the other scientists but for a different reason. Usually, she wouldn't have let John-Paul stand there gazing out into the sky as she had done earlier when the Range Rovers arrived, but she was eager to get into the cars and on her way, so she rushed over and jumped inside. But this was something else.

Michelle got John-Paul's attention quietly. "John-Paul," she whispered, "do you see that?"

John Paul said, "I'm not sure what I am looking at, or rather what am I looking for?" He scanned the sky in the general direction that Michelle had been looking, but there was nothing there. He looked at the temple, around the temple and over the temple, but he had no idea what his wife was talking about. The two of them stared at the temple as though it had some mystical power over them. Michelle could not take her eyes of it in case the thing she thought she had seen would reappear. John-Paul was looking intently to try to see what had so clearly spooked his wife.

Now Michelle's and John Paul's attention towards the temple was seen by Dr. Lee and Dr. Phillips. The rest of the scientists turned to look towards the temple. The large dark area in the sky over the temple was so large that nearly half of the stars in the sky in the direction of the temple appeared to be missing. What was once a clear sky filled with a sea of brightly flashing stars had changed, and so had the atmosphere.

There was no noise, there was no animal sounds or insect sounds, just the crackling of the campfire. The noises of the Bolivian plain that had been so clear only a minute before had disappeared. John-Paul thought that the lack of animal sounds would please his wife, but the fact that they were missing was more concerning than comforting. By now, even the local Bolivian porters had turned to see the same image the scientists were looking at. But their reaction was much different. They froze in horror. It was not something that they had ever seen before. Their legs told them to run, their etiquette told them to protect their masters, but no matter what signals they were getting, they were simply unable to move.

Suddenly, out over the temple grounds, a shaft of light came from the center of the dark spot towards the ground. As everyone watched the light shaft move along the ground, it lit up different objects. First, some trees and then a wall and then more random objects. Then the light went off, and it would come back on in a different location. The random movements of the light were a mesmerizing sight. The whole group stood as one with their eyes to the sky. They had no idea what was happening. Their scientific minds were in overdrive, trying to figure out what in the world was going on. Dr. Phillips thought back to earlier in the day. His thoughts of the rocks maybe being cut by aliens didn't seem so farfetched all of a sudden. Whatever it was, he wanted it to stop.

The scientists looked at each other, not knowing exactly how to react. Each looked towards the rest of the group for answers. Each offered no clues in their facial expressions that they had any idea what was going on. Some of the greatest scientific minds in the world were reduced to looking at each other in the same way that they would look to their parents for guidance when they were young.

Before the scientists could decide what, their next move would be that the dark area was now directly over the campfire. And within a split second, the circle of chairs, the scientists, and the campfire were washed with a brilliant white light. But the Bolivian porters were not within that brilliant light circle. The scientists became buoyant and started floating upwards, and within seconds, the light was gone, and so were the scientists. This sight brought about a panicked response from the team of porters. It was more than they could take. The porters ran in terror and never once looked back to see if the light was still there.

At the same time on the other side of the world from Bolivia, a team of archeologists were continuing to excavate the Göbekli Tepe near the city of Sanliurfa, Turkey. This site predates Stonehenge by six thousand years and is a site that is revered by scientists the world over. The team was headed up by a young Chinese archaeologist named Liu Xiang. Accompanying Dr. Xiang is her trusted aide and PhD student, Shu Yi Chang. This site, along with Puma Punku, had become some of the most recent archaeological studies that pushed the knowledge of human culture to a limit never before imagined. Only a few years before, the information that these two sites were able to deliver was unheard of. Scientists had to guess what had happened in these areas before the sites were uncovered and studied. But now with the rich information that these sites had given up, it was possible to see how these ancient cultures had lived.

The site of Göbekli Tepe is nearly two and a half thousand feet above sea level with massive stones that are not usually found in the area. It was first discovered and explored by the University of Istanbul in the 1960s, but it hasn't been until the advanced scientific methods of today that the true origins of the area were able to be explored in any detail. In all the years of exploration, both amateur and professional, there had been no graves found at the site, which was unusual for ancient sites. I was as though Göbekli Tepe was a cathedral on top of the hill, a site for meeting and praying together.

Dr. Xiang and Ms. Chang had planned their trip to Göbekli Tepe for some time. It was their first research trip in Europe, and they were very excited to be able to lead the team. They went into the trip with a very open mind of what they might find. Dr. Xiang always worked this way. She felt that doing all the research before an expedition led to a narrow mind when they arrived at the location. They would be prepared but make no prejudgments on what they would discover. This meant that they could leave all the research work for when they were at the site and when they got back to China.

The two women waited outside their hotel for the transport to arrive and take them to the site. Dr. Xiang wanted to start early, so they were up and ready before five in the morning. The jet lag still hadn't worn off from the flight over from China the day before, so their bodies didn't really know whether they should be awake or asleep. But their minds were racing. The excitement had built over the previous months to a frenzied level. The two colleagues were very professional in what they did, but they could not hide the joy they felt in being able to start the research work that they were able to carry out. They were both as giddy as schoolgirls at the prospect of spending some time in a foreign country and going to one of the most revered archaeological sites in the world. The excitement had been evident on the flight over as the two talked incessantly about their trip, and it was all going to start in less than an hour's time.

It was 5:11 a.m., and Dr. Xiang and Ms. Chang were picked up by very dirty Ford vans from a hotel in Urfa. The team headed out for a thirty-minute drive to a grassy hill where barbed wire protected a corrugated steel roof and the main excavation site. In the pits, standing stones or pillars were arranged in circles. Beyond on the hillside were other rings of partially excavated pillars. Each ring had a layout that resembled the next. Large stone T-shaped pillars encircled by slightly smaller stones facing inward were the typical arrangement.

So far, the tallest pillars powered sixteen feet in the air, and Dr. Xiang calculated the weight between seven to ten tons each. Dr. Xiang took in the whole sight at once and thought about the task ahead.

How on earth did they get them here? These stones would be difficult to move with today's technology. I can't comprehend how this might have happened. I have an open mind when it comes to this research, so I must consider all possibilities. It sounds weird for a scientist to think this, but there is something otherworldly about this place. It doesn't feel as though it fits on this planet. I must get organized and get all of my team ready for the task ahead. It will soon be time to start.

There was dust everywhere. The work that was being carried out on this ancient site had disturbed the soil that had grown over much of Göbekli Tepe in the years since it had been abandoned. The dust rose in small clouds from each area of excavation but joined together in the atmosphere above the site. As they had approached the area, Shu Yi could see it rising above the hills. It reminded her of the worst days of smog that she had experienced back home in Beijing. She had been born and raised in the city, and although she loved it, she was aware that the sheer number of people living and working in this one place was causing problems. Shu Yi was happy to be away from her home at times, especially when she read the news reports of the smog enveloping her home. It was bringing health problems to many people, and it was the one thing that she wanted to change about her city. She sometimes dreamed that one day she would become rich from her research and then be able to set up a research party into reducing the smog in Beijing and then the rest of the world. She feared that the only answer would be to have fewer people.

As the early morning cool, damp air began to warm up, a light breeze blew up the hillside. Many of the team members were busy excavating the various posts. While Dr. Xiang and Shu Yi discussed the day's planned activities, a commotion in the neighboring excavation caught their attention. They heard a voice call out, "Dr. Xiang, please come here." She was the lead archaeologist so had to be called whenever something of interest was found, but this call sounded different. There was something else in the voice of the caller. It was as though he had found something completely unexpected.

It was a short walk to where the voice was coming from, so Dr. Xiang and Shu Yi broke off from their planning to see what the fuss was about. It was not uncommon on digs for someone to get overly excited about something only for an expert to arrive and it be quickly dismissed as nothing of significance. Archaeological digs took thousands of items out of the ground. It was only really by sifting through them back in the comfort of the laboratory that they could be properly assessed. Uninterrupted study was the key to scientific discovery, not the more romantic notion of laying your hands on something and immediately knowing what it was all about.

Shu Yi and Dr. Xiang made their way to the other excavation pit where the voice had come from. As they arrived, the leader of that team, Dr. Kadir, an archaeologist from the University of Istanbul, motioned for Dr. Xiang and Shu Yi to look at these new columns.

Dr. Kadir was a small man who had worked in science all his life. He was approaching what most people would consider to be a retirement age, but he had no intention of stopping his work. He was as fascinated with the world around him today as he was when he was a small boy. As a Turkish man, he had heard stories about the Göbekli Tepe ruins when he was younger from members of his family. They used to tell stories of a city that was abandoned and empty. Little did he know then that he would one day stand in that city as the chief archaeologist on a major excavation to find out more about this city than had ever been learned before. The family that used to tell these tall tales to him when he was young had all passed away, but he still had his own children, all grown-up now, to tell about what he found in his work. They listened intently. Dr. Kadir was still unsure whether they listened out of genuine interest or out of the politeness he had taught then when they were young. Either way, they listened, and that was what was important to him.

Dr. Kadir pointed out that the carvings on the columns in this circular excavation were different from the carvings on other large columns found in the other circular excavations.

Dr. Xiang said, "What's so interesting about these carvings, Dr. Kadir?"

RASHURE CODEX

The look on Dr. Kadir's face expressed his astonishment about what he was looking at. He had never seen anything like it in all his years of research. This is why he continued to come to Göbekli Tepe. He wanted to find things that nobody else had seen before, at least, nobody in many hundreds of years. The site was surrounded by rumor and speculation all over the world, especially in the scientific community. Göbekli Tepe was heralded by some as the answer to many riddles about ancient civilizations and how they lived. Dr. Kadir was someone that saw the world in black and white rather than any shades of gray. Once he decided on something, then it was near impossible to get him to change his mind. What he had seen on that column had him convinced that he was dealing with something that was not made by the people of this area but centuries before. The problem was that he was busy at this time trying to convince himself that this was not true.

Dr. Kadir began to explain to Dr. Xiang, "I am an archaeologist, but before I became someone that looks for old things in the dirt, I looked to the stars as a graduate student astrophysicist." He continued to explain as he walked around the nearest stone columns, pointing out and touching the face of the carvings. He asked Dr. Xiang, "Have you ever heard of a West African tribe called the Dogon?"

"Yes, I think I have," commented Dr. Xiang. Shu Yi nodded her head; she too had also heard about the Dogon. It was a tribe that had received a lot of attention about eighteen months previously in the news and on the television. Many people had heard about the Dogon.

"Well," said Dr. Kadir, "the Dogon believe they are descendants from a star called Sirius B, and they arrived on the earth in the year three thousand two hundred BC. It wasn't until 1930 that the world became aware of the Dogon and their acclaimed history. Because in the nineteen thirties, the world was not aware of this star that circled Sirius A yet, but the Dogon somehow already knew before astrologers and scientists that Sirius B orbited Sirius A." Dr. Kadir continued, "Finally, in the nineteen seventies, a large telescope photographed Sirius B for the first time."

In the 1970s, this caused some astonishment in the world of astronomy. The tribe had their beliefs dismissed as a fake because it surrounded a star that as far as the rest of the world was concerned did not exist. But when it was photographed, the tribe were suddenly to be believed. They had beliefs that were mocked one day and then studied at length the next. The Dogon people had no access to any astronomical devices yet knew about a star that was not visible to the human eye and took a very powerful telescope to detect. Their beliefs posed as many questions as they answered, and the tribe were generally left alone to live their lives until a few years ago when they were "uncovered" again and made the subject of a television documentary. It was dismissed as nothing more than an attempt to tap into *The X-Files* fan base, and the world moved on.

Dr. Xiang looked at Shu Yi with a confused look on her face. "Okay, very interesting. What does this have to do with this site and this timeframe in history?"

"Look at these markings on these columns," directed Dr. Kadir. "These are diagrams of the stars and specifically Sirius A and Sirius B."

Shu Yi said in a very soft but unnerved voice, "So, how do the inhabitants of Göbekli Tepe know about this star and all these other star charts?" Shu Yi had a knack of getting straight to the point. In any conversation, she was the one that was asking all the pertinent questions, even if she didn't speak with a great deal of confidence. Dr. Xiang had faith that this confidence would come in time.

"That is very curious, Shu Yi, I don't know the answer to that yet." Just as everyone started to drift off into their own thoughts, Dr. Xiang continued, "And this culture predates the Dogon by over ten thousand years. Is there any way these carvings could be fake?"

"We have tested them, and they appear to be authentic."

This sentence seemed to stop the three of them where they stood. Each was lost in their own thoughts. The research that each of them did here might lead to greater success in the future. Dr. Kadir had dreams of winning international awards for his work. As he had grown older, his thoughts had moved from earning money to being recognized for the work he had put in. He wanted his children to see him collect an award for excellence in his field.

Dr. Xiang wanted to expand the work that Beijing University was doing and by finding artifacts of great significance, she could attract more investment and more top researchers like Shu Yi. Her colleague, Shu Yi, wanted to fight the smog problem of Beijing. All three of them wanted this big find to be something that helped their careers and helped the people around them. They all stood together, but they could have been a thousand miles apart, as they were so lost in their thoughts. While they were lost in their own minds, the world immediately around them was changing.

In their excitement, the three of them did not perceive the gathering storm clouds over the hill. Many of the workers had covered their faces and started to head for shelter. The dust was so strong that it was difficult to see through it to usher anyone else to safety. The local people that worked on the site were as confused as the visitors from other countries. In this dry and arid landscape, there were often clouds of dust, but none looked anything like this before. It left everyone confused and frightened of what might be about to happen. An exposed hillside was no place to be in a storm.

It wasn't until the wind began to pick up the dust from the dig site that the three of them realized the locals in their team had already left. Dr. Kadir began to call out for his dig supervisors but found that no one answered. They had all moved to a safer place. The wind continued to grow in strength. The clouds above them were beginning to swirl. Dr. Kadir thought that they were about to experience a tornado. So, he yelled to Dr. Xiang and Dr. Chang to take cover behind the large stone pillars. But in the sky, there was no tornado, but the clouds were beginning to grow darker. And suddenly, the wind went calm. It was as though the storm had been stopped in midtrack by an invisible force.

As the three of them shook off a lot of the dust from their head and eyes, they could begin to hear a low hum. Shu Yi looked into the sky towards the dark clouds, which installed the beginnings of a large black craft floating out of the dark clouds. As that Star Craft came towards the dig site on the hill, the three scientists watched in amazement.

The experience made the three of them stand closer together. They were unable to speak or move at this point. All had seen something move above them in the sky. None could explain what it was that they had witnessed. The thoughts of glory, fame, and money had all faded from their minds that were in survival mode, but their bodies were still frozen to the spot. The three of them looked overhead to see if they could make out any detail and determine exactly what it was they were looking at.

The craft had a geometric-looking surface structure to it. It hovered towards the hill. Suddenly, it stopped directly above the three scientists. Since the clouds made the light of day turn to dark of night in an instant, the black Star Craft was easily disguised. A shaft of light came from the center of the Star Craft. As the craft floated towards the center of the hill where the archaeological dig site was at, the shaft of light was on the ground, moving across the side of the hill towards the three scientists. Dr. Xiang turned to Shu Yi and in Chinese told her that everything would be fine. Now the shaft of light was directly over the three scientists, and they became buoyant, and within an instant, they were gone.

After the darkness had receded and all signs of a storm were gone, the rest of the people on the dig at Göbekli Tepe moved out of the places they had taken shelter. As the site was now a complete mess, they looked for the leaders of the expedition to tell them what to do and how to proceed. None of the three leaders were anywhere to be seen.

Chapter 3

The Astrophysicists

Earlier that same day, high in the Cerro Paranal of Chile, the sun was at its highest point in the cobalt blue sky. The Cerro Paranal observatory is situated in the middle of the Atacama Desert, so the heat that is generated in the middle of the day is stifling. The reason that the observatory is situated here is because of the lack of light pollution. It is around ninety miles south of the nearest city, Antofagasta, so there are no streetlights to have any effect on the VLT that the observatory houses. Scientists love their abbreviations, and they usually refer to long-winded and technical. For example, the simple term DNA is an abbreviation for deoxyribonucleic acid. It comes as a bit of a surprise to people then when they find out that the abbreviation VLT stands for Very Large Telescope. The astronomical community likes to poke fun at itself, and this is just one example of the way that they do this.

In the heat, it was not yet time for her shift at the observatory to start, but sitting alone in the café of the ESO Hotel was an Italian astrophysicist whose name was Abrianna Nucci. She was sipping her freshly brewed coffee. As an Italian, she considered herself an authority on coffee. On the streets of Roma, many an argument has ensued because the person who has consumed the coffee does not feel that it was up to standard, while the purveyor of the coffee feels that it is excellent. In true Italian style, they will have a loud and demonstrative conversation before moving on with their day. The coffee that Abrianna was drinking was a reasonable attempt at an Americano, and with the fact that she was no longer in Italy and the heat being oppressive, she felt that a heated conversation was not the right way to go. If she was drinking this coffee in Roma, on the other hand, then the outcome might have been different.

It was about this time when her friend from University of California walked over and asked, "Is this seat taken?"

Abrianna peered through the steam from her hot, strong coffee and, through her long silky black hair, smiled. "Yes, this seat is taken, but this morning it is yours." Abrianna loved to play this game with people. Back home this would be taken as a joke, but when she met other people from different cultures, she liked to see how they reacted.

Dr. Mariska Kalas grabbed the chair and sat down. Mariska asked as she spread cream cheese on a hot toasted bagel, "You cannot sleep again?"

Abrianna did not look up but answered, "Yes, but not very long and not very often." Abrianna had been having a terrible time sleeping in her new surroundings. Although she had been there for a few weeks now, she had just never settled. She couldn't really put her finger on exactly why. In the first few days, she blamed it on the jet lag, but she knew what jet lag felt like as a regular traveler and never really believed that to be true. Trying to sleep in the extreme heat of the day or the extreme cold of the night, depending on what shift she was working, was another possible explanation that she had mulled over and discarded. But there was a reason that she was not sleeping very well, a reason that she wanted to forget. It was something that she had discussed only with Mariska.

Mariska smiled without taking her eyes off her bagel. "Perhaps you are too lonely on top of this mountain, or maybe you are having those dreams again?" As soon as she said the words, she knew that she had spoken out of turn.

"Those dreams are between us!" Abrianna snapped at Dr. Kalas. She was obviously very angry at this being mentioned. As she snapped, her hair swooshed forward and partially covered her face. She brushed it away, and Dr. Kalas could see that her cheeks were red with a mix of anger and embarrassment. To Abrianna, anger was not a natural thing. Many people mistake the Italian passion and volume for anger, but it isn't so. They live life to the full and display exuberance at every potential occasion, but anger is not a part of the natural Italian psyche. Abrianna wanted the world to swallow her up. The last thing she wanted was a confrontation.

"I confided in you, and you promised to keep our conversations to yourself," she said softly but sternly, looking around the café.

"Okay, Okay . . . let's talk about our plan today and tonight at the observatory, Dr. Nucci." Abrianna Nucci was happy that the matter seemed closed. She had no reason to fall out with her friend and needed someone that she could trust to confide in. Hopefully, that would be Dr. Mariska Kalas. Ever since the days of her childhood, Abrianna had needed someone to confide in. Her mother was that person until she tragically died when Abrianna was only twelve years old. She needed someone else to take over that role, and Abrianna's aunt became her trusted friend. Throughout her school days, Abrianna had only one fried that she would spend as much of her time with as possible. They were inseparable, and Abrianna and her friend, Lucia, shared all their secrets. That friendship went on until the two of them went off to university to study different things. It wasn't that their friendship died, but the closeness and the confidentiality had disappeared. Abrianna had been looking for a replacement ever since. She believed that she had found this in Mariska. The two of them had signed up for a three-year placement at Cerro Paranal, and they both needed someone to spend time with. They were roughly the same age, both worked in the same department at the observatory, and both had a passion for music. It seemed like a perfect match.

Abrianna thought about the work that she would carry out that night. "R136a1: VY Canis Majoris," Dr. Nucci began, "is where I plan to start tonight. My thoughts are if this blue hypergiant star goes supernova, we need to watch out on this side of the galaxy." Dr. Kalas nodded her head in approval. Nucci continued, "If my theory is halfway correct, we should see marked increase in the ambient light generated by the lesser star as it is consumed by the parent star, thus setting up a supernova, or perhaps even something more dynamic—the birth of a black hole." Abrianna knew her stuff, and she should. It had taken many years of study and work to get to the level she was at now. The two colleagues were heading to the top of their field through their intelligence and hard work. Both felt able to bounce ideas off the other. It was great for the two of them that they had each other in the observatory. It could be a lonely place to spend time in if you had nobody to talk to.

Both doctors start gathering their belongings while they continued talking and planning. "Shall we catch the next shuttle to the observatory?" asked Dr. Kalas, nodding her head while she finished her muffin and swung her backpack around to her back. "I would also like to take new readings on Eta Carinae and WR104 while we have the facility under our direction tonight." The two doctors made their way to the shuttle station just outside of the hotel. All the while, they talked about the plans they had for that night's work and the sequence in which they would carry it out. It was still hot in the street, and the pair of them were both looking forward to working in the air-conditioned luxury of the observatory. The money that had been spent of developing this place to study in the middle of the desert was mind-blowing. Every need was catered for from the scores of washrooms to the staff canteen. It was a comforting place for those that were inevitably many miles from home.

Abrianna looked up towards the mountaintop and saw the roofs of the VLT complex where the shuttle was to take them. Then she looked straight up into the very clear blue sky. "Now faith is the substance of things hoped for, the evidence of things not seen," Abrianna whispered to the sky but loud enough for Mariska to overhear.

"What was that?" asked Mariska.

"Hebrews chapter eleven, verse one," whispered Abrianna.

"You're a scientist, Dr. Nucci."

"Yes, and I am also a child of my God. I firmly believe you can be a scientist and a Christian or a believer in a Creator. In my short career, the amazing things I have seen and other astrophysicists have seen and discovered in the cosmos prove to me that there was a supreme entity that organized and planned the universe to support humanity. There are too many instances that could not be an accident or happenstance. But I could go on and on. When I was a little girl growing up in Roma, my mother would take me and my four sisters to church nearly every day, and now that my mother has passed, I know she is in heaven watching over me." The way that Abrianna was brought up had a lot to do with the determination that she had to make a success of her career. Her mother had died way before her time, and this left Abrianna feeling as though she had to cram as much in as she could every day of her life. She didn't want to die in her forties like her mother and have not achieved everything she wanted. All of her sisters were the same. No matter what field they worked in, health care and medicine mainly, the sisters were all heading to the very top. Each had a burning desire to achieve as much as they could from the life that was set out before them.

As the VLT shuttle bus pulled up, a group of scientists in white coats stepped off the bus. One of the scientists saw Dr. Nucci standing and waiting to get on the bus. "Abrianna." He spoke out and waved. "Good morning . . . oh no, good afternoon!"

Abrianna and Mariska looked around and smiled at the same time as they recognized their friend, Dr. Chico, Aldo Chico. "Ola!" exclaimed Abrianna. It was good to see others from their work outside of the observatory, even if it was for a few glancing seconds. It made them feel as though they were living in the real world. They stopped to talk quickly. Abrianna asked Aldo, "Are you off work or just coming down to hotel for dinner?"

Aldo said, "Dinner and a quick visit with the general and then back up the mountain for tonight's observations."

As Dr. Nucci and Dr. Kalas stepped on to the bus, they replied, "We'll see you up there. *Ciao!*"

As the bus pulled out of the complex and headed up the mountain, Dr. Nucci and Dr. Kalas sat back for a nice relaxing twenty-minute ride. The whole area had really grown up around the observatory. In what was once a part of the desert, a new town had sprung up consisting of a hotel, some shops, a grocery store, a coffee shop, and the bus stop. It was a strange sight to behold if you passed over by air, as it was the only sign of any life for hundreds of square miles until you reached the big city. These were new buses. Abrianna could remember the older, less comfortable buses they used when she was a graduate student. As they came around the last bend in the road, the VLT complex came into full view. It was an imposing building. The observatory appeared as though it had risen out of the hill rather than being built there. It seemed like something organic that had decided to grow just there on that spot.

But the two doctors loved working there. It gave them a chance to meet new people and further their interest in astronomy. Abrianna and Mariska collected all of their belongings before getting off the bus. They both had earphones hanging from their ears as they listened to their favorite music. It was their way of preparing for the night ahead and the work that they were due to carry out.

They walked into the initial building and passed the cafeteria and dining room, which connected to a large stairwell and elevator to the second, third, and fourth floors of the building. It was a large building that confused everyone when they arrived there for the very first time. Every room and corridor was a clinical white, and this made moving around the place even more difficult for the uninitiated. Coffee breaks that were due to take only fifteen minutes often saw newcomers disappear for anything up to an hour. But it was both expected and accepted by those that had worked there for a long time. If possible, they didn't let any new recruits go on a break on their own for the first month. But when people knew their way around, it became second nature. The first journey that they learned off by heart was from their work station to the cafeteria.

Abrianna said to Mariska, "The aromas here on the first floor always get me excited to be here. That along with the prospect of discovering something new every night." The challenge of working through the night on a meticulous level was offset by the fact it was the most fascinating job that either of the two colleagues could imagine doing. Abrianna bristled with excitement and the work she had planned for herself that night.

Little did she know that tonight she was beginning a journey of learning that would compare to nothing she could imagine. But before anything like this could happen, she had to climb the stairs she climbed every day to reach the scientists' lounge. There was an elevator, but none of the people that worked there really used it. A combination of the reputation it had for reliability and the fact that they all wanted to stay fit was the reason behind it. On their tours around the building, the new team members were never taken up and down the floors in the elevators, so it was a habit that everyone picked up straight away.

The two of them arrived at the scientists' lounge. Abrianna was on a mission that night, so she got there a few steps in front of Mariska. As she opened the door to the lounge, an older gentleman in a wheelchair came through the door. Abrianna spoke as she held the door open. "Dr. St. John, good to see you. We just arrived."

"That's great. I was just heading up to the office to begin the sequencing of tonight's observations for you and Dr. Kalas." Dr. St. John was always the first in his team to arrive. He was the most organized person that anyone knew. He always had the plans for the day set out so that everyone knew what it was that was expected of them. He took the details from the rest of the team about what it was they wanted to study that shift and set out the equipment so that they could just come in and get on with their tasks. This way of working was highly valued by the rest of the team. They loved having him around to make their life easier as a colleague, but his way with people left most, if not all, of his colleagues feeling cold.

"Thank you, we should be up there in the next few minutes. When will you be ready for us to start?" asked Abrianna. She was more eager than ever to get started on that evening. She had not been this excited about working on a particular night for a long time. She loved her job and never struggled to get motivated about her work, but this was different. She was raring to go. She had no particular reason to feel like this, but Abrianna felt that something different was going to happen tonight. She felt that the hard work she had put in recently would lead her to a discovery soon. Perhaps that night would be the night.

Mariska was feeling differently.

I don't really know where to start tonight. I wish I had plans like Abrianna. She seems to know exactly where she wants to look every shift, but I can't think like that. I have set out the areas I want to look in to Dr. St. John, but they are just the next part of the sky along from where I looked last night. I can be methodical, and I hope that this gets results, but Abrianna seems to have the knack of knowing where she wants to look. There seems no method to it, but she works on a hunch that she might find something really interesting. I think that she is going to be a brilliant scientist.

Dr. St. John said to the two of them, "Give me about a half an hour to get things in position. I had already received your message outlining tonight's observation coordinates. It should be very interesting tonight." Dr. St. John was one of the longest-serving scientists at the VLT. He was respected by everyone there, but he was difficult to like. Everything about the way he worked was about the work itself. He loved to get things organized to get all of the tasks in order, and he would rather have worked with robots that carried out their daily tasks in a silent and efficient manner than people who had the tendency to talk and waste time. Dr. St. John wanted to map out the whole of the sky in a matter of days through clinical analysis rather than look at interesting features and discuss them with colleagues. Tonight, he was working with two colleagues that he knew how to handle. They worked well together, and when he could see them flagging and be tempted to talk, it was easy for him to suggest a coffee break, get everyone recharged, and then start again in relative quiet.

Of all the people he worked with, Dr. St. John liked to work with Dr. Nucci and Dr. Kalas the most.

Mariska and Abrianna sat together in the scientists' lounge. They chatted for a while about the things that made them smile. They recalled how they first met on their very first day at the observatory and the fun times that they had shared since. Surprisingly, there were fewer people working in the observatory at night than in the day, so the people that were present at night had a freer run of the place. The cleaners, porters, and many of the security and catering staff worked during the day and left a skeleton crew at night to look after the few scientists that were working on the telescope. All meetings took place during the day, as did the teaching and research classes that were run for graduates and new recruits. At night, it was a bit of a playground, and the stories that the two women had to tell included playing hide-and-seek as well as racing along the corridors on wheeled chairs. Although the entire complex was covered by CCTV cameras, the purpose of those was to replay if any incidents happened and not to monitor the workplace behavior of the people on duty. As long as the work was carried out, then everyone was happy. The fun usually came during break times. As the two colleagues sat and spoke, the night outside took on a mysterious air. The stars in the sky seemed to shine brighter than ever before, and the desert remained completely still. It was as though the desert was preparing for something to happen. It was as though the desert knew something that those inside the observatory had no idea about.

Thirty-five minutes after the two colleagues had started talking, Dr. Kalas and Dr. Nucci reached the observation laboratory. As they approached, they could hear some music playing through the glass doors. Dr. St. John loved to listen to Stevie Ray Vaughan, specifically "Tin Pan Alley." It seemed to fit Dr. St. John's character and his life in a wheelchair. It was a very bluesy song for a very bluesy man.

As the two girls walked into the doors, Dr. St. John caught them out of the corner of his eye and seemed a little startled and embarrassed as he reached for the volume to the music. "Oh, don't turn it down. This is the good part," said Abrianna. It immediately lightened the mood and relieved Dr. St. John of his embarrassment, and they were all ready to work together.

The three of them settled in for the night's observations of R136a1: VY Canis Majoris. There was an excitement in the air that what they were seeing was rewriting history. Canis Majoris activity was spiking. Or at least, it was reaching levels never recorded before. Each time new data was coming on to the screen, the three scientists would smile at each other while rubbing their eyes in disbelief. The beliefs of Abrianna that something special might happen on that night were starting to feel as though they were correct.

"Let's take an evening break," said Dr. St. John. They all went down the hallway, and they could overhear a lot of loud voices coming from one of the other observation labs. They stepped into the room to see if anyone wanted to join them for a break. When the group around the monitor turned around to see Dr. Kalas and Dr. Nucci, one voice said, "Come see this." It was Dr. Chico and his team. Dr. Chico ran the lab along the corridor from where the three were working. They were a great team to work alongside, and the energy in the team always made the night shift more interesting. It was good to work near Dr. Chico.

So, they walked over to the group where they were looking at some NASA video footage from one of the solar satellites positioned to take photos of the sun and its corona. This particular video observation was absolutely amazing. "What are we looking at?" said Dr. Nucci. She stared at the screen but couldn't really make out what it was they were watching.

The lab technician sitting at the monitor said, "We are not sure, but it looks as if a black sphere maneuvered close to the sun and allowed one of the solar prominences to connect, as if the sphere was feeding off of it." Nothing that anyone could say by way of explanation felt right. They were all trying to process it in their heads, but the words had not yet been invented to fully describe the events that appeared to be unfolding on the screen in front of them.

"Or the sphere was recharging its fuel somehow," said one of the other technicians. Dr. Kalas looked at Dr. Nucci with a little disbelief. The whole room was filled with disbelief. They had all seen some weird and wonderful things in their time from events that only powerful telescopes could detect to some pretty elaborate hoaxes. It wasn't clear which of these they were witnessing.

She said with a wink to Dr. Nucci, "What are we looking at again? Are you sure this is real and not fake?" suggested Dr. Kalas. As they were looking at the NASA footage, the black sphere stayed in place for about thirty seconds, and then it slowly disappeared into the blackness of space. There was a buzz of excitement around the room as everyone took in what they were seeing. Dr. Nucci and Dr. Kalas could feel the energy radiating off the other team. It made the hairs on the back of the neck stand on end. Surely, NASA don't release videos of fakes? What was happening here?

"Okay, folks, I think it is past time to have an evening break," said Dr. St. John. "There's been more excitement in the last three hours than I've seen on station here in the last three years." Dr. Kalas and Dr. Nucci both nodded their heads. They wore smiles from ear to ear. So, the three of them left the observation lab to go to the dining room and take a break.

The dining room was located on the first floor but under a glass roof overlooking the mountain range and the valley. It was one of the very few concessions that the architect of the building made for the people that would eventually work there. Just about everything else was about the function of the building as an observatory. The walls were six feet thick so that no sound would echo through the building from outside and have any chance of affecting the work that went on inside. There were no windows in any of the workspaces so that people were forced to focus purely on what was going on in front of them rather than see what the wider world was up to. It was a similar trick to the one that casinos use in Las Vegas. There is no reference to the outside world, so people would spend hours and hours inside the casino without knowing if it was light or dark outside. In the vast majority of the observatory, people were only alerted to the passing of time in the outside world by a glance at their watches or by the beeps that signaled the end of their shift. Back in the cafeteria, the three colleagues were settling down with their thoughts. They all had a buzz about the events of that evening, and all sat staring up through the glass roof. At this high-altitude, deep visual observation of the stars in the sky at night was amazing and inspiring, to add to the amazing and inspiring events that they had already seen that night.

They were all ready to eat and drink and refuel for what promised to be a very interesting night. There were several tables of scientists in the dining area. However, one side of the dining area was fairly empty. This is where Dr. St. John in his wheelchair led Abrianna and Mariska to his favorite, quiet table under the stars. He liked the table for two main reasons. The first was that it afforded him the best view of the stars. Being in a wheelchair, he was unable to move himself to the far corners of the room, which gave the fullest view of the sky. The table that Dr. St. John had chosen was as close as he could get. It still allowed him to see most of the sky, and he positioned his wheelchair at the end of the table so that he could view the area of the sky that they had been observing earlier on the shift and would be returning to later. It was not that he could see anything with the naked eye, but he felt strangely drawn to that part of the sky. The second reason was that it was at the quiet end of the room. Dr. St. John preferred the company of himself whenever he could manage it, and for some reason, that end of the cafeteria was not as popular as the other side. It gave him the solace that he needed, although on that night, he was happy to share that solace with the two other doctors he had been working with. Somehow, he felt that all they had seen that night would produce more thinking from them than speech.

The waitress came over and took their orders. The three of them had coffee. Abrianna smiled at the waitress; they had developed a bond over the coffee that was served here over the years. The waitress often worked the same night shift as Abrianna and knew exactly how the Italian liked her coffee. She would pay care and attention to making sure it was just perfect. The conversations that did break out were all focused on astrophysics, but they were few and far between. A hush had grown over the three scientists because they were all in awe of the events they had been privileged to witness that night.

But during the conversation, Abrianna kept looking up at the stars. She was in a reflective mood. "You know I never get tired of the brilliance of the stars here on top of this mountain," commented

Abrianna. The others sat silently, but Abrianna knew they were not being rude. It was hard for all three of them to absorb all that had happened on that shift, but they were barely through the shift, and there was much more to come.

Dr. St. John glanced at his watch, it was eleven in the evening. Even though the moon was full, the stars were still so brilliant at this elevation. The moonlight was coming in through the glass, creating a shadow on the floor and the table. They all joined Abrianna and took a look up at the sky. The night outside was calm. This was very much in contrast to the excitement both they and Dr. Chico's team had felt within the confines of the observatory.

But the strangest thing started happening, some of the stars overhead were disappearing as a dark spot in the sky came out from behind the observation building slowly. The three scientists were immediately puzzled. This wasn't a natural phenomenon that they were aware of. They stopped drinking their coffee and just stared at the sky above. Abrianna was completely lost in her thoughts. Nothing could have broken her from them at that moment.

Could this be linked to the events that we have already seen tonight? O Lord, please give me the strength to understand what is going on. I work hard every day, and now an opportunity has presented itself in front of me. I am worried that I will be unable to make sense of it. Please guide me through this night, and I will dedicate my findings to you.'

Eventually, the dark spot filled half the sky. Abrianna pointed out suddenly to the other two. "Look up, the stars are gone!" They both looked up, and within a second, a brilliant light filled the room but was focused over their table. They looked down at the light on the table and, within an instant, started becoming buoyant. Only the three of them were beginning to float out of their chairs. And suddenly, as quickly as it appeared, the light went off, but the three of them were gone.

Chapter 4

The Union

A peaceful feeling of floating in a warm but dark space came over Simon, Daniel, and Sierra. They were able to see the outline of each other as they floated up away from the ground slowly, and they could hear each other too. "Stay calm," yelled Simon to Sierra and Daniel.

Sierra was crying. "Daddy, I'm scared!" Simon was scared too, but all he wanted at that moment was to look after his daughter. He could not reach her; she was a blurry shadow that appeared too small to be anywhere close. So, he tried to comfort her with his words.

"Close your eyes and pray Sierra, I will catch up to you soon." Simon comforted. As he said those words, Simon glanced towards Daniel. He had not heard anything from Daniel. Simon yelled, "Daniel, are you okay?"

Daniel's arms were stretched out like bird wings. "I'm just enjoying the flight. I have never felt so light since I was a baby," claimed Daniel.

Simon smiled and said, "That's my Daniel, always positive." Even in the most terrifying of situations, Daniel had been able to lighten the mood. He always helped Simon at funeral services, and his deftness of touch with people shone through. Funerals were a pleasure to conduct with Daniel around because he allowed people to think positively. Many people fear that in a funeral, they must cry and look downbeat because that is what is expected of them. But in many cases, people are put out of their suffering when they die, or they are able to look back on a happy and fulfilled life. Daniel's words and actions gave people the permission to look back with joy that had been a part of this fulfilled life rather than the pain of it ending.

It was the same here. The father and daughter were scared of the situation they found themselves in, but Daniel had allowed them to see the positive side of it. Simon and Sierra loved to have Daniel around.

The lights on the ground were getting smaller as they all floated higher in the air, but Simon was still not sure why they were in the air, anyway. Simon was himself getting nervous about the height. In his mind, he replayed the thought, What goes up, must come down. What goes up must come down. What goes up . . .

All he could think about at that moment was the basic training he had done for a charity parachute jump about five years previously. He had listened intently to the instructors because he was doing something new and wanted to be able to recount the tale to all of those that had sponsored him to take the jump. Part of the role of leader of the church was to raise funds to keep the church in good repair and to help out those in the community that needed a hand up. Simon took this part of his role seriously and set out every summer to have one big charity event to not only raise funds but also raise the profile of the church and all the good work it was doing with the local media. In fact, on this parachute event, he had managed to get the local news anchor and a reporter from the local newspaper to jump with him and twelve members of the church. The money that had been raised was more than $20,000, and he was sure that this would allow the church to start up a soup kitchen that winter in the nearby city. Simon was pleased and proud of the work they had done.

The oddest part of the induction with the parachute instructors was when they told everyone what to do if the parachute and backup parachute failed. Although there was only a minute chance of this happening and, if it did happen, only a minute chance of survival, the procedures had to be discussed. Simon found it strange that they had a room of people that were excited and nervous in equal measures, and part of the way that they would coax the nervous side to get into a plane and throw themselves out of it was to talk about both parachutes failing! The first step would be to look for someone else with a functioning parachute. No luck on that count! Then you were to look for open water or an area of trees, something that would help to break the fall. Without much in the way of visibility, Simon hadn't much idea where they were at this particular point, but he knew that they were probably not far away from Lake Palestine, so there was a source of water and trees if they needed it. Their best bet was to approach the area together and then split up close to impact. This was not what Simon thought he would be doing at that time of the day. In fact, when he was listening to the parachute instructors talking about a failed parachute and a free-fall landing, he hoped that it was advice he never needed to use.

Plan for the worst, hope for the best. And the three of them continued to rise.

But he did not want to alarm the others since there was nothing they could do but trust that the outcome would not be tragic. Faith would have to take over now. The three of them were in the hands of something that they knew nothing about and would just have to face the consequences.

Up until this point, Simon had been looking down or out towards the others. For the first time, Simon looked up. It was one of the paradoxes that Simon felt in his faith. The traditional view of God is in the sky, overlooking everything that we are doing, but whenever we pray, we look down to the ground. It had become a natural reaction for Simon to look down to the ground whenever he was thinking or whenever he trusted his faith. Years of looking downwards at the moments in his life when he stopped to reach out to God had left him looking down at this very moment.

Until now. He turned his head and looked to what was above him. There were no stars, no moon, nothing that could be seen. All that was there was just a deep, empty blackness above them.

Simon closed his eyes and prayed, this time while facing upwards. "Lord Jesus, protect us. We trust in you, all that we are and all that we have. Please hear this prayer tonight. We need your protection. If you cannot save all of us, take me and save them. I ask this blessing in your holy name. Amen." And Simon opened his eyes to whatever it was that was above him. He took it all in and thought.

Is this the thing that produced the light we saw? Am I dreaming? This is an unworldly event that just cannot be happening to me. It is far more vivid and realistic than any dream I have ever had. My mind is telling me that this must be a dream because this cannot happen, but it is far too realistic to be anything other than reality. All of my experiences and all of my faith still leave me petrified at this moment, so I cannot think what it might be doing to my beloved Sierra. I want to be able to reassure her that everything will be all right, but I don't believe that myself. So, how could I possibly try to convince someone I love?

At that moment, the three of them came closer together. It was still too far to reach each other, but the fact that they became closer gave them all a strange feeling of reassurance. Here they were floating in the sky above their home under an object that none of them had even imagined, let alone seen before, and they all felt comfort by the fact that they were a little bit closer to each other. These were strange times indeed.

Above them, a rectangle-shaped light came on, and the three of them floated through it. They gently landed on their feet on a solid surface. Daniel said, "Where are my jeans and boots?" Simon looked at Daniel and Sierra. Then he looked down towards his feet. They were, all three, in a type of cream white robe that flowed beneath them. None of them had noticed the exact time that they had transformed from their own clothes into the robes, and there was a little silenced embarrassment between them that they had been disrobed and redressed in the presence of each other. It took them all some time to regain their composure and look around to see what had happened.

The air was crisp and filled with the fragrance of flowers, but there was nothing in sight that was the obvious source of the smell. The light in the room was low, but again there was no indication of a light source. There seemed to be no explanation for anything. Things just were. Simon whispered, "We were just floating above the city, now we are standing on something firm. What has happened, and where are we?"

Now that Simon, Sierra, and Daniel were together again, they began to calm down. It was a comfort to Sierra to finally be surrounded by the two men that she trusted the most in the world. Her feeling was that if anyone could get them out of this situation, then it was her father and Daniel. And the warm light that was washing the room seemed to also calm their feelings.

"Where are our clothes?" whispered Daniel. They were all three standing in cream-colored robes that reached to the floor of this room. The fabric was lightweight and silky to the touch with a slight luminous quality too. At once, all three of them noticed that each one was feeling their robes. It was like no material known to man, and it pricked their curiosity just to be wearing it.

Sierra seemed to love the way it flowed. "Look, Daddy," Sierra said as she slowly spun around, watching the robe billow out. "Doesn't this look beautiful?" Sierra smiled as though the beauty of the robe had erased the memory of the situation they were in.

"Yes, sweetheart." Then Simon looked over at Daniel; he too was spinning to let his robe billow out. "Daniel!" Simon softly yelled. "Be careful, you might fall." Simon was concerned that Daniel's false leg could cause him to stumble. The last thing they needed was a medical emergency right now. All three had to be alert to whatever might happen next. "We need to stay focused on what just happened to us."

Daniel said with a puzzled look on his face, "This is not heaven?"

"Daddy, did we die?" Sierra asked with fear in her voice.

"No, we did not die. I don't think so . . ." The ambiguity in Simon's words was not matched by the confidence in his voice. He was sure that they were still alive, and he hadn't even contemplated that the three of them were dead until Daniel and Sierra had mentioned it.

Daniel then attracted their attention. "Guys, wait." He reached down to pull up his robe to look at his leg. Sierra and Simon gasped. Daniel revealed that both his legs were fine! Miraculously, his shattered, amputated leg was no longer gone. And Daniel looked thinner too. Sierra asked, "Daddy, what happened?" as she held on to Simon in fear.

Daniel whispered in amazement, "Yes, my Lord, what just happened?" He had the use of his leg again after many years without it. The news almost knocked him off his feet. He shed a tear as he rejoiced inside at the revelation. His leg was back, and Daniel was happy and confused.

At that moment, a woman's voice spoke from behind them. "Welcome." The three of them looked at each other in a startled manner before turning to see where the voice was coming from. Standing across this round-shaped room was a woman wearing the same type of cream-colored robe as they had found themselves in. The color of the robe contrasted with her long black hair, and she stood around ten feet from them. Her manner was soothing to the three confused friends who wanted answers to the questions, not only the ones that they had asked each other but also the ones that they mulled over in their head. "Daniel, this is not heaven. And, Sierra, you have nothing to fear. This is about the safest place you have ever been in your life." Try as they might, the three of them could not get the surprised look off their faces. They were stunned to see someone else here, and even more stunned that this woman standing in front of them had calm answers to their questions. The surprise had glued them all to the spot. None were able to move in any direction, look at each other, or move their lips. It was as though their bodies needed time to take in the woman. She was one surprise on top of many others, and the cumulative effect might have been too much for them. The place was silent.

After what felt like several minutes had passed, Simon was finally able to mutter a question. "How do you know our names?" Then Simon remembered he had many questions. "And where are we? And who are you?" Then Daniel joined in with the questions. "And where are our clothes? And can I keep this leg?" That last question put a smile on Sierra's face as she looked up at Simon.

"Yes, Simon, I know you have many questions, and most of the questions you have not thought of yet. It's okay. I am called Marta." Now a man's voice spoke from behind them as they faced Marta. "And I am Hozai." The three of them turned again slowly to see a blonde-haired man in a long cream-colored robe standing behind them. They were now all standing in a circle, all looking inwards.

Daniel looked startled. "Oh my, how many of you folks are there?" Sierra grabbed Simon's hand a little tighter. "We are many," answered Hozai. "But we are all here to keep you safe. We will begin to answer all your questions in time. Please follow me to the gathering place."

The five of them started walking towards the far edge of the round room. There was no apparent exit to this room until Hozai raised his hand. At this moment, a large opening in the wall just appeared. *Lord, what is next?* thought Simon. He didn't mind admitting to himself that his faith was a little shaken.

Things were happening so fast, and this whole experience was becoming hard to believe for Simon, given his religious background and how he was raised. Simon knew deep down that what he was witnessing was a series of miracles, but on the surface, he was skeptical of the people he had just met.

Through the large opening, they could see a gathering of people inside of a very large room. These people seemed to be waiting for something . . . or someone. All of these people were wearing the same cream-colored robes. This struck Simon as being odd. But Hozai and Marta led them into this large room that was lit with a soft white light. It seemed to be very quiet in comparison to the large amount of people standing in this room, as though they had all just arrived there and were as stunned as Simon, Daniel, and Sierra. The hush was palpable, but the three newcomers seemed to be the only ones that noticed it.

As Simon, Daniel, and Sierra followed Hozai and Marta, Simon began to recognize a few of the people standing around, talking to each other. Simon said to Daniel in a whisper, "That looks like our state representative and our senator."

Daniel said, "You know, Simon, I think you're right." Sierra was looking in the other direction and recognized some celebrities that she had seen on television and in gossip magazines.

Hozai and Marta led the three of them to the edge of some large steps that led upward to a platform. Everyone was standing below the platform. The edges of the room were dark, and it wasn't quite possible to get a feeling of how big this room was. Hozai and Marta turned around and told Simon, Daniel, and Sierra to wait there. Then Hozai and Marta walked up the steps to the top of the platform that overlooked the crowd of people.

They began. "We are sorry to have brought everyone here in this way, but it is important that we get our message to everyone in a manner that all of the people on the planet will understand, respect, and believe. They must believe what you will tell them from this meeting."

Within the crowd were the various scientists from Cerro Paranal in Chile, Puma Punku in Bolivian, and Göbekli Tepe in Turkey. They all had experienced exactly what Simon, Daniel, and Sierra did by floating up to the Star Craft.

As this scene was unfolding far up in the sky, the rest of the people on the planet were unaware of what was happening. Down on the ground, only the people that had seen the light and fled knew that something strange was happening, but even these people had no idea what it actually was. Nobody had seen anything like this before.

Across the planet, things went on as normal. Everyday lives were unaffected by the events that Simon, Daniel, Sierra, and the others were experiencing. People were getting up as usual and going about their daily lives. Commutes were being endured, deals were being done, and children were going to school. Across the United States, people were going out shopping, driving around in their cars, and conducting their normal meetings.

One such meeting was happening in a small room in a big building in Washington, D.C. The White House had been the home of all American Presidents since 1800 when John Adams took up residence. The exterior had seen attacks by the British in 1812 and many additions to the building commissioned by former presidents. The inside had seen some of the most important meetings that the country of America had ever faced. Some were now out in the open such as the discussions over the Cuban Missile Crisis and much of the scandal surrounding Watergate, while most are still unknown to anyone that was not present. The current meeting was one such meeting that was classified as top secret, and the details were destined to never leave the room.

The President was a suspicious man. This had started when he was running for the nomination of his party and had continued right throughout his election campaign and his presidency. Those around him knew that he had to be constantly reassured and backed in order to keep him happy. Nobody was quite sure why he operated in this climate of suspicion; nobody was safe from the President's mood. He looked upon everyone from both sides of the political spectrum as people that could undermine him at any given opportunity. They say that it is an almost impossible job to be President of the United States of America, but this man was sure that it was other people that made it so difficult.

"Mr. President, there have been reports of unusual activity near some historic sites in different parts of the world. Although there are always reports of the paranormal around this time of the year, we are looking into it," the Chief of Staff reported. He knew that the Internet was responsible for wild speculation at the best of times, but in the run up to Halloween, it just went wild with speculation. Kids going back to school and getting together to start new pranks, people with too much time on their hands as the evenings grew darker, and those without a job were the main culprits. He was sure that the Internet was responsible for many good things, but the conspiracies that it brought were nothing short of a pain.

"Let the security services deal with it. There are always new reports of this kind. I suspect that the security services get to see thousands of these every day. Get them to monitor it closely and report back to me if they find anything in it. Always keep me in the loop," said the President. The rest of the people present knew that he meant exactly that. Nothing got past him. He was always on alert.

Not since the attacks of 9-11 had any President put those around him on such an alert as this President. It was as though he could see something coming that nobody else had any idea about. It was as though he was able to sniff out problems before anyone else, like a dog that was trained to find drugs in luggage at the airport. He thought that he could sniff out potential danger when nobody else was aware of what was going on. He felt that this was an essential part of his job.

"Will do, Mr. President," said the Chief of Staff. He knew that he would be asked about this over the coming days. He knew that he would have to gather all the information that he could and report it back. He knew that the President would jump all over him for the finer details of this situation and any others that would be brought up during the meeting.

"Let's move on to the next item," responded the President. But he hadn't moved on in his mind. He felt a threat with this news. It wasn't something that would usually cause any other President of the United States to feel this way, but this was no ordinary President. In fact, this President was so self-absorbed and acted so beneath the office of the President, and many people that voted for him now regretted voting for him. But so many of those people that voted for him always said, "Give another chance, he is different." Most people in the country and around the world knew this President had a mental and emotional problem that has only grown the longer he was President.

The rest of the meeting passed by in the normal manner. Each of the items on the agenda was discussed, and then the President always finished with, "Keep me in the loop." He had said it so much that they all knew it was coming. None of them had worked as hard for any other President before this one. They were constantly looking into things and reporting back, not just the major issues that they felt needed the President's attention but also insignificant items that they wouldn't normally discuss. This man wanted to know everything about everything. They were all sure he never slept. There were phone calls at all times of the day and night from him. He had placed multiscreen TVs throughout the White House so he could monitor all new channels. He was so self-absorbed his focus most of the time was on people that would criticize him rather than on fixing the problems he promised during his election. He was either looking for updates on some minor issue that they had discussed days or weeks earlier, or he was asking if they had seen a minor news item from an obscure news Web site. Nothing escaped his sight.

Through working with the President, the Chief of Staff had become suspicious himself. He wasn't sure whether that was a result of all the suspicion flying around or he had a point. This President was starting to make him nervous. This President was very different, he thought.

As the meeting was ending, the President looked towards the windows and commented, "There is something happening, but I'm not sure what it is. Do you feel it?"

Chapter 5

The Revel

Hozai and Marta walked to opposite sides of the platform, which allowed a large hologram of the Earth to materialize. Simon, Daniel, and Sierra looked at the hologram. It brought back to them the events of the day. Only a short while ago, they were standing outside the church at home, going about their normal daily activities. It had been a typical weekend day in the life of the three—fishing, talking, and helping people. It was what they all loved to do. But now, they were standing here in a place that they knew nothing about.

Simon was concerned for his daughter. She was bright and took everything in, but there was just too much here to make sense of. He worried about how she would react to the unfolding events. And he also worried about his wife back at home, who saw them disappear. How was she coping with all of this?

Daniel was happy at the fact his leg was back with him but had no idea what was going on. He had resigned himself to a life of struggling with his balance, but all of a sudden, he was back with two legs and perfect balance again. It was a miracle, but with this great gift he had received, there was a small tinge of doubt. He believed in the power of God but had never heard it manifest in this way before.

Sierra was numbed. So much had happened in such a short time that she had not taken it all in. She was not a typical young girl in the way that she went about her life and her faith, but this was too much to get her head around. She was sure that this was the workings of God, her faith was that strong, but she was confused. She stood there and went through the events in her own thoughts to try to catch up with where she was now.

We were just standing there. We were outside the church after a long day. I was with Daniel and my dad when a light appeared. That's it—a bright light that seemed to randomly move around in the sky. It was as though it was searching for something or for someone. Maybe it was actually searching for us. I can't believe that we just started floating up into the sky. Then there was a blank, it must have only been a few seconds, and we were here in these robes. I hope that Dad or Daniel didn't see me undressed. That would be really weird. Now we are here with other people looking at a hologram of the world. I hope that Daniel's leg is here to stay. He looks so happy that he has it back, and I know that he and Dad will look after me.

The crowd that Simon, Daniel, and Sierra were standing in was about three thousand people or possibly more. As it became apparent to Simon, the people that were in the crowd were influential individuals from around the world. He started thinking to himself, *Why were we selected? We are not influential to the level most people in this crowd are.* Simon just had to think and pray, *It is God's will that we are here and safe in this place, wherever this place is. We are as safe as we can be right now. I'm sure that there is a purpose to us being here, and my faith will guide me through.*

The feeling in this room was peaceful and not threatening at all. Otherwise, Simon thought everyone would be angry and yelling, that they were brought to this place. If a crowd of people were taken to somewhere that they knew nothing about on earth, then there would be panic and confusion. People would be trying to escape, and the noise levels would be unbearable. But that was not the case. On the contrary, everyone seemed to be in a state of respect and awe, and almost as if the air itself was calming. Nobody showed any signs of being upset or angry. They all looked serenely around the Star Craft with a gentle smile on their face. There was no sign of what was going on outside the Star Craft except the holographic representation of their home planet. The three companions did not know how long they had been up there, or whether the storms or clouds that they saw were still going on—or even if it was night or day out there. They had no idea what was happening with their loved ones back on the ground, but they had the faith that seemed to be present in the rest of the room. Everyone was serene and confident that they were safe there.

The room was a safe place. None of the occupants knew yet, but they were in a place that had been safe for a very long time. It carried a cargo that needed protection. The fact was that the Star Craft instilled confidence in people. It was one of those places that people just accepted for what it was. The Star Craft was somewhere that all those in it were able to stand in quiet contemplation. It was like St. Peters in Roma or St. Marks in Venice. As soon as you walked through the doors, you just stopped all the worries and thoughts of the world and stood there in a mix of awe and inspiration. The Star Craft had the same magical quality, and you could see it etched on the faces of all those that stood in it at that moment.

Simon, Daniel, and Sierra by now had joined the group and also stood silently, but they were looking around at the people that were standing near them and the massive space they were in. They had become reassured and were calm.

Hozai and Marta began to speak. They captured the attention of the room immediately by just standing there. They stood with a smile and immediately got the attention of every single person in the room; it was as though the smile had worked its way around the room and let everyone know that something interesting or important was about to be said. They say that a smile works wonders in communication, but that is for a one-on-one conversation. These two smiles—one from Marta and one from Hozai—had gotten everyone to look in their direction and wait for what they had to say.

As Marta and Hozai were talking, the anticipation by everyone was palatable. Hozai began by saying, "We have several issues to share with you. First, as you are now aware, you are not alone in this universe," Hozai said this with an even bigger smile on his face. He knew that the people they had selected would take this news in the way in which it was intended. He knew that with many people on the planet Earth, all of this would have panicked them or caused them to attack or to run away. But they had done their homework and chosen people that could take this news and the rest of what they were about to be told. Hozai was thankful that they had been given the right direction when it came to selecting the people they had gathered on the Star Craft.

He continued, "And we know your people for many years have pondered the question, 'Are we alone for many years?' Secondly, yes, we look similar to you because you are us and we are you. Basically, you are our seed. You all may be thinking, why contact us now if you have always known about us? This is a good question, and the answer is like this—you are our seed, and we have been watching your development for millennia." Hozai was now in full flow.

"Our culture, our beliefs are very similar. We believe in one supreme God that created everything just like you do. However, this planet is not your origin. This is the third planet your people have lived on. The reason you all don't remember the first two planets is because your development had not reached that cultural memory or advancement needed to remember," Hozai explained. He wanted to reach out to everyone in the room individually, but they did not have time. After waiting for thousands of years, the time was now right, and the people that were gathered in front of him had work to do.

Simon and Daniel looked at each other with a slight surprise on their faces and their mouths half-open. Daniel silently mouthed,

"No way." Simon's thoughts immediately went to the Bible and what it says about the creation. He thought for a few moments about how the words of Hozai fit with the words of God he had followed all of his life. As Simon looked across again at Daniel, he could see that his friend stood there with his eyes closed in deep thought. Simon could only assume that Daniel was also matching his beliefs with what he had just heard. So, this statement from Hozai was received with a large amount of doubt from Simon and Daniel. They could only assume that the rest of the room was going through the same thought process. Even though the room was silent, you could sense different moods existing within the silence. When they had first entered the room, it was obvious that there was an air of serenity and quiet contemplation. Simon knew this sound from the quieter moments in church. Silent prayer within his congregation had a similar feeling. As Hozai and Marta started to speak, the air was filled with expectation, even though there were still no sounds. Then it was possible to feel another change in the atmosphere of the room, again even though there was no change in the sounds being made. It was obvious to all that the people gathered there were working out what they had been told and referencing it against their own experiences and beliefs. Hozai and Marta seemed to be tapped into this too, and they fell silent for a minute or two so that the people in front of them could process the information they had just received. They wanted people to listen to what they had to say and work with them. They knew that the delivery of this information was vitally important.

After a short while had passed, Marta spoke up. "I know this is a lot to process in a short time, but there is more we need to share." Marta turned to the hologram, and as she turned around, the hologram changed from a representation of the planet Earth to a three-dimensional image of the Milky Way galaxy. The rest of the room turned with her, and at once all eyes were fixed on this holographic image. The attention of the room had gone back from processing information to listening intently to what Marta had to say.

She said, "You call this the Milky Way, but we have always known this galaxy by a different name, Osdai. But to communicate to your people, we will use the names you are familiar with until you all are taught the historic names for places in the universe." Marta knew that time was short but also knew that unless she presented this information in the right way, confusion would result. She again paused for a few seconds so that everyone would follow her on the next step.

Now Dr. Kalas and Dr. Nucci looked at each other with their mouths wide open in surprise. Dr. Nucci said softly, "That is so cool." She had a strong feeling that the night would uncover something special, but never in her wildest dreams had she imagined she would be standing here listening to this.

Marta continued pointing at the hologram, and the area in the galaxy our solar system resides became highlighted. She still had the full attention of the room. Everyone wanted to know what would be said next. Marta looked blankly as she spoke.

"The one reason we are here now," Marta explained, "is that we have detected a tragedy about to happen that will impact this planet just like other catastrophes that occurred on the other planets that caused us to relocate you thousands of years ago."

"I know the longer we talk," Hozai announced, "you all get more and more questions entering your heads. Do not worry. We are here to answer all of them." He knew that there would be questions, but he had also planned everything that they would say to the finest detail to keep them to a minimum. The people they had gathered together in the Star Craft were intelligent enough to read between the lines. The scientists among them would ask enough relevant questions for the rest of them to understand what was going on and to follow the requests that Hozai and Marta were about to make.

Dr. St. John, now standing tall without his wheelchair, spoke up. "What is the tragedy?" Individuals in the crowd murmured and added, "Yes."

Marta continued, "Thank you," as she acknowledged Dr. St. John. "Here in the **Sagittarius** constellation, seven thousand five hundred light-years from here"—it lit up on the galaxy hologram—"there is a twin star that is about to create a gamma-ray burst directed towards this planet. You call it WR 104."

This was Dr. Kalas's area of expertise. She had wondered why she was aboard this Star Craft up until that point, but the events of her evening were all starting to make sense now. She would be able to help people understand what was going on. Dr. Kalas spoke up. "Yes, we have been aware of WR 104 for many years." She wanted the others in the room to know that the words coming from Marta and Hozai had relevance to what she and her colleagues had been studying. She stood next to Dr. Nucci, and the two of them felt closer than ever. The fact that she knew about the dreams Dr. Nucci had been having was a step towards a closer friendship. The unprecedented events they had seen in the observatory that evening brought them even closer and the rise to the Star Craft another step. But the fact that all of these things were actually connected brought another dimension to the situation they were in. Dr. Kalas wondered if her colleague would tell Hozai, Marta, and the rest of the group about her dreams, but after the rebuke she had received earlier, she dared not bring it up herself.

Hozai remarked, "We know, but we are here to do something about it."

One of the European leaders from England spoke up. "I say, what is the danger? Our planet has weathered many meteors and sun storms in the recent years. We have a strong scientific community that can deal with the threats of the universe." The English are proud of their scientific heritage and had grown a sense of belief over the last ten years or so that science can heal almost anything. They ploughed money into research on cures for cancer and diabetes. They had developed drought-resistant grain that they hoped would help feed the starving. The luminary universities of Oxford and Cambridge led the way in world scientific research, and he was confident that this was the right time to mention the healing power of these institutions. He hadn't banked on the reply.

"Sterilization of life on this planet," firmly stated Marta. It stopped most people in their tracks, and the English leader looked like he was going to pass out.

Dr. St. John and the other astrophysicists agreed with Marta. A hologram of Earth appeared again. Dr. St. John said to the crowd, stepping up two steps and turning around to face the crowd, "If a direct hit of a gamma-ray burst happened here on Earth, life will end, our atmosphere will be blown away, and then without an atmosphere, our sun will fry the surface with ultraviolet rays." As Dr. St. John explained, the hologram displayed what he was saying to give the crowd a visual picture. Daniel said to Simon, "That would be a bad day on the ranch." He knew how to sum up a situation and retain as much humor as he could.

Marta overheard and acknowledged Daniel, "Daniel, it would be the end of the ranch." The two of them shared a smile not dissimilar to the one that the *Mona Lisa* displayed on the wall of the Louvre Museum in Paris. Neither could read it, maybe they were nervous, but the expression matched from one face to the other.

Hozai now spoke up. "Okay, now with this knowledge, what do we need you to do as leaders of your communities? Convince everyone that we are here to rescue the entire population. You all have the most difficult task to keep everyone calm until we can get everyone on our Star Craft."

Now the hologram showed the Earth and the moon. Coming out from behind the moon was a dark sphere nearly the size of the moon. Then on the surface of this dark sphere, about five triangular pieces flew off the surface towards Earth. Marta pointed towards the hologram. "This is the Star Craft." She was pointing at the dark sphere. When she was certain that the rest of the room were with her, she continued, "Our landing craft is docked on the surface of the sphere as triangular vehicles. One of these landing craft brought you all to the Star Craft. We will do the same to everyone else, but our landing craft we will be moving close to the surface to load everyone."

Marta paused before the next sentence. She wanted it to have maximum impact and wanted everyone to understand.

"But the experiences you all had arriving on the Star Craft will happen to everyone else. Our Star Craft has a need to heal. This is why our environment automatically affects all of us this way. It is why those of you that arrived here with afflictions have been cured."

Sierra hugged Simon tightly because she was still feeling a little scared and starting to miss her mother. Sierra was a daddy's girl at heart, but when she needed some comfort, it was easier to go to her mother. As with many family relationships, Sierra went to her father for solutions and her mother for sympathy. Right at that moment, she could not see any solutions to the situation they found themselves in, except for the ones that Hozai and Marta were speaking about, so she felt in need of sympathy. Her father would do for now, but she longed to see her mother again. Until only a few minutes ago, she wondered whether or not she would ever see her mother again, but the calm words of Hozai and Marta had reassured her that she would return to earth again to help educate people on the dangers they faced and the solution that had been presented. Although she was sure she would go home again, Sierra had no idea how long it would be.

She whispered up to Simon, "Daddy, when can we go home?" Simon paused before answering. He hadn't thought about this with everything else that was going on, and he didn't really have an answer.

A new and deep but calming voice spoke to Sierra. "My child, it is all going to be okay. Fear not but trust in the Lord our God. He will forever protect and guide you."

Sierra looked around Simon to a man that had knelt down as he spoke to her. His robe was different than everyone else's. It had light blue and cream-colored stripes. The man had gray and white-streaked hair and long gray beard that made him appear as though he was well into his seventies, if not beyond. But the appearance didn't make sense when matched with the rest of the man. His smile and voice were youthful in stark contrast to his external appearance. Sierra felt reassured by the man and the way he spoke to her. He carried an authority in his gentle voice that calmed her fears immediately. If this man could so calmly and confidently tell her that everything was going to be okay, then who was she to judge? She looked up at to see if anyone else had heard what the man had said.

Simon and Daniel heard his comments to Sierra too. Acknowledging God in that way was refreshing to Simon and calming, given all that they had been through and had heard over the past few hours. Time had been muddled up in all the events, excitement, wonder, and curiosity of what was happening to them. Simon hazarded a guess that they had been on this adventure for hours, but the hours could have been days by now. It was almost impossible to tell. In the next few seconds that passed, it was as though the new man that they were speaking to had pressed the pause button in their lives. No movement was made, no sound was heard. They all froze on the spot to consider the words they had heard. It was the most comforting thing that had happened to any of the three all evening. They were all satisfied that things would be fine by the very words, "It is all going to be okay," that were uttered by this man.

As the world un-paused for the three people, Simon said to this new man, "Hozai says we share the same beliefs of one God. We are Christians too, we also believe in Christ that was the son of that one God." In a way, Simon was seeking for some more information from this man. He was different. He wore different robes to the rest of the people on board the Star Craft, but there was more to him that set him apart from the rest. Simon reckoned him a man of faith, so his question was designed to see how deep that faith was. But the answer he received certainly wasn't any of the ones he had been expecting.

The new man answered Simon without speaking. Simon, Daniel, and Sierra heard his voice in their minds saying, *Yes, my son, all that you have learned about me is true.*

At that moment, Simon, Daniel, and Sierra froze as they stood with a little confusion on their face. But all at once, they realized what had just happened. In unison, they bowed their heads and slowly bent down to their knees. Daniel was overcome by the situation, and he began to weep. He took a few moments with his thoughts.

First the leg and now this! I can't take anymore! I did not think that my faith could ever be tested or strengthened, and I have experienced both on the same day. I had questions when Hozai and Marta were speaking, but now I know I must follow their plans. All of my prayers have led up to this day, and I am eternally thankful for what the Lord has delivered. I will follow my savior in whatever path he sees fit.

As Daniel slowly raised his eyes to his friend, he saw a tear run down Simon's face. The new man reached out for Sierra to walk to him so he could comfort her. Simon and Daniel noticed his wrist above his hands had the marks of the crucifixion. They could no longer contain themselves and bowed their heads to him again. "Lord!" Simon said softly. Other people in the crowd also saw what was happening and also heard the words in their heads. Sierra felt privileged to be kneeling beside Jesus Christ.

The group all looked over at Jesus and the young girl he was kneeling with. They all wanted to crowd round and have an audience with the great man, to touch him, but they retained their calmness. The serenity of the Star Craft was still working its magic on all of those inside.

Jesus walked round with Sierra towards the stage where Hozai and Marta stood. Simon and Daniel were close behind, watching in awe as Sierra walked with Christ. As he reached the place where Hozai and Marta were standing, Sierra stepped back to let him enter the stage on his own. It was clear that he had something to say.

"You have all been selected to be here. We have chosen each of you to be messengers, specifically to help us with the next steps of the evacuation of your planet. It will not be safe to be there over the coming months, so we need to move the population of the earth to a safe place. You are all my children, and I need your help to protect the rest of my flock that are not here right now. Not all of you have been chosen because of your religious outlook. Some of you are here because of your influence, some of you are here because of your scientific knowledge, and some because you will be able to spread the Word to a great number of people in a short span of time. We need the help of each and every one of you to save the people of the planet." Jesus spoke slowly. He wanted the message to be taken in by all of those around him. It reminded him of a time several thousands of years ago when he spoke to a mass of people on a regular basis. He had always had the ability to speak to a crowd of people without the need to shout or gesture wildly. He had their attention.

Once again, the room had a change in atmosphere. The three thousand or more people listened as though they were one person, one face, one pair of ears. The message that was delivered was succinct and explicit. It was their role to save the people of earth. It was their role to help people understand what was happening and to deliver them to safety, but each of them knew that this could be a difficult task. In a world full of information, it was a hard job to get a message across. The Internet was full of conspiracy theorists and people that would probably mock what they had to say. There were those in power who had a vested interest in there being no change at all in the world order. It created an atmosphere of deep thought.

Mariska turned to Abrianna and said, "Jesus? I thought he was crucified two thousand years ago. This cannot be him."

Abrianna responded, "Yes, but he rose and walked on earth for forty days before ascending to be with God. So, Jesus lives as we have all said." Then Dr. St. John stated after overhearing their conversation, "Do you remember Einstein? Of course, you do. His theory of time travel and relativity may have just been proven."

Many of the people on the Star Craft were already turning their thoughts to the task in hand—how they would first speak to their trusted friends and family and then start to speak to those in their community before reaching out to more and more people over the coming hours, days, and weeks, if they had that long. The scenes of serenity and calmness aboard the Star Craft would more than likely not be recreated on earth. A sense of panic and mass hysteria might prevail when a large number of people are moved from one area to another to avoid a potential threat. The message would need to be delivered in the right way to avoid people coming to harm.

Jesus spoke again to ensure that the room stayed mindful to his instructions rather than think about their next actions. He looked to his left and found Hozai looking up at him with a positive expression that confirmed to Jesus that he was the right person to help him on this path. As he looked to the right, he already knew that Marta would have the same expression, giving him the same confidence in her ability. He was right. "I know that the task you face may be tough. I know that you may find people along the way that will doubt you, that will mock you, that will try to stop you. Have faith that you are doing the right thing. If each of you carries out your task, then we can save the people together. You have been chosen because we know you are strong. We know that you will keep on going, even when things are tough. I have faith in all of you. However, God gave humans the ability to choose, so some people may choose to not be rescued."

His next words were not clear to most except to Simon. "I have sent to earth a communication that is just now being uncovered. One of you have this in your possession but are not aware. Use this to tell and convince the skeptics of the words we bring to be from love." Simon immediately remembered the meteorite he left with the scientist.

These final words brought tears to the eyes of many in the room. To be told by Jesus that he had faith in them was an overwhelming moment for so many of the people. The effect of the words was to take everything that had been said away from a technical instruction about how to let people know and get them to safety to a spiritual instruction about how their faith will get them through what was bound to be a difficult time. Simon thought about his faith as Jesus paused for a few moments. If he could get through the day that they had just experienced, then he was sure to be able to harness these events into an even stronger faith when he returned to work. He already had the support of his friend, Daniel, who could make sense of any situation, and his daughter, Sierra, who was passionate and levelheaded. Then his friends and congregation at church would be among the first to be told, and he was certain that he could count on their support. He steeled himself for the path ahead. Although at this point he did not know when he would return to his earth, his family, his friends, and his congregation, he wanted to be ready at a moment's notice. Simon was ready for the task ahead.

Jesus began again, "I say that your quest will not be an easy one. I know that putting these words into actions will take a lot of courage. People will try to undermine you. They will look at you and say that you are crazy. People are resistant to change. They are happy to go along with their normal lives without thinking about the bigger picture. You will need to be persuasive. When you look at this through the eyes of a skeptic, then you can see how it may look to them. You will be telling them that they are insignificant and imminent danger, and to save themselves, they must get on board a spaceship with aliens. Of course, this will bring doubts and mockery from some, but do not judge them. They will be frightened, and they will approach this situation with closed minds. It is your job to comfort them, to tell them everything will be fine, and to open their minds. Once you have gained their trust, then you can lead them to safety."

Daniel thought about all of this for a moment. He warmed to the task that had been set out in front of him. He was a great communicator, and he had a large circle of friends and acquaintances that he could start with to spread the Word. But it wasn't those that he knew that worried him; it was those that he did not know. There were many people that he had met that entered into any conversation about their spirituality with a closed mind. He had tried to start conversations about the church with some of his old army buddies but received nothing but abuse. He was concerned that this might be the reception he got from many people now.

He knew that once he had the people that would believe and work with him, then he would be able to use them as well to help spread the message of hope and salvation. If Jesus had chosen him to be one of the people to spread the Word, then he must have faith that he was capable of doing it. He gained inner strength for the journey ahead, but he wasn't ready for the next words spoken.

"When we look at the Bible," Jesus said, "it states that the earth is ruled by the devil. It states that Satan is the god of the world. It was true in the days when I walked the earth. My message of peace and tolerance did not fit with the rule of the Romans and their vengeful beliefs. I was cast aside as a heretic. I was labeled as a bad influence on anyone that dared to listen to me. I am the way, the truth, and the light, and no one shall get to the Father except through me, as was written in your Bible. I was crucified to stop my message from becoming widely known." At this point, Jesus lifted his arms. He did this to ensure that the full attention of the room was on him, although the action was not necessary. What it did do was expose the marks on his wrists from the crucifixion. It focused the attention of those in the Star Craft on the fact that Jesus had died to save people before. It made them all realize that the journey they were about to follow as not just difficult. It was potentially life-threatening.

Jesus lowered his arms and continued, "I was seen as a threat and as such had to be snuffed out. The forces of evil on the planet Earth at that time were strong. They were powerful, and they controlled all of the important parts of daily life. Don't make the mistake of thinking that times have changed. The devil still rules over the earth and still has control of power. You will find the influence of the devil at the higher levels of politics. You will find the influence of the devil in the media, controlling what people think, say, and do. You will find the influence of the devil anywhere that simple people have not opened their mind to the teachings of the Bible. The devil finds willing servants in all walks of life. These people are not willing servants not because they embrace the devil himself but because they do not embrace my love and leave a space in their heart for hatred."

Simon thought of the Bible. He remembered the words of 2 Corinthians 4:4, "In whom the god of this world hath blinded the minds of them which believe not, lest the light of the glorious gospel of Christ, who is the image of God, should shine unto them." He had spoken these words in his sermons more than once, but the impact of them on his congregation had never been at the same level of impact he felt at that exact time. He had spoken them before, but much of his teaching in church felt abstract to many of the people much of the time. When he used the words of the Bible and then put them into an everyday context, it resonated with the people he was speaking to. He was able to make a connection with their everyday lives, and then they sat up and took notice. But the words of 2 Corinthians 4:4 had eluded his connection to real life until now. He knew that the people in his congregation would now be able to make the link between this quote and the situation they were about to learn that they faced. He listened as Jesus began to speak again.

"Money has made the devil powerful. It has given him the ability to control the parts of life that he can. He has developed a pyramid of power by influencing the elite in many parts of life. From the few, he can filter down his message of evil to the rest of the population that he seeks to control. He influences people's lifestyle in many ways. He creates evil and then watches as it rips through parts of the world unchecked. He will try to stand in your way. He will try to stop you."

Jesus followed a now familiar pattern for all the people on board the Star Craft. He would speak a few sentences and then pause for a few moments to let it sink in. He knew that what these people were being told would be difficult to take in, so he made it as easy as he could. He was impressed. Jesus thought that the people that had been chosen displayed great patience and restraint in the face of such challenging news.

"At this time, I cannot set foot on the earth. While the devil rules the earth, it is full of sin and evil for me to be there. I have met you in the sky for now. If I return, then conflict will ensue, and I want to resolve this with peace. I trust you to deliver my message of peace."

The room turned from an awed silence to a murmur. People were talking to those that stood close to them, people that they knew, people that they had been brought on to the Star Craft with. The mood in the air was electrifying as the group of people absorbed the request for help from Jesus Christ. Then people started crossing over to other groups and talking to them. Larger and larger groups formed as people spoke of their desire to help. The whole room was prepared to tackle whatever lay in front of them to help out the savior and the human race.

Daniel, Simon, and Sierra were talking to the astrophysicists, Dr. Nucci, Dr. Kalas, and Dr. St. John. They were talking about how liberating an experience it was to see the man that they had worshipped for so long. Daniel and Dr. St John were united in their experience of being healed. Both had a newfound pair of legs, and both were determined to repay Jesus for the healing that he had enacted on their body. Both were ready to go back to earth at that moment. There were still questions to be asked and answers to be given, but the main thrust of the information had been given. Then Marta spoke. "Our plan is to start Rashure within thirty days. This time schedule could be modified depending on conditions on the planet."

Daniel turned to Simon with a confused look and said, "Did she say Rapture?"

Simon responded slowly, "I don't think so."

It was time for the messengers to deliver the message to the people of earth.

Chapter 6

Sharing the News

After speaking, Jesus left the main area of the Star Craft. He had said his part and his presence had inspired people to go about their business and set out to save the people of earth. He was not needed for the next part. It was time for people to ask questions.

Hozai and Marta knew that people would have questions. Many of the answers were already planned and outlined in advance because they had been working on this for many, many years. They were prepared for many of the questions and were able to answer them quickly. In order to save time and make the process more efficient, people were grouped up with others that they would be sharing a craft back to earth with. This would allow the groups to form naturally and start conversing with each other so that Hozai and Mart did not end up answering the same questions over again.

Some of the questions were not ones that Hozai or Marta had the answer to. Questions such as "How am I going to do it?" or even "What do I do?" were not ones that they were prepared to answer. Hozai reassured everyone. "Do your best and be ready to leave when it is your time. We know we will not convince everyone to be rescued. The Lord will still be with those that chose to remain behind."

Each person had to find their own way to communicate with others and to spread the Word to as many people as they could. Each person would find their own method once they arrived back on earth. Some of the celebrities had huge followings on social media or through their television shows. Many of the politicians were able to call on their government structures to be able to speak to their whole nation in one go. People like Simon, Daniel, and Sierra would be able to have meaningful conversations with people on a one-on-one basis to make sure that the message was understood and spread through word of mouth. Nothing had been left to chance. The three thousand-plus people that were aboard the Star Craft were there because of their positive intentions and because they each had an effective way of reaching out to others.

Once all of the questions were answered and the people were ready to do the work of the Lord, then the groups were taken to separate transport craft to be taken back to their own part of the world. From high above at the top of the main room of the Star Craft, it must have looked like quite a scene. There were more than three thousand people all making their orderly way to their respective parts of the Star Craft to begin their journey back to Earth. They looked like a determined bunch of people that had all come together for one purpose. You could tell just by looking at the group that they would do everything within their power to achieve the aim that they had been set. Just by looking at the group, you could see that they would give their all. But as with many teams, there was an overriding feeling that they were far more than the sum of their parts. On the face of it all, it seemed impossible that an army of three thousand could instigate an evacuation of seven billion people, give or take. Breaking down the task into pure numbers made it look impossible to anyone, even those with the most faith and most energy in the world. But with the collective power that they felt and the backing of Jesus and his faith in their ability, the groups that were forming to return to carry out the task in their own part of the world were confident that they could achieve this mammoth feat. They were ready to save the people of the planet Earth.

It was an army in any other name. An army without guns, planes, or tanks. An army that didn't have generals or the latest battlefield technology. An army that wasn't setting out to destroy, hurt, or maim the people that they were seeking out. The only things that they wanted to destroy, hurt, or maim was evil, distrust, and indifference. These were the enemies now. These were the things that would finish the human race and leave the future of mankind in jeopardy.

The groups of people filed towards the areas they had been allocated to when speaking to Hozai and Marta. Each had been given a letter, and each letter represented a part of the Star Craft that they would go to in order to get their ride back home. Once they arrived home, then their missions began. People patiently boarded their own craft, and as each one was fully loaded, the doors were closed, and the ships started their countdown to leave. Hozai and Marta stood in the center of the room where everyone was gathered before, and as the spacecrafts were filled and the doors closed, they returned to the normality that they had lived their lives in for many years before. But they knew that their normal life was coming to an end, and the mission that they had been selected for was about to begin. It was soon to be the beginning of their time for action. Both bristled with excitement at the future that lay in front of them. Both knew that they had delivered the first part of their task to the best of their ability. Both knew to a degree that the future of the human race was now out of their hands, at least, for the next phase of Rashure.

On spacecraft number 1, Dr. Liu Xiang and her PhD student, Shu Yi Chang, sat together. They had been side by side from the moment they left China for their trip to Göbekli Tepe. They had not left each other at all during their elevation from the site at Göbekli Tepe to the Star Craft, and they sat next to each other. During the whole trip from China to Turkey to space and back to China again, they would probably never have been more than a few feet apart. They both looked around when they were in the Star Craft and saw people that looked like they knew each other by standing in groups. They thought that people had been chosen in groups of two or three so that they had someone to share the experience with. Now that they were returning to Earth to spread the Word, they felt that people had been chosen in small groups to support each other and maybe to protect each other too.

Shu Yi Chang thought that she was going home to enact her wish in a roundabout way. With dreams of cutting the smog in Beijing, a lifetime ambition, she was saving the people of Beijing from the smog but not in exactly the way she had planned. In fact, she hadn't planned anything at all—just dreamed. That was part of the issue. There were no real ways in which to deal with smog that were presently known to science, so this would be the quickest way to deliver them to safety.

On board with them was the Premier of China. He was a small man with the hopes of a large nation resting on his shoulders. Shu Yi Chang had always thought that he looked as though he was being dragged towards the ground every time she had seen him in the news. But in the flesh, he was different. He looked as though he could carry the weight of the world on those shoulders. Maybe it was the experience that he had been through and the faith that Jesus had shown in them all, but he felt different now to Shu Yi. She had also noticed Dr. Wang Lee on the spaceship. He was an eminent scientist and well known in Chinese research circles. Shu Yi had never met him before, but her companion, Dr. Xiang, had.

"Shu Yi, allow me to introduce you to Dr. Wang Lee," said Dr. Xiang. She was a little in awe of the other doctor because he was world-renowned for his work in the field of archaeology. All three looked at each other, bowed their head slightly, and smiled.

"And as we are introducing people, I would like you both to meet our Premier," replied Dr. Wang Lee. Shu Yi Chang and Dr Liu Xiang stood forward and shook hands with the Premier. In their normal society, they probably would not have done this, but the world seemed a different place now. The reverence that was reserved for people of authority in the Communist Party in China no longer seemed appropriate.

The four of them spoke for a few minutes about the situation they found themselves in and how they would go about delivering the message to the people. The Premier asked the three scientists if they had any idea why they were chosen to be on the Star Craft in the first place. The conversation moved on to how the three of them worked in the field, and it clicked to them all that some of these ancient monuments had links to the events that had unfolded. The Premier wanted the three of them to join him in speaking to other members of the party, as he felt that their background and research would prove influential.

"I would be honored if you can help me explain to the rest of my party and to the people of our glorious nation the importance of taking the right action at this time. Our country has always taken what it believes to be the right steps for ourselves. It is now the right time to help ourselves and the rest of the world at the same time. We have much influence in Africa and across the rest of Asia. Once we have secured the safety of our people, we will help to secure the safety of our allies," said the Premier.

Dr. Wang Lee spoke for the three of them; from the conversation he already had been involved with for his fellow scientists, he already knew that they would have the same feelings as him. "We will help you in whatever way we can. As scientists, we are compelled to help others. All of our research has been to move forward the knowledge of the human race so that we can learn lessons for the future. That will not stop now we know the earth is in danger. We will continue to spend every waking hour helping others. You have our backing." Shu Yi Yang and Dr. Liu Xiang both nodded in agreement. They would help the evacuation of the planet Earth in any way they could. This agreement and action was replicated across all the other transport ships that were taking people back to their regions. People from vastly different backgrounds and sometimes from across the other side of the political spectrum were coming together to plan united action. The chosen people were coming together in the way that Jesus had wished for. They were coming together to enact his plan.

Once they arrived back in China, the Premier would grant the three scientists and all other Chinese citizens on board immediate membership of the top echelons of the Chinese Communist Party. They would have access to all state secrets and all the information and resources they would need to help him. The Chinese government was a closed group of party officials that had worked their way up the ranks. The Premier was unsure how the rest of the higher echelon would take these newcomers, but he had no option but to enlist the help of the others that had been on the Star Craft with him. He had no option but to use all the power and influence he could muster to get the message out to the billion or more people that lived in his country.

The Premier had seen the country grow from a backwater to a superpower over his lifetime. Although many of the people in China still lived off the land in relative poverty, the country had grown into a huge economy over the last years. The leaders of the country had seen the impact that their plentiful supply of cheap labor could do for an economy, and they opened up trade with the rest of the world. It kick-started when they took over Hong Kong from the British in 1997, and the country never looked back from there. Hong Kong gave the Chinese a trading link to the rest of the world, and this grew and grew until they were the only economy with the might to stand up to the American juggernaut. The last fifteen years had seen massive investment in the cities of China. They were eating up resources at high speed, and all of this was fueled by the trade links they had made in Asia, across Australasia, and into Africa and Europe.

His party had worked hard to give their people a standing on the world stage. He wasn't about to relinquish that now. He was determined that China would convince their population first and would lead the way for the rest of the world. China would be moral leaders as well as financial ones in the new Earth.

As the ship bound for China made its way from its docking station, another spacecraft was still boarding. It was headed for the Old Persian area of the world, and the people heading home there were waiting patiently to get on board. One of the first to board was Dr. Kadir. He had said good-bye to his colleagues from Göbekli Tepe and wished them well in their quest. Even when Shu Yi Chang and Dr. Liu Xiang were talking to the Premier of China, they still had Dr. Kadir in their minds. His part of the world was a much more difficult place to get a unified message across. It was a melting pot of races and religions, and the varied leaders would need to be united and strong to help all of their people. Any religious leader in that part of the world that even as much as shared a stage with a leader from another religion was looked upon with a degree of suspicion by many of their followers. It would be a time that needed conciliation and peace like no other in the recent history of the region. Dr. Kadir sat in his seat aboard the transport craft and reflected on the day that he had just been through and the potential of the days ahead of him. He was filled with positivity and enthusiasm every time he looked backwards into time. The audience with Jesus and the other people around him filled him with the belief that they can achieve something that looked impossible from the outside. He knew that the strength of character in the people he would be working with was something that was brought out by the words of Christ. But when he looked forward it didn't seem as straightforward. The inspiration and hope of the message was one thing. Actually, applying that on the ground surrounded by all the problems of being on his own city of Istanbul, not only his own country of Turkey but the whole region.

J.R. PHILLIPS

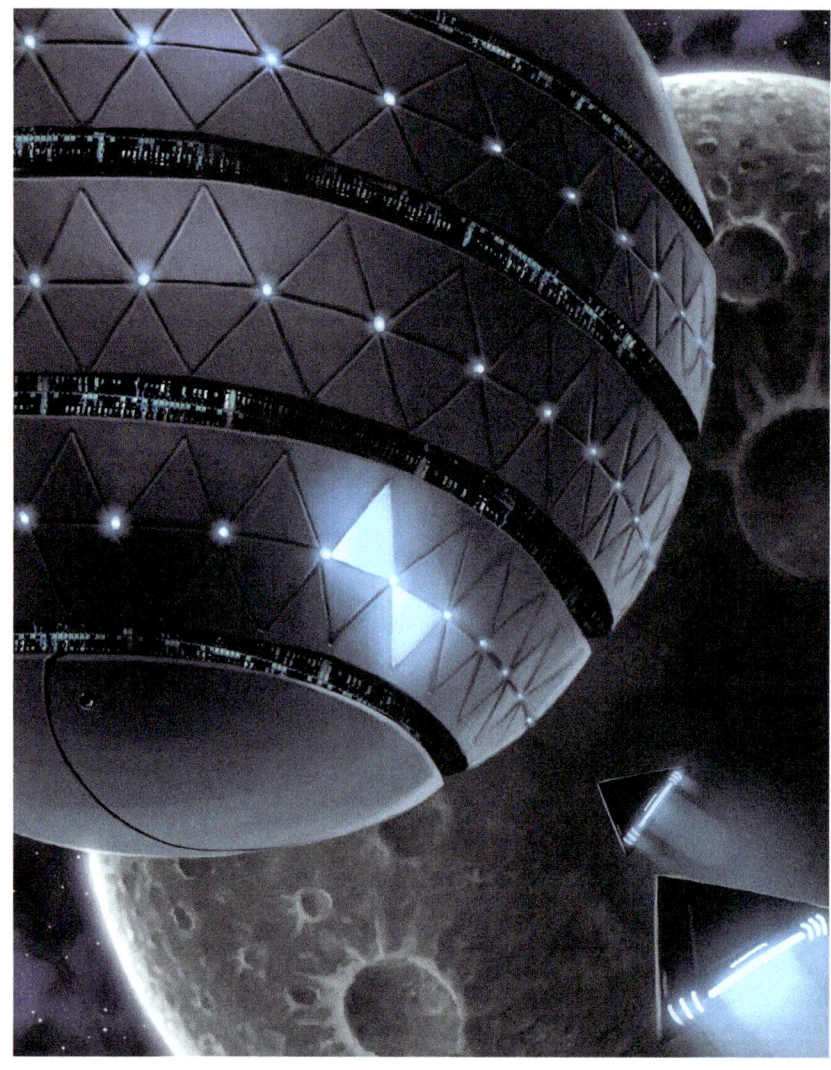

Istanbul had long been known at the gateway between East and West. In the early days of international trade, it saw spices, tea, silks, and opium travel from East to West in exchange for money. With half the city in Asia and the other half in Europe, it was at the center of the most important trading route in the world. The bazaars and souks of Istanbul were still full of wonders from all parts of that trading route when Dr. Kadir left his home a couple of weeks earlier. He had no reason to believe that it would look any different on his return. But he wasn't returning to the souks and bazaars; he was returning to spread the message that would save his people. Turkey was a mix of religions and a mix of people. It was working towards joining the European Union on its Western borders and keeping a keen eye on the wars of the Arab countries to its East. It was uniquely positioned to look both East and West and help to provide safety for people on both sides. But the Turkish government found movement very difficult to do in such a situation. Every time it looked to forge ties with the West, it lost ground in the East and vice versa.

Dr. Kadir knew that this would be a tough task. He hoped that the other people getting on board the spacecraft would have the power to unite and inspire. His hopes were answered when he saw the people entering after him.

The next person to enter the spacecraft after Dr. Kadir was the Dalai Lama. He was the spiritual leader of many people and had been formally recognized as the fourteenth Dalai Lama as far back as 1939 when he was only four years old, although his reign didn't officially start until his fifteenth birthday. Before taking over as the spiritual leader, he was a monk at the Gelug School in Tibet. He was renowned throughout the world as someone who practiced peace and had been given an audience with all the world leaders, and even addressed the United Nations in New York. Dr. Kadir knew that the Dalai Lama would have a great influence over peace-loving people, especially Buddhists in the region, and have a reach to the greater world.

Following behind the Dalai Lama was another figure that Dr. Kadir immediately recognized. It was the Crown Prince of Saudi Arabia, the second most important man in the House of Saud. Like

Turkey, Saudi Arabia had an influential position in world politics. They were the most Western-looking Muslim nation and had forged strong links with the United States of America and many countries in Europe. They would be important allies in spreading the word through the Muslim parts of the region and keeping the lines of communication open with the Western powers. Saudi Arabia sat on vast oil fields and allowed US air forces the use of their airports during both Gulf Wars. This made them friends in the West and some enemies in the Gulf, but their immense wealth had allowed them to build bridges with their neighbors again. Dr. Kadir had seen the huge mansions and fleets of expensive cars that the Crown Prince owned on television shows back home in Turkey. He was seen by the rest of the world as a bit of a playboy, but he had a smart head on his shoulders and kept a fine balance between doing business and cultivating relationships. Dr. Kadir could see why the Crown Prince of Saudi Arabia was chosen to be on the Star Craft. He could see his money and influence saving a lot of lives if used in the right way.

The Prime Minister of Israel was the next man to step aboard the transport craft that was headed for the Old Persian area and took a seat next to Dr. Kadir. He introduced himself to Dr. Kadir, but the introductions were not necessary. The Prime Minister of Israel was big news in Turkey, and nobody would have missed his visit to the city of Istanbul recently. He was on an ambassadorial trip to grow a strong relationship with Turkey before their journey to becoming a full member of the European Union. Israel could do no trade with its neighbors in the region because of the political tensions that existed there. So, the Prime Minister of Israel saw a future opportunity to follow Turkey into the European Union and become a string trading partner for Europe. His visit was treated in the same way as one would from the Queen of England or the President of the United States. Turkey knew the benefits of bringing Israel into the European Union club with them, so they laid out the red carpet for the Israeli Prime Minister. It was all over the news, there were processions along the main streets of Istanbul and the capital of Turkey, Ankara. He was another heavyweight world leader that was born just after the World War II. Many nations were led by people that were born at that time, and it often meant that they were wary of others. The climate after World War II and as the Cold War began, its freeze was one of suspicion and fear. The leaders that were young at this time were suspicious and fearful as a result.

Dr. Kadir asked, "Do you think that your people will listen? They have made a migration to safety once in the last seventy years. Are they ready to do it again?"

The Prime Minister of Israel paused. He mulled over his thoughts and replied, "The people of my country have been handed down the stories from their parents and grandparents of the evil in Europe and their flight to the promised land. They will be ready to follow the same course of action that protected their ancestors, but they will leave our home with a heavy heart." He seemed convinced that he was able to persuade his people to leave their home. "If I can communicate what I just experienced and heard from my heart, most will listen."

Dr. Kadir smiled, and the Israeli Prime minister smiled back. They were both glad to be on their way home, but both were also eager to see who would board their spacecraft next. In the eyes of Dr. Kadir, they were forming quite a group. He hadn't taken much time to look around the large room when they were in the Star Craft because he was making sure that his colleagues, Dr. Liu Xiang, and her PhD student, Shu Yi Chang, were okay. He had only met them a few hours earlier, but he felt as though he had a need to protect them like a father. Dr. Kadir wanted to make sure that they were coping with the events that were unfolding. For the Turkish doctor, it was a coping mechanism. The more he focused on the needs of his two Chinese colleagues, then the less he thought about his own situation. In a bizarre way, thinking about the fact that these two women had been plucked from the earth by a strange light and were now on board a spacecraft receiving instructions on their role in saving the population of the planet helped him forget that he had also gone through the exact same experience. With his attention firmly fixed on Shu Yi and Dr. Xiang, he didn't know who would be joining him and the others on the transport craft headed for his home region.

There seemed to be a delay in people entering the spacecraft. Dr. Kadir had sat in a seat that was facing the entrance, partly because he was a bad traveler and partly because he wanted to see people as they boarded. But from his position, he could only see people as they actually entered the transport craft, not as they approached. So, for a few minutes, as nobody else came through the door to start the journey, Dr. Kadir thought that this might be it. There seemed to be nobody else coming on to the transport craft. He started to wonder if there were enough people. Sure enough, those that had boarded that he had recognized were influential and he was sure were chosen wisely. But in his home region, surely there was a need for far more people than this. His worries were eased after a couple of minutes. With no explanation for the holdup, the Prime Minister of India arrived, stopped in the doorway, scanned the transport craft for faces, and then took a seat at the rear of the craft.

It was as though he was looking for acknowledgment as he walked through the door onto their craft. The Prime Minister of India was used to being recognized and fawned over. As the head of the government in a country of a billion people, he had his every whim catered for. After the founders of the county in Gandhi and Nehru, he was considered the most important man in India, certainly the most important living man. He was taking India along a similar path to the one that China had forged a few decades earlier. With a massive population and low wages, the Indians were able to compete on the world stage once they got their infrastructure in the right place. Indian universities delivered up to another two million graduates every year to their mobile and educated workforce. The Prime Minister wanted to use the massive resources of the country to become a global superpower. So, because of his radical program of reforms, he became a central figure in Indian life. Those that were benefitting from his early reforms and becoming wildly rich treated him as another god. They waited for his every word, and in their eyes, he could do no wrong. This sector of India society would be easy to deliver the message to. They would listen to him and follow.

But the rest of India was largely concentrated in the rural areas and had little access to the media, to political discussion, or to big business. In rural India, the only global company that gained any traction was Coca-Cola. Somehow, there was Coke branding on billboards, on the side of local eateries, and on T-shirts. Nothing else had the power to infiltrate like a Coke. In his election campaign, he had to cover his vast county for eighteen hours a day. It seemed to him that he was visiting the rural parts of India village by village. This strategy worked, and he won an overwhelming majority, particularly from the rural parts of India. He might need to employ the same tactics on his return.

There was a steady flow of people entering the transport craft now headed for the Old Persian region of the world. Dr. Kadir didn't recognize all of them, but each walked on to the craft with a sense of serenity and a sense of purpose. He could feel it in the air as each arrived, looked around, and took a seat. In his position near the door, Dr. Kadir received a smile from all of the people that walked on board. He was given a great deal of determination by the human contact that he received while seated there. At times during the events of the last few hours (he was sure it was only a few hours, but it could have been any amount of time—his body and brain had no idea how long it was since he stood at Göbekli Tepe), he had wondered if the people of earth were worth saving. Having had a view of the terrors of the world from his television screen and computer, he saw some of the deeds that mankind had brought to the world and thought twice if saving the people would bring about a change in the way they were. He looked through the television news every evening wherever he was in the world and was often filled with a despair of how humanity was. Murders, rapes, drugs, gun crime, prostitution, war, and famine filled his evening TV news screen on a daily basis. Was there really a future for a race of people that inflicted this on each other or stood by while it was happening?

But the words of Jesus started him on the train of thought that there was a lot of good in the world. These people were weak rather than evil. They had been caught up in the devil's plan for the world and enacted his sins. Once the teachings of Christ were back in the forefront of people's minds, then they would turn against sin and embrace a good life. Then as each of the messengers entered the spacecraft and looked at Dr. Kadir in a connected way, he was surer than ever that they would prevail. Every person that boarded that spacecraft made Dr. Kadir feel as though he was part of something real, something that was worth saving. There was no alternative. The other option was to not try, to leave the human race to perish. That was as big a sin as any that he had seen on the news over the years.

As the doors were closing, the last person on their craft stepped inside. Dr. Kadir had a feeling that one person was missing when he scanned the room, and the call went out for the doors to close. And it made him wonder about why that person was excluded. Over the years, successive American presidents had been vocal about the evils of Iran. There had been scandals, controversy, and incidents between the United States and Iran since the overthrow of the Shah in the late 1970s. The incumbent president always had something to say about Iran at the United Nations, during NATO meetings, and whenever an atrocity happened somewhere in the world. They were part of George W. Bush's axis of terror, even though there was no evidence linking them at that time to 9-11 or sponsoring terrorism. When Dr. Kadir looked around the spacecraft, this was the only person that he knew he would recognize that was missing from the selection of people assembled with him. Maybe the presidents were right? Maybe the leader of Iran is evil? Maybe they have been excluded because they are on the side of the devil?

The countdown to the doors closing began. Ten . . . nine . . . eight . . . seven . . . six . . . As it reached five, the last figure walked in. It was the Supreme Leader of Iran—the Ayatollah. This was the figure that much of the Presidents' wrath had been aimed at. This was the man that represented the unacceptable face of Islam if the succession of American Presidents since 1979 had aimed their attacks. But he didn't seem evil at all. He was the last to board the spacecraft, and he stopped and smiled with Dr. Kadir as all of the others had done. He made a human connection, and Dr. Kadir felt no evil in his presence.

The Ayatollah was the second Supreme Leader of Iran since the country was run by Muslim clerics. He had been in command of Iran since 1989 and had made such contacts throughout the world with the notable exception of the United States. The Ayatollah was seen as the spiritual leader of the country and rarely left the state of Iran. There was also a President who dealt with external affairs, but the spiritual leadership of the people of Iran was all under the influence of the Ayatollah. As was the control of the military. Dr. Kadir had thought until that point that a major regional power was unrepresented on the transport craft. Now he knew that the immense spiritual pull that the Ayatollah had over his people would be more than likely to follow and be led to safety away from the earth and the threats that it would soon face.

As Dr. Kadir and the rest of the people that populated his transport craft left the Star Craft and headed back to their home, their thoughts were all on their region. For the doctor and his country, it meant a new period in their history where they looked to the East. The immediate West was covered by a transport craft that was leaving the other side of the Star Craft at exactly the same time.

Michelle Moreau rested her head on her husband's shoulder. The two of them had rarely been apart since they first met in their home city of Paris, and they were determined to face this side by side. She had grown tired from the intensity of the time since they had been transported from the site at Puma Punku. She wanted to rest her eyes for a few minutes. She was sure that there would be a lot of discussion as the transport craft approached Europe and took them home, so she needed to rest her head and gather her thoughts before this happened.

I am so glad that I have my husband, John-Paul, and my faith. Without these two things, I think I would be pulling my hair out right now. I am blessed to be married to a calm and generous man like John-Paul. He made sure that I was okay throughout everything we have been through without a thought for himself. With anyone else, I would be unable to face the task that lies ahead, but with John-Paul by my side, I am certain that we can succeed. It sounds crazy, there are so few of us and so many people to convince, but I am absolutely sure that with this man, I can do anything. Today I have seen Jesus. I have spent all of my life looking to this man for inspiration in the knowledge that I would never see or hear from him. How could I? He died thousands of years ago.

He died for our sins. But today not only have I seen Christ, I have also heard him speak. I have been told by him that he has faith in me. That gives me more power than I have ever had. That gives me the confidence I need to deliver his message.

John-Paul Moreau sat upright with his eyes open. He had a role to play. He knew that his wife would be concerned about the path that lay ahead, so he had to be the strong one. It was a role that he had played for their whole relationship. They had been through some adversity during their time together, and he had always stepped up to the plate. A few years earlier, they were trying to have a baby. It hadn't happened naturally, so they went off to the fertility clinic attached to the Paris-Sorbonne University where they both worked. After some initial tests and procedures, the fertility doctors were sure that they could help. After two rounds of fertility treatment, Michelle fell pregnant. The two of them were as happy as anyone could be. But this happiness was not to last. Michelle lost the baby, and in the procedure to remove the unborn child from her, she also lost any hope of ever conceiving again. They were devastated, but John-Paul had to be the strong one, the one that saw the light at the end of the tunnel, even though he wasn't even looking in that direction. He wanted to wallow in his own self-pity at that time but had to focus all of his attention on his wife and the pain that she was going through.

He had been strong before that and strong ever since but had never needed to tap into his great resources of resilience and focus as he had at that time until now. He knew that every part of this was going to need all of his will for them to get through what lay ahead, and he would have to support his wife through it as well. She was his world, and he could only think of how it might affect her. He would carry out his duty to the rest of the planet, but his primary concern was the welfare of his beautiful wife. No sooner had the transport craft taken off then, John-Paul's will was needed.

"I propose that the European Union headed by Germany takes care of this," said the German Chancellor. "We have led the people of Europe to a period of peace longer than any our continent has ever known. We are the ideal people to lead the people of Europe to safety." The German Chancellor was the biggest beast in the craft.

She had been chancellor for as long as anyone could remember and was the only current European leader that would stand up on the world stage with the likes of the American President and the Premier of China.

"There are too many diverse people to just stand in front of a television camera and tell people what to do," replied the British Prime Minister. "Our people are deeply skeptical of the European Union and may not react well to being dictated to by the powers that be. I think that we need a coordinated plan."

The German Chancellor looked towards her natural allies. In the years since the formation of the European Union Germany, France, Belgium, The Netherlands, and Italy had been at the forefront of the project. Along with Luxembourg, these were the founders of the European Union. But she did not get the support that perhaps she was looking for. The British Prime Minister had a point.

"We are many people. There are so many religions, so many belief systems in Europe that we need the input of all the leaders to stand a chance of making this evacuation as efficient as possible," said the French President. The German Chancellor had not been expecting any resistance from the French at all. They had been the main partners in turning the EU from an economic project to one that was social and political. This was a break in relations that was not anticipated at this moment in time.

Europe was indeed made up of many religions and subreligions. Even under the umbrella of Christianity, there were separate parts of the church in each country such as Lutheranism, Anglicanism, and Calvinism. The one thing they could agree of was the words of God. Everything else seemed to be up for debate. To make this work, there needed to be religious and nonreligious leaders called to listen to the message and then trusted to deliver it to their own followers.

"We should work together on a plan that will lead people to the right conclusions themselves rather than try to impose it on them. The people of Europe are able to make up their own minds as long as the facts are conveyed in a convincing way," said the British Prime Minister, fresh to the job but looking forward to the challenge.

John-Paul saw this as his opportunity to add the view of the common man, "I don't have the power and influence that all of you carry but I have something to say. We are all children of God but the diverse religions of Europe see themselves as belonging to their own part of that. We must unite the religious leaders of Europe and deliver the message to them. But we must also look to the number of people in Europe that have no religion. Their views and faith will change once they hear the message and are saved by the Lord Jesus Christ but we need to reach them too."

Michelle was incredibly proud of her husband. Not many people would have stood up to the leaders of Europe and given their opinion. But John-Paul was different to most people. He wanted to help, he wanted to get the right thing done, but most of all, he wanted to protect her.

As John-Paul looked around, he could see the military leaders of Europe standing close to each other. He suspected that before their visit to the Star Craft, they would have approached a situation like this with a plan of attack. They would have briefed their commanders-in-chief that military intervention was the only way to operate. Now, after an audience with Jesus and being faced with a situation as this, all the bombs, warplanes, and destroyers in the world could not solve this crisis. They all had to rethink the way that they viewed the world. Perhaps they were considering how to make a new life without weapons in the new world they would all soon inhabit. Whatever thoughts were running through their heads, John-Paul was sure it did not involve their armies doing anything other than helping to evacuate people.

The discussions continued throughout the journey from the Star Craft to home. The leaders all agreed that the way John-Paul had described things was the right way to go about it. They had to pull together and gain consensus. Any other way could lead to panic and confusion. The evacuation had to be managed in a controlled and orderly fashion so there was no risk to the lives of the people that they were trying to save.

The leaders agreed to meet again as soon as they were on the ground. Then they could have access to the information they needed and start plans to mobilize their resources. Europe was going to be a tough nut to crack, but they were all sure that they were going about it the right way. The faith that Jesus had shown in them had to be repaid.

Another transport craft was loaded with passengers and had started to move away from the large Star Craft that had housed all the messengers of Jesus. The voices that could be heard throughout this spacecraft all had American accent, and they all wanted to be heard. Luckily for them, the journey would give people a chance to have their say.

Simon stood by a floor-to-ceiling window looking down at the earth beneath. He had been standing there silently since he had been the first one to board the spacecraft with his daughter, Sierra, and his good friend, Daniel. All three had stood there looking out of the window from the moment they arrived. None spoke to each other for all this time. They were all comfortable enough in each other's company to stand in silence for long periods. They all knew what each other was thinking anyway after the long journey that had started at the church and had brought them to this window, the window that looked back towards where the journey had started. The three of them wanted to go home. None were afraid after the encounter with their savior, but they wanted a few minutes alone with their loved ones before the work started on saving the people of planet Earth.

Both Simon and Sierra wanted to see Sierra's mom. They were a close family that spent a lot of time together. Sierra was growing up fast, and the way that she spoke with confidence to the others at church that night made her mom realize that she wouldn't be her little girl forever. She was growing up fast and would have her own ideas about the world and what she wanted to do.

Simon was a typical father. He didn't see all of this in his little girl and thought that she would stay this way forever. He just adored spending time with Sierra and was so happy that she had an interest in the things that interested him, especially church and fishing! As time went by, he involved her in more aspects of the church. He could see her making a wonderful preacher just like him and his father. He wasn't making plans for her but wanted to see her gifts put to good use. All of that was up in the air in the situation they now faced. He had no idea what the new world would do for the prospects of his daughter or anyone else he would meet from now on. All he could think about was saving as many people as possible with the help of those he loved. Once Sierra was safe, then he could worry about her future. Without a safe passage, away from the threatened Earth, she would have no future. He was desperate to see his wife as well. She was the rock that their marriage, church, and community was founded on. She made sure that there were people in the church and that all the preparations were made. While the three were out fishing, it was Simon's wife that organized to clean the church, set out all the tables, made sure those that were invited were still coming, and generally made the evening a success. They made a great team, and Simon wanted her by his side every step of the way when it came to rescuing the people they would meet.

Daniel had few friends and family outside of the church; he just didn't have the time. His brother lived in the next town, and he wanted to get home and tell him first of what had happened, especially with his leg and what was about to happen. His brother was the only family that Daniel had left, and he wanted to be able to look him in the eye and warn him about the danger that he faced. It was the least he could do.

Simon turned around to see the vast number of people on board the transport craft headed back home. The focus of the conversation seemed to be on the bank balances of all involved rather than their lives being in danger. Simon moved closer so he could listen some more.

"The Senate will pass a bill that prevents a run on the banks. We will do whatever we have to if a time comes to support the stock market. We know that the news will provoke panic, and we will put all necessary measures in place to protect our financial standing in the world," said a large senator that Simon recognized from the television. He knew the face but not the name. The senator was short, shorter even than he looked on TV, and had lost most of his hair. In a style that Simon had never understood, he had swept the remaining hair from one side of his head over and across in what looked like some vain attempt to hide his almost-baldness. Simon smiled.

The senator looked across at a group of men that had stood closely together. It looked as though they were trying to form some sort of power group by standing in a line, all looking in the same direction at the same time. One of the group spoke. "We heard all of this with the financial meltdown that happened in two thousand eight. You can't protect anyone from this situation because the markets don't lie, and people will draw their own conclusions. You can't postpone panic. It will happen tomorrow or the next day, but the only thing that is certain is panic. Nothing affects the markets like panic. Politicians are not the right people to deal with a financial crisis." The atmosphere was not strained, but the opinions being offered were forthright. It was the type of conversation that politicians and businesspeople had all the time behind closed doors but rarely had in front of an audience. Simon was intrigued. He listened on.

"So, who are the right people to deal with this?" asked a young blonde woman. She looked as though the robes had been designed specifically for her. Simon thought that this could have been her fashion shoot. Although he vaguely recognized her, he had no idea where it was from or indeed who she was, although it struck him that she would probably be thinking the same about him if he spoke up but without vaguely recognizing him at all. At this time, Sierra walked the few steps to join her father. She had no interest in the conversation but wanted to be close to him. She recognized the speaker as someone from her celebrity magazines.

"We, the journalists, have the ability to reach many people in a short space of time. We have more trust from the public than any of you in business and all of you politicians put together," said a man with a white beard that clashed with his dark hair. Sierra thought that he looked as though he had gotten halfway through dyeing his hair and was just about to move on to his beard when he was taken by the white light that had taken her, her father, and Daniel. He was a tall man and had an air of authority that captured the room when he spoke. His voice was loud, but he wasn't shouting. Sierra listened and thought that he was the type of person that had no need to shout.

"But there are some of us here that can reach tens of millions of people in thirty seconds flat with one tweet. We can reach across the globe and speak to people whether they trust politicians or not, whether they care about the stock market or not, and whether they watch your TV programs or not." This person was diminutively short and spoke quietly. If there was one thing that everyone else in the room had learned from their time in the Star Craft, then it was to respect the right of others to speak. In a normal business or political environment, or even in a television studio, when someone was speaking this softly, they would have just been talked over and ignored. Here on the transport craft, every opinion was respected. Jesus had chosen all the people on board to be messengers, and all the people had a right to put forward their suggestions. Sierra and Simon both knew who she was. She was one of the biggest stars in the world. They had both seen her on television and on billboards, and Sierra followed her on Twitter.

The conversation went on in this vein for a little while before Daniel stepped forward. Simon had been so engrossed in having a front row seat for the debate that he had forgotten about his friend standing at the window. Daniel hadn't listened to all that was going on from start to finish, but he had heard enough to prompt him to speak. "Can't you see that you are all right? The solution here isn't to give the responsibility to a bunch of politicians or to rely on the fact that the celebrities have billions of social media followers. We were *all* chosen. We all have a part to play. The politicians need to pass whatever laws will help, gain the consensus of the government, and speak to the people in their own states. The businesspeople have the ability to speak to their employees and reassure them that things will be fine. The celebrities can reach people that business and politics leave behind. A united approach will give is the strength to succeed. It is the will of Jesus that we succeed."

Daniel's words sent a wave of calm across the room. The realization that they could not do this alone hit every one of them. The world needed thousands of heroes, not just one. There needed to be a coordinated plan that was out into practice as soon as possible to avoid panic.

Daniel was still riding the wave of euphoria from his little speech when the three of them were dropped off by the transport craft. It was making multiple drops across the country so that people could go home and start their task of saving the people. Simon and Sierra said good-bye to Daniel. They knew that they would see him again soon, but they just wanted to be home for a while. It was nighttime. Simon was sure that one day had passed since they were taken by the bright light, but he could not be sure. Daniel had insisted that the spacecraft drop him off with Simon and Sierra, although his intended journey was to the next town to see his brother, Mike. He was itching to use his new leg, and nobody could talk him out of it. Daniel knew that when he reached his brother's house, his wife would be there too. His wife would know that the best person to turn to in a time like this was Mike. He was more sensible than anyone else either of them knew. In any crisis, Mike was the right person to turn to, and all the family would do the same. Daniel's brother would understand the emotions of Daniel regaining his leg. His brother had also served his country and had seen some of his colleagues lose limbs in battle.

Simon and Sierra held hands as they walked up the road to their home. They felt closer than ever after the experience. Although they were both walking quickly to get home, the last few moments together as the only people in their family that knew what was going on were precious.

"Dad, we are going to be okay, aren't we?" Sierra asked. She knew that her father would respond with nothing but positivity, but she wanted to hear it all the same.

"We will be just fine. If Jesus has faith in us, then we can't go wrong, now can we?"

It was just what Sierra wanted to hear. She knew there was no option but to try everything to save the people that she knew and loved and the rest of the planet too. She felt that Daniel, her father, and herself were small and insignificant compared to all the other people on their transport craft. She wondered why they had been chosen to stand along so many political and business leaders, but when Daniel spoke, she felt all of that wash away. In the same clothes as the rest and with equal right to speak, she knew that this was a mission that Jesus had set for them all.

"Dad, how are we going to do this? Where on earth will we start? Literally?"

"With the ones that we love. With our family, friends, and church family," replied Simon with the certainty that gave Sierra belief that he had a plan. Their home was at the top of a hill along a narrow road. They could see it from about a mile away and never took their eyes off their house for the entire walk. Like Daniel, they had been dropped off some way from their home. The transport craft needed somewhere large to hover, and to avoid causing panic, they found open spaces where the chances of others seeing were highly limited. Their transport craft had been spotted by one eagle-eyed young man who was sitting in the attic of his parents' house looking out of his telescope. He had seen the craft pass by his home in the direction of Lake Palestine and was already typing away on his computer, uploading what he saw and a blurry image to a Web site that specialized in UFO sightings. It was another upload to a site that received thousand every year, so it caused no panic. It gained no traction with anyone other than those that visited the site on a regular basis.

As Simon and Sierra reached the edge of their property, their walk slowed. The excitement of seeing the woman that they shared their life with was tinged with some trepidation of the news that they knew they had to deliver. As Simon and Sierra walked to their house as the sun was going down, the typical first star of the evening sky was shining, and a full moon was rising in the east. Sierra even commented how beautiful it was to see the big orange moon rising. Then in a flash, a new bright white star started shining next to the moon.

Unknown to Simon, Sierra and all the messengers, Marta, and Hozai had given the command to move the Star Craft out from behind the moon and then illuminate the Star Craft so as to support the messengers and give the people of Earth some evidence of their presence.

The light of the illuminated Star Craft took on the brilliance of the old biblical "star of David" that reportedly shone in the sky, heralding the birth of Jesus over two thousand years old. This new star gave Simon more confidence that the task at hand would be successful.

The house was lit up. There were lights on in the living room and the kitchen that could be seen from the road as well as a bedroom upstairs. They both wondered what she had been going through during the time they had been away. She was bound to be frightened, but had she called the police? Had she informed relatives? Was she out looking for them? Simon scanned the house and yard. He noticed all the small details that made the home different. The streetlight shone in the direction of their home. He saw the patched-up part of the roof that had tiles of a very slightly different color to the rest. The original tiles were no longer in production, and he had to settle for those because they were as close a match as he could find. He saw the earth patch at the edge of the lawn where they had buried the family pet cat a few years earlier. Even though the years had passed, it was still obvious where their pet kitty lay to rest. He saw the guttering above Sierra's bedroom where a storm had caused so much rain that it gave way under the weight. The new guttering was larger and stronger, and old Jimmy in the hardware store in town that had sold it to him said that it would last longer than either of them. It had seen some storms since, and the gutter showed no sign of giving way.

The front door was open. As Simon opened the door, he ushered Sierra to walk through first. He knew that she was desperate to see her mother and wanted nothing to stand in her way. As Sierra stepped inside the living room, she saw her mother, and they ran towards each other with beaming smiles, tears in their eyes, and their arms wide open. Simon watched this scene unfold with his eyes welling up with tears of his own. He loved them both dearly and was so happy to be a part of this family.

"Mom, we're okay!" Sierra wailed. "We're okay, we're okay, we're okay!"

"My sweetheart, I have been so worried. What happened to you? Where have you been?" asked her mother but without expecting a reply. As she held her daughter tight, she opened her eyes and saw over Sierra's shoulder her husband, Simon. She cried some more as

Simon moved over to the two of them and wrapped his arms around them both.

At that time, the three of them felt as close as they could be. They all wanted a bit of normality for a while. Sierra wanted this most of all. She wanted the three of them to sit together on the sofa and watch TV. She wanted to watch *America's Funniest Home Videos* in her PJs while drinking hot chocolate that her mother had lovingly made for her. She wanted to eat cookies and drink warm milk before going to bed. She wanted to wake up in the morning and have breakfast together around the table while her father made fun of her mother and got them all to laugh. She knew that a different life lay ahead, so she wanted a last night of her old life.

Simon heard a rustle coming from the kitchen. He broke off from the hug with a little suspicion and looked in the direction of the kitchen at the back of their home. As he looked, the door opened, and several members of the family walked through. His wife had let people know that the two of them were missing, and they had all come to help look for the two of them by day and to keep her company at night. His mother-in-law, brother-in-law, his wife, and two grown-up children were standing there with his uncle and his two sisters and their husbands and children. He was always filled with joy to see them, and the occasion made it even more emotional.

Simon and Sierra spent the evening telling the others about their experience. They started with the day fishing on Lake Palestine for those that they had not seen in a while. They told them about the day on the serene lake through the mist and how they could not have imagined at that point where events could possibly have taken them. Sierra spoke about the evening in church and the way that her friends had doubted the existence of Christ. Everyone listened intently, but they all knew that the big event was coming up. Even though Sierra and Simon were great storytellers, the whole room wanted them to move on from the beginning of the story to the events that had brought them to the house. Sierra's mother had told the rest of the family a little, but they all wanted to hear what happened from the point of view of Sierra and Simon.

"We were taken from the ground by a bright light. It seemed to seek us out and then lift us from the ground. At first, the movement of the light on the land seemed random, but we now know that it was looking for us—Sierra, Daniel, and me." Simon took over the story from his daughter. They took it in turns throughout their retelling like a baton being passed back and forth in a relay race. When one ran out of steam, the other took the baton and charged forward with the story. All the others in the room were now completely hooked and hung on their every word, predicting when one would take over from the other in their minds.

It wasn't time to change. Simon continued, "It was as though the light was lifting us. With the storm swirling around too, it was difficult to see the others. I was scared."

"I was scared too, Daddy," Sierra added. It was her turn to talk. "We moved upwards, but it all felt like we moved quite slowly. We were rising rather than racing. It felt like it took half an hour, but it could have been thirty seconds. It could have been several hours. Then all of a sudden, we were on a spacecraft. Our clothes had gone, and we were dressed in these robes." Sierra blushed again as she remembered her thoughts on the Star Craft. She could still not work out how she had been undressed and placed in these robes in almost an instant, and she felt embarrassed that her father or Daniel might have seen her. But at the same time, she knew that she hadn't seen either of them, so she assured herself that there was nothing to worry about.

Simon continued to speak as Sierra thought. He told them the most amazing thing, "Daniel got his leg back! The Star Craft that we were taken to had healing properties, and Daniel lifted his robe to show us his two legs. He is walking over to see his brother now."

The rest of the family was all amazed. They all knew Daniel through the church and knew the story of how he had lost his leg. They found it hard to believe that Daniel had been healed, but they had never found a reason to doubt Simon in their life and were not about to start now. Simon carried on, "On the Star Craft, there were thousands of people from senators to politicians, businesspeople, and celebrities that Sierra instantly recognized, and I had no idea who they were. Everyone was dressed in the same robes as us. We were all gathered together to be told something, but as we were heading there and Sierra became upset, the most incredible thing happened." He looked at his daughter, and their eyes twinkled at each other.

"I met Jesus," Sierra exclaimed.

The whole room took a gasp at the same time. The sentence that Sierra just blurted out had taken them all by surprise. Sierra's mother asked, "How could this be?"

Simon spoke up. "I'm not sure, but I am sure it was our Lord. He spoke to us all without speaking."

"I held his hand and walked with him in the Star Craft. He spoke to us all. It was the most incredible thing that I have ever witnessed in my life. Christ spoke quietly, and a room of thousands of people listened intently to his every word without a murmur. He spoke to us as equals. He told us that he had faith in us," Sierra continued in an excited way. Her father watched the absolute euphoria on his daughter's face as she spoke. He also gauged the room for their reaction as he wiped tears from his eyes.

"He has faith in you to do what?" asked he mother. She had listened to every word and wouldn't doubt her husband or daughter under any circumstances. "What does he want you to do that needs his faith?" she asked the same question in a slightly different way, as though the first time around she had asked it in a foreign language.

"We have work to do. A change is about to come. Jesus has asked us to help him," said Simon. He asked everyone to sit down in the house before he spoke again. He knew that there would be some confusion and a lot of questions, so he wanted everyone to be comfortable when they received the news.

"The planet is in grave danger . . ." Simon started to speak. What followed was almost word for word what they had been told by Hozai and Marta on the Star Craft. He looked into the eyes of each of the family members that were gathered in front of him as he spoke. He wanted them to understand that he wasn't just letting them know about the task that he, Sierra, and Daniel were given—he also wanted them to realize that he was recruiting them to help him take the first steps to delivering the message and saving the people of this planet. In his mind, they were to start with the church and then spread the message one place at a time. Rather than the television messages that others on their spacecraft were planning, Simon knew how to communicate on a one-on-one basis, and this would be the way that he and his people would deliver a message of hope and salvation rather than one of fear and panic.

There were questions, plenty of them. Simon, now assisted by Sierra, answered each of them in a calm manner, inspired by the way that Jesus, Hozai, and Marta spoke to people on the Star Craft. Simon took a few moments to think while the others took in the news.

He has always been my inspiration. Whenever I felt weak or lost, he always gave me strength and found me again. Now when I am delivering distressing and life-changing news to my loved ones, he is there again. I can feel him in my words. I can sense him in my faith. I can feel my determination and positivity springing from the determination and positivity of our Lord. I am thankful that it is me that has received the blessing of this task. I will carry it out to the wishes of Jesus. I will lead my family, my friends, and everyone else I can reach to safety.

The questions came for what seemed like hours, but Simon and Sierra answered the last one with the same reassurance and calm as the first. They could tell immediately that the questions were not about disbelief—they had complete faith in Simon and Sierra. But the questions were all to ensure that they understood what was going on and how they could play a role in it. Sierra answered all the questions about feeling.

"What was it like to meet Jesus?"

"How did it make you feel?"

"Did he have an aura?"

"Were people crying? Were they praying? Did they kneel before him?"

Simon answered all the questions about the practical side of things. He asked them all, had they seen the new star tonight? Everyone look puzzled. No, they all muttered. Simon and Sierra stood up and asked them all to come out on the front porch. As they all stood on the front porch, Simon pointed up towards the full moon. "See that brilliant star next to the Moon? That is not a star but the Star Craft that Sierra, Daniel, and I were on," stated Simon. "Now I know what you all are thinking. But you know me, Sierra, and Daniel, we don't make up wild stories," Simon exclaimed. Finally, in a quivering voice, he said, "And that is where we met Jesus." Simon was still trying to get his mind around all that he had just experienced.

"How long do we have?"

"What is it we can do to help?"

"When will you be speaking to your congregation?"

"Will the political leaders make an announcement soon?"

After all the questions and answers, the rest of the family made their way to bed. It was a large house, and there were plenty of spare rooms to house all the guests. Sierra's mom loved to have a lot of people around to stay. She had grown up as one of three sisters and two brothers, so a busy house was all that she knew. She missed the days of the big family occasions of her childhood, such as Thanksgiving where there would be scores of people all under the same roof enjoying the company of each other. Whenever she woke up in the house on the times that Simon and Sierra had gone out fishing or on one of the meteorite field trips, she felt as though it was a waste of a big home. There was so much space, and they all had so much love to give that waking up in a large house all alone felt to her like she always needed to fill the space. So, she took the opportunity to open her house to needy families or single moms that needed help at times. She knew this was a gift and that she had to give God the glory. She closed her eyes and wished that when she opened them up again, the house would be filled in every room with people, like her parents' home when she was young.

After everyone had gone to bed, there was just Simon and Sierra sitting in the living room next to each other. A fire in the fireplace was crackling. It was the only home that Sierra had known. She looked around and studied the room in great detail. It was filled with things that confirmed their life together. There were family photographs, pictures bought from their trips to other parts of the country, thank-you cards from the people of the church that they had helped, and ornaments passed down from past generations. This was the building of their lives. All that had gone before had led them here, to this living room full of their mementos. This showed anyone who cared to look what the family had done so far. But what it could never tell was what was going to happen in the future. Sierra had never thought about her timeline before. As someone who hadn't reached her teenage years yet, she had just enjoyed life every day. She had lived it to the fullest, as all the inspirational posters teach. But now she was more aware than ever that the point she was at right now was the pivot point of her life. Every moment is a pivot point between the past and the future. Some are insignificant and do very little to change the timeline of a life. Some are momentous and contain the decisions that will spin the future in one direction or the other. Sierra thought that the last day and the coming weeks would be filled with momentous decisions that would decide her future.

"Daddy, nothing will ever be the same again, will it?" asked Sierra.

Simon didn't answer. They both got up and made their way upstairs to bed. Simon kissed Sierra on the top of her head and said, "Good night, baby, see you in the morning." Then Simon walked over to his Bible study room filled with mounted pictures of family and fishing and of them hunting for meteorites all around the world. He stood at a glass cabinet filled with meteorites and other rare minerals. But one of his favorites was still with the professor at Texas A&M University. This was the one he found on a field trip near the Holy Land over ten years earlier. He had always felt it was special and now realized he had to get in contact with the professor the next day. Simon expected this special meteorite may be the message that Jesus referred to just before they left the Star Craft.

It was special, of course; where he found it made it special to him. But what also made it different was its appearance. It was pitted from the heat as it fell from outer space, but the melting of the iron rock as it fell through the Earth's atmosphere seemed to partially unveil a different metal object that appeared to be embedded in the rock. Simon knew that this was odd. He had not shared this meteorite with the public, but after all that had happened, he felt like the time to reveal it was now.

When Sierra arose the next morning, she could sense activity in the house. She was the last one up, and everyone else was assembled in the large kitchen. There was movement everywhere as Sierra opened the door. People were darting backwards and forwards, fixing breakfast. There was a pan of milk on the stove, the coffeepot was churning out hot fresh coffee, and people were searching through cupboards to find food and then get it ready for the table. It was a wonderful sight for Sierra to see. She had not slept particularly well, but she did feel rested and ready to face the day. The sight of her family all rallying round and helping each other turned her readiness up a notch or two.

When the breakfast was ready, they all sat down at the table. Sierra hadn't seen a breakfast like it before. There was such a selection she didn't know where to start. She looked up and down the table, searching for a suitable place to begin this food journey, but it all looked so good that she didn't make a decision for a few minutes. In the meantime, she watched as the hands of the rest of her family flew around the table, grabbing the food that they wanted and returning it to their plate. Sierra decided that the next hand she saw arrive at a choice she would follow and make that the start of her first breakfast since she knew about the terrible threat to the world. It was her mother's hand. Good choice! The hesitation quickly washed away from Sierra, and she ate a hearty breakfast. As the rush to be fed subsided and everyone sat with their drinks at the end of the meal, the television became more of a focus. It had been on in the background for the whole time, but now with the quiet coming over the room, it was heard for the first time.

The television presenter said those familiar words that preceded all major events. "We interrupt this broadcast to bring you breaking news . . ."

The screen turned from a television studio to the inside of the United Nations. The United Nations was housed in a building on the

East Side of Manhattan Island, New York. It was founded in the wake of World War II with the primary aim of stopping another conflict like that from ever happening. In the modern, more peaceful day, it debated the major topics of concern to the world, including climate change, international security, and delivery of aid to those in need. But on this day, there was another more pressing issue to be discussed.

Simon and Sierra recognized the senator that stepped forward to make comment. He was one of the people that had travelled back from the Star Craft on the transport craft with them. He had been standing right next to Daniel when he spoke up and seemed to be in more agreement with the things Daniel had to say than any of the other politicians that were assembled on the return to Earth. As Daniel spoke, the senator had a determined look in his eyes and nodded uncontrollably as though the force of Daniel's message was making it happen.

At the UN, the senator was clearing his throat, ready to speak. A murmur moved its way across the assembly room, as people could sense this was going to be an important announcement. It was always like that with big assemblies. People that had been around them for a long time could automatically sense when something out of the ordinary was unfolding. Some of the UN members in the room already knew what the senator was about to say and at this point joined him on the stage. Simon and Sierra recognized some of these as people that were also on board the Star Craft. In the next town, Daniel was watching the television with his brother. At this point, all the news TV channels were broadcasting the United Nations speech that was about to happen.

However, the main news channel, CNN, leads the UN live story with a report from a journalist outside of the UN building in New York City. The reporter addressed the CNN anchor, Wolf Blitzer, back in Atlanta by saying, "Wolf, this morning, here in New York and around the world, it has been pointed out that a bright object has appeared in the sky. Some are saying it is a new star or possibly a supernova in a nearby solar system. Before we go to Dr. Cooper at the Palomar Observatory in California for a report, it looks like the UN Assembly is starting." Wolf Blitzer said, "Let's go to the UN General Assembly for a special announcement."

J.R. PHILLIPS

A second murmur washed over the hall as the group assembled alongside the senator. It was against protocol to have more than one person standing on the main stage at the microphone at one time. People were now sure that something major was happening. An interested onlooker noted that the senator had recently been working on a radical new climate change bill in the American Senate, and he had been looking for international support for it. Maybe they had reached a breakthrough, but the fact that it was being announced at the United Nations didn't make sense to the onlooker. Then the second murmur died down, and the senator let them know he was ready to speak. He looked down at his watch. It was a Casio digital watch that he had worn since he was very young. He had taken such good care of it that it had lasted him many years. He couldn't picture life without it. He looked down at the watch, and the time was eleven o'clock in the morning. He pressed the button on the top right of the watch, and the date was confirmed as 11-11. He stared at the numbers for a few seconds before beginning to speak. Unbeknownst to people on earth, a subliminal message was being sent by the Star Craft that the planet was in its eleventh hour of existence.

"All of us here have just experienced an amazing and life-affirming event. We have all been asked to be a messenger of this event and the information shared with us of the pending catastrophe," he said as the whole of the United Nations and the people of the world watched silently. He looked straight into the barrel of the camera lens as he spoke. The words came out slowly and deliberately for all to hear. The group of people standing alongside him all wore the same robes as he did. They all looked out of place in the setting of the United Nations.

"Many of you know me from my office in the US Senate, and many of you have only known me from my wheelchair. And as you can see, I am no longer in that wheelchair but standing here in front of you to testify and share the following information. We have been warned of a mortal danger to the planet Earth, an event that has been confirmed as a distinct possibility by scientists and researchers that are here with us when we found out. We have been given the task of leading you all to safety. We don't know how much time we actually have, but an orderly process will ensure that we can all be saved from this disaster." He paused again for effect. The last line that he would deliver in the speech that morning was going to be the one that turned all the heads. It would be the line that people would see on the news bulletins later and the one that would be reported in all the newspapers that afternoon. It was going to be an immortal line in world history, as immortal as Neil Armstrong's "One small step for man, one giant leap for mankind," or "I have a dream . . ." by Martin Luther King.

He continued, "In order to save the human race, we will have to evacuate the Earth." It drew the gasps that he expected from the people assembled in the United Nations. It drew gasps from people watching all over America. Everyone who had been watching the television at that time of the day were now tuned into the events from the United Nations because every television channel had switched whatever they were showing to live events from the United Nations. There were gasps even from Simon, Sierra, and the rest of the family because the rest of the world now knew what they had known. There were gasps from people in front of television sets all over the world. People who could speak no English gasped a few seconds later when they read the subtitles that confirmed the news. The senator could feel the gasps of the entire world blow towards the United States of America, past the Statue of Liberty on their way to Manhattan. He could feel the gasps grow stronger as they gathered together through the streets of New York and arrive at the door of the United Nations building. He could feel them blow through the doors and then down the vast corridors of this building of power towards the assembly hall. The gasps shook him to the core. He had been the one to deliver this news to the world. He was the one to put the events in place on the planet. He handed over the stage to the highest-ranking astrophysicist group in the world. He introduced them and asked everyone to listen to what they had to say.

He turned the podium over to them and stepped aside just to the left of the group so the rest of the room, the rest of the world could see that they had his full backing and that they were part of the solution.

The lead scientist stepped forward. He was much taller than the senator and had a messy hairstyle that reminded you of Einstein's head of hair. He would have been what many people would have expected an astrophysicist to look like if they were asked. He looked as though he had spent all of his life behind either a microscope or a telescope. He demanded respect. He began by confirming that the statements of the impending catastrophe were verifiable. "The reason we had not seen this to date," he stated, "is our limited technology and historical knowledge of a star system like Eta Carinae and WR 104. We are aware of the visual observations but have no knowledge of the thresholds and limits it will reach before blasting our solar system with a gamma burst." The science was complex enough that people had to really sit up and listen but not too complex that people switched off. The senator was pleased with the way that this was going. He wanted the astrophysicist to help confirm in people's minds that this was something that they really needed to deal with rather than another politician's weasel words to score political points or achieve a small victory over the other party. Like Daniel had said on the transport craft, "A united approach will give us the best chance to succeed. We are all on the same team this time."

The astrophysicist continued to give some more details about the constellation that they had been observing and how recent activity was cause for a large degree of alarm. People in the general counsel chambers were making copious notes with every new sentence so that they had all the information they needed to look back over what was said and how they needed to react. When the chief astrophysicist had finished, he looked at the audience. He was aware that his words would be seen by not only those assembled in front of him but also those around the world that had tuned in to their television sets. He spoke slowly yet firmly, "Ladies and gentlemen, we need to work together now for the good of humankind." He stepped away from the podium, looking to the entire world as someone who had used up all their energy. He looked weary and ready to collapse, but his inner strength kept him standing upright as the senator stepped back to the podium.

The senator began the final part of his message with the words, "A big part of our message is the salvation handed to the human race." He wanted to end on the most positive of notes. "We have all seen miracles over the past twenty-four hours. As you can see, I am proof. We have all been in the presence of Jesus. I will say that again, we have all been in the presence of Jesus Christ." The senator pointed to the group on stage in the robes from the Star Craft and continued, "He told us that we can save all of the people of the planet Earth if we all deliver a peaceful message and leave the planet. There is another safe planet already waiting for us. It is our refuge and our chance to begin again. We must use this opportunity to spread a message of hope. We must remain calm and support each other through the tough times ahead. I cannot lie to you, moving to a new planet will not be a simple task. There are seven billion people here on earth, and moving that many people will take time. But you are all assured a safe passage to our new home, our new Earth. If there are any lingering doubts, just walk outside and look up. The presence of the Star Craft is now shining in the sky. May God be with us all."

The senator laid his hands on the podium to demonstrate that he was finished speaking. He then turned to all of the others standing in the robes and smiled. He looked along the line of people and mouthed the words "thank you" one by one. The support that they had given him had filled him with the strength to make the speech and alert the world that action needed to be taken. In many ways, this was the easy part. The hard road still lay ahead.

At Simon's home, everyone that just witnessed the television news were speechless. Simon went to the phone to call the professor that had the meteorite. Once the professor knew he had Simon on the phone, he began to yell. "Simon, Simon, where have you been!" he exclaimed. "You have to get here as soon as possible so we can show you what we have found!"

Simon, still in his white robe, took a few family members and drove the hour to the university.

Chapter 7

The Chaos Begins

The gasp of breath that had reverberated around the world was changing. It was changing from a gasp of shock to a gasp of panic. The news that something big was being announced in the United Nations was spreading quickly via the Internet and SMS messaging on smartphones. As a consequence, there were billions of people watching the senator and the astrophysicist speaking on their television sets sitting in different parts of the world. In the major cities of the world, people stopped what they were doing and searched out a TV. They were huddled around sets in cafes, restaurants, and bars. They were gathered in train stations, bus stations, gas stations, and pretty much anyplace they could find a TV. As the words came out of the television set and into their ears, they took a little time to process. Like all of the people on the Star Craft, they had received the news slowly, and they had been given a few seconds to take it all in before the next piece of information was delivered. But unlike the people of the Star Craft, the people of planet Earth took the news badly. They didn't receive it with the calm that the senator hoped his early announcement would deliver.

In the city of New York, home to the United Nations, there was an instant reaction. New Yorkers are known for making their feelings heard, and in a coffee shop under the shadow of the Empire State Building, panic erupted immediately. Angry customers started looting the coffee beans from behind the counter, pushing and shoving the people working there out of the way so that they could fill their bags with coffee. It was an irrational reaction to the news, as if coffee was going to save them from the fate that had been foretold. One man saw this as an opportunity to smash open the cash register and make off with all the money inside. Chairs were thrown, windows were smashed, and people staggered out into the street with broken teeth and streams of blood running down their faces. If they thought that the street was a safer place than the coffee shop then they were wrong. The scene was repeated in every establishment that had been a meeting place for those that wanted to watch the United Nations speech. Panic was the initial thought that went through peoples' minds and then people turned that panic into a violent knee-jerk reaction. The irrational acts of hoarding freshly baked pastries or herbal tea bags had nothing to do with preparing for the imminent destruction of the planet Earth. It was an outlet for all the anger and fear that the people of New York felt at that moment. But it wasn't just in New York that panic was spreading.

Over in Paris, France, the Eiffel Tower gave the perfect viewpoint for American tourist Henry Mills to see something he just hadn't bargained for when setting out his itinerary for a vacation to the City of Lights. In every direction he looked, there were fires. Cars had been overturned, and the streets seemed to be filled with waves of people moving in random directions. As one wave of people crashed into another, bodies flew against buildings and then fell onto the floor. From the height of the Eiffel Tower, the people seemed lifeless as they lay there. Over to the south, Henry saw the building housing the tomb of Napoleon emitting a combination of smoke and flames.

Henry was a medic in the army when he was younger, and his natural instinct was to get down there and help. But the lifts were shut down by equally panicked staff members who had just shut the whole thing down and disappeared. All over the city, there were posts abandoned and people running in terror and chaos. Henry looked over to the Louvre, the museum that was filled with some of the most desired treasures in the world, including the *Mona Lisa* and the *Venus De Milo*. He could see hordes of people walking out of the museum with works of art under their arms. It was the most orderly sight in the whole of his range of vision but at the same time the most culturally destructive. Henry had been up the Eiffel Tower for over an hour and had no idea what was going on. Perhaps France was having another civil war? Perhaps there had been a coup from the French army, and they were taking over? Little did Henry Mills know that this wasn't a scene restricted to Paris, or even France; it was being played out all over the world.

Roma was a city that had seen some history, to put it mildly. From the times where the Roman Empire ruled the known world to the fascist movement of Mussolini during the Second World War, Roma had been at the center of their own universe. Roma was a passionate city that attracted people from all over the planet to spend time there and take in all the beautiful sights such as the Trevi Fountain, the Spanish Steps, and the Coliseum. The Coliseum was built two thousand years earlier to showcase the gladiatorial battles and other public spectacles of the time. It had stood through the ages as a testament to the power of old Roma and what it stood for. But on that day, it housed another battle that was far from gladiatorial but just as brutal. People had formed two "sides" and were attacking each other as though they were in the stands of the Stadio Olimpico. It had changed from the original days when the fights took place in the main Coliseum amphitheater and the stands were a safe place to watch the violence.

The fight had broken out between the Ultra soccer hooligans of the city's two teams, Lazio and Roma. The tensions between the two sets of supporters had grown to outright animosity over the years, and now the news about the end of the planet was the trigger for the animosity to turn into hostility. Groups of Ultras wore either the sky blue of their beloved Lazio or the burgundy of their famous team Roma. The battles were as bloody as most seen in the Coliseum over the centuries except there were no weapons. These gladiators used their fists and pieces of the Coliseum walls that they managed to break off. The building had stood for two thousand years. It had survived the vast modifications to turn it into a castle in medieval times, an earthquake in 1349, being lived in, being neglected, and two world wars, but it was now being torn apart by people that wanted to use its two-thousand-year-old bricks as weapons to bludgeon their fellow Romans that just happened to follow a different soccer team. It was a horrific sight to see.

In Beijing, it was past midnight when they received the news. It was a country that managed to have order and tranquility, even though there were a billion people living within its borders. Social media was booming with the middle classes in China, especially in the cities, so the fact that a major world announcement was about to be made in the United Nations spread like wildfire. Bars and restaurants were traditionally open all night in the center of Beijing, so there were people sitting around the television or watching on their smartphones as the senator gave his speech. China was in danger. All the work that the country had done since the Cultural Revolution was designed to stand apart from the rest of the world. They had grown a powerhouse nation, and it was now under threat. The people reacted with absolute astonishment. China had developed an insular attitude. The people of China had been taught that the fate of China was in their hands and was the most important part of their lives. They supported China against everything else in the world.

Hang Mai was sitting in his Beijing apartment on Wangfujing Street when the news broke. He watched on his own in his living room. His family was all from the countryside. He was the first of his people to leave the paddy fields and seek his living where the bright lights of Beijing drew him. He was one of the first to support and defend China against whatever the rest of the world was dong. He sat on his sofa, thinking about what had just been said.

Here is a time when the different countries of the world should look inwardly. We as a Chinese people need to look after the interests of China before we look at the interest of the rest of the world. But this politician seems to be suggesting that we look out for the other nations of the world as much as we look after our own. If there is to be a new planet, then our first task must be to make sure that China has a leading role on that planet. This can only be achieved by getting Chinese people on the new planet first and by setting the rules ourselves. We must be at the forefront of the race to the new world.

His thoughts were not echoed by the rest of Beijing that he could see out of his window. He lived on the fourth floor of a tower block that had views across to the main squares of restaurants, bars, and cafes in downtown Beijing. The number 4 has connotations of bad luck in China because in sound, it is almost identical to the word for death. This meant that the fourth floor of tower blocks were always the cheapest to live in. Hang Mai turned up in the city with almost nothing to his name and had only been there for around a year so at this point in his life, a one-bedroom apartment on the fourth floor of a tower block was all he could afford. The fact that most Chinese people turned away from anything with the number 4 was probably the only reason he had been able to find anywhere to live in Beijing. It was his third home in the city. He first lived at number 4 on a dark seedy street in the worst neighborhood in the city. His next move was to block four of the newly built towers on the outskirts of the financial district. It was built by an overseas company that didn't have any knowledge about Chinese superstition. As a result, Hang Mai could live in block 4 on the fourth floor in apartment 44 because nobody else really wanted to stay there. It was the last apartment to be rented out, and he drove a hard bargain.

Now from his third residence in the city, he was watching as buses were being driven at speeds through red traffic lights, smashing into parked cars and other vehicles moving through the green light at the other side. He was watching windows being broken out on all the banks in his view as people vainly attempted to gain access to the money inside, maybe not knowing that it was locked up in high security vaults that they could never access with bare hands. He could see people drinking sake to excess and vomiting on the pavements below. There was a light rain that washed this vomit into the gutters of the street where it was lit up by the lights coming from the restaurants and bars that had been abandoned by their owners. Beijing was in turmoil.

Across to the southern end of China, a similar scene was happening. Hong Kong was a beautiful city built on an island that was really too small to house it all. They had at first crammed as many buildings on the island as possible and then built up when all the available space was filled. It was a financial hub of the world and attracted money from every corner of the globe. But there was one place that dictated much of how Hong Kong operated and made money. They say that when America sneezes, the rest of the world catches a cold. Well, when America sneezes, Hong Kong is bedridden with pneumonia and is lucky to pull out of the other side. This was going to be the mother of all sneezes.

Like the financiers and businesspeople on the transport craft heading back to the United States, the people of Hong Kong were mainly concerned about how all of this might affect their wealth. They lived shoulder to shoulder with other people on this island to make money. They were not living in the constant traffic and noise for any other reason. When the news broke from the United Nations' general counsel chambers, the people of Hong Kong looked at their bank balances. They wondered what would happen when trading opened on their stock exchange the next day.

As with the other parts of the world, this turned to a panic within minutes. Windows were smashed on apartments high in the Hong Kong night sky, and a shower of glass rained down on the streets below. Many of the skyscrapers in Hong Kong had communal viewing areas on each floor. The buildings were owned by multinational corporations, and an anger to the way that the world looked at that exact point led people to kick these windows out, smash them with whatever they could find, and shower the streets with glass. It was another irrational act that people in different corners of the world were enacting on the things they saw around them. Nothing escaped the carnage. Buildings, cars, possessions, banks, cafes, restaurants, bars, shops, and even other people were all at risk from the panic that boiled over into anger and frustration across the world.

In Sydney, Australia, the beautiful and iconic Sydney Opera House was ablaze. It was a building that was instantly recognized as one of the modern wonders of the world. The building was completed in the early 1970s after years of planning and construction and was known as distinctive beacon of Australia's arrival on the world stage. But now it was being destroyed from the inside by a fire that was lit by people that wanted to see the world burn. The panic and confusion that the news had brought reached every faraway corner of the world no matter what time of day or night it was. From the Sydney Harbor Bridge, you could see the building that had represented so much hope to the Australian people wouldn't make it through the night.

Known as a relaxed and civilized city, Sydney was home to people from all over the world. It was a popular choice for people that wanted to emigrate and start a new life. In much the way that the United States grew on its immigrant population in the 1800's, Australia (and Sydney in particular) had seen a population explosion from immigration in the 1900's. And it was still growing. In Sydney, you could find people from just about any part of the world. And they all brought their cuisines and lifestyle with them so you could find Greek neighborhoods nestled next to a small Croatian district and then cross a few city blocks to find an Irish community all living together. If you wanted to eat food from a different part of the world every night, then Sydney rivaled New York for choice.

But now each neighborhood was afraid of the next. Barricades had been made from cars, trucks, furniture, wood, trees, and whatever else people could lay their hands on. Each part of Sydney was now divided as each separate community turned on their neighbors and boxed themselves in. They thought that if they were trying to survive, then they would stand their best chance with their own people. Groups of young men guarded each barricade to make sure that no outsiders were able to enter. Everyone who approached was treated with suspicion until they could be identified. If they were part of their own community, then they would be welcomed with open arms. If they were from another, then they were sent away with harsh words or sometimes with more than words thrown at them. The streets of Sydney were a dangerous place to walk on that night.

While the world was in a state of panic, the senator and the others in robes that had joined him on the stage sat in a small room in the United Nations building and prayed.

In New York, there was a crew of about three hundred workers constructing a new tall building that was going to have shops on the lower floors, offices on the next ten or so floors, and then homes on the upper floors. It was another in a long line of skyscrapers that New York was famous for. Ever since the Empire State Building was declared the world's tallest building in 1930, New York architects had developed a passion for building on a grand scale. After the events of 9-11 and the attacks on the twin towers of the World Trade Center building, tall buildings went out of fashion for a while. But with this new building among seventeen earmarked for construction in the coming years, skyscrapers were back on the agenda again.

The construction crew had been listening to the daily safety briefing when they were interrupted by one of the foremen who told them all to come into the office and listen to what was about to unfold in the United Nations only around half a mile away. It was strange for the workers to see events that they could walk to in ten minutes, being transmitted into their lives via a television set in an office, but they listened intently. After everything had been said, the will to work drained out of the construction workers. One spoke up. "What would be the point of doing any more work on this building?" There were shouts of "Yeah" and "What's the point?" to accompany what he had said while the foremen and supervisors looked at each other for an answer. Income, family security . . . but no one could confirm that they all would continue to be paid.

After a standoff that lasted a couple of minutes with the foremen trying to block the exit of the workers that were at the forefront of the protest, everyone decided that it was time to leave. A big shove from the whole group sent the supervisors and foremen flying in all directions like bowling pins, and the construction workers abandoned their posts. They went back to the area that had been set aside, got changed, gathered their things, and made their way back through the streets of New York. John Adamczak had worked in construction all of his life, and he had never seen the people rise up together like that before. He was excited that this might mean the people of the world could come together and be saved. He spoke to the guy standing next to him, who was clearing out his locker. "That was great. Where are you going now? I just have to get home to see my family."

The man standing next to John said, "Same. I need to see my kids," and left before John could continue the conversation.

John left the building site on 5th Avenue overlooking Central Park and headed home. He pulled up the collar on his coat and attached his earphones to his phone. He scrolled through a few options and then pressed play. As the music began, he looked at the time on his phone. It said 9:11 a.m.

God, I'm down here on my knees, 'cause it's the last place left to fall,
Begging for another chance, if there's any chance at all,
That you might still be listening,
Lovin' and forgivin' guys like me . . .

As he stepped outside the safe zone of the construction site, he noticed a lot of noise coming from the streets of Manhattan mall around him. John didn't know at this time, but he had walked into the panicked situation that was gripping different parts of the world all at the same time. He walked carefully along the road at the side of his building and checked the corner of the blocks that intersected to the south of him. It was clear. He had to make his way back to Brooklyn to see his family. He was aware of unrest in the city and made his way to the nearest subway station to get the train back home. The station had the shutters across the entrance that John used every day. He had been working on this building site for a few months now and always travelled the same way backwards and forwards from home in Brooklyn on the corner of East 39th Street and Avenue I to work in Manhattan. He walked across the street to check the other subway entrances. The same.

They were both locked. There was nothing else to do but to begin walking. He attempted to call home using his cell phone, and it worked. He spoke to his oldest son and told him to keep all the family indoors until he got home. The thought that his phone or other utilities like electricity might stop working scared him. He headed downtown to see if the next stop on his line was open. It wasn't that far, and it was in the right direction. Around ten minutes later, John arrived within view of the next subway station, and he could see from a distance that it was shuttered too. At this point, he was not walking alone. Many people were trying to make their way home by walking. He knew that what he had seen on the television screen would cause concern for people, but what he hadn't realized was how quickly it would happen. Like the rest of his colleagues at the construction site, the subway workers had seen little point in continuing what they were doing. They all simply closed up the entire New York subway system and went home to their families. There were thousands upon thousands of New York workers walking the streets from their work they had abandoned to their home. John knew at that point that he would have to walk down Manhattan to the Brooklyn Bridge and cross there. It would only be a short walk of less than an hour, and he was prepared to make his way back home to see his family.

After around twenty minutes, John was walking close to the financial district. Down Wall Street, there was a lot going on. John walked past the New York Stock Exchange on his way back home. As he walked past the Stock Exchange, he pictured a flurry of activity inside. He expected the floor of the stock exchange to be teeming with people all shouting over one another to be heard and make their money. It seemed to John that no matter what the crisis, some in banking would always make their money. It was the same in the aftermath of 9-11 and the same as Lehman Brothers' collapse in 2008.

The image that John had in his head as he made his way past the New York Stock Exchange was as far from the truth as anyone could be. During the time that the senator was speaking, the floor was completely silent. As with anyone else on the planet, the stock brokers in the Exchange were totally engrossed with what was being said across town. When the speeches finished, the people that worked in the NYSE expected to go straight back to work and to see some major trades on the back of the news. As they made their way back from standing in groups near the available TV screens and returned to their desks, another silence fell over the Stock Exchange. All of the screens had the same message scrolling across: "Trading has been suspended."

It was unprecedented. As with the construction workers farther up the island of Manhattan and the subway workers all over New York, the bankers were clearing up their desks, getting their coats back on, and making their way out of the building. By this time, New York had pretty much shut down for business. Grocery stores were all closed, and some had even taken the step of boarding up their store windows and taking home as many groceries as they could carry. All of the banks had closed down for the day to protect the money in their vaults as well as the lives of the people that worked there. People were headed out onto dangerous streets to add to the panic and confusion that was already present. The authorities saw the banks as a target that would attract potential looters once they realized that they were unmanned. With the city in the first stages of meltdown, it wouldn't take long before criminal and opportunists took to the streets in search of easy money.

All of this had been coordinated by the senator and his contacts in the New York Police Department. There were teams of armed police positioned in front of banks and many other essential businesses needed for survival before the rescue started. There would be a need to keep people warm, clothed, and fed in the run up to leaving the planet, and nothing was left to chance with this. The police had been given a list of businesses that they had to guard, and all leave was canceled. This was going to be an around-the-clock situation, and as such they needed all the police officers that they could lay their hands on. Even the chiefs and superintendents that would usually spend all of their day behind a desk were not spared from this duty. It was going to be vital to a peaceful next few days and an orderly evacuation of the city of New York. The cold November air blew against the exposed skin on the faces of the two police officers sitting outside the bank nearest the United Nations. They had been outside the building when the senator had given his speech. There were around two hundred police officers stationed there in case there was an uprising against the institution, but the panic that played out on the streets of New York was random rather than organized. People may have gathered to protest outside the United Nations building if they had any idea of what was going to be said, but with the words coming so unexpectedly, the chaos was sporadic rather than orchestrated. Once it was clear that the United Nations building was safe and not going to be the target of attacks, most of the two hundred officers were redeployed.

"What are we doing here?" asked one of the officers. "Most people will be at home with their family. There is nothing here to protect."

This wasn't the first time that the officer had sat moaning about his assignment that day. He hadn't been happy when asked to report for duty at the United Nations building. He hadn't been happy when asked to go and guard a bank. His partner, Officer John McFarland, a third generation NYPD officer from the 52nd Precinct, was tired of listening to it. He replied with a snap, "You must know by now that we don't work as police officers to deal with most people. Most people don't commit crime. It is the few undesirables that we have to guard this from. You know how important all of the locations the NYPD have been asked to guard are going to be in the next few days. Be happy that you are helping humanity."

And humanity looked at that point like it needed all the help it could get. The world was in chaos. All over the world, people had jumped into their cars and headed away. The people that lived in the city felt that it would be safer to be away from the city. There were thousands of cars clogging up every major road out of every major city in the world. Families had all developed the same idea and fled the city that they lived in. Some new others in parts of the countryside would go and stay with them. Some were prepared to sleep in their cars and live life day by day as long as they were away from the dangers that they saw in their home city. Others had no plan at all but to just get out. They had seen what panic had done to the streets of where they lived and worked. They had seen the television news reports of looting and violence. They wanted to get their family out of harm's way and into a position of as much safety as they could find on the planet right now. They had no idea what might lie in store for them away from the city, but they were sure that it would give them a better chance of survival than to stay put.

The mass exodus caused gridlock on the streets of the world. The estimates were that around half of the world's population lived in urban areas at that time, and it felt to those on the road that those billions of people were trying to leave all at the same time. Every road became a parking lot as people turned off their engines to save gas. Many slept in their cars on the roads they hoped would lead to their escape from the urban jungle to a more tranquil existence in the rural areas close to their home. While families sat in their cars for hours, the car became a place to eat, a place to sleep, a place to play, and a place to pray for huge numbers of people.

As this situation unfolded across the world, another person of power was getting ready to make a television address. He was notable by his absence on the Star Craft, and the fact that he was excluded was not an accident. He was not chosen to be one of the messengers, even though he had a great power and influence over the people of the world. As he prepared to give his speech live on television, he sat there with his eyes closed, mentally preparing himself. He went through the opening line of his speech in his head over and over again.

Americans and people of the world, Americans and people of the world, Americans and people of the world . . .

He knew that the impact of his words would be felt around the world, and it was now time to take back the spotlight and influence from those that had tried to undermine him at the United Nations in his mind. The senator at the United Nations, however, was aware that the US President was not on the Star Craft. So, in the senator's preparations, he quietly scheduled his presentation by contacting his friends at the United Nations.

The US President became aware of the UN speech when his aids asked him to watch the UN speech on the White House TV. By that time, it was too late to put his machinations into action and put a stop to it. He was powerful and had influence to shut something like this down, but he just didn't have enough time to make the calls that would have enacted it. Now he had a population in front of him that was starting to believe the salvation. He had to put a stop to it.

The man preparing to make the speech was not the evil one that Jesus had warned about but an evil person nonetheless. He was hell-bent on destruction and didn't want a bunch of do-gooders saving the people that he was there to rule over. He was not the demonic President but the demonic prelude to the anti-Christ. It was his role to keep the people of the earth under his thumb. The evil that he had spread throughout the world was going to continue as he tapped into the right emotions to see the people turn against these messengers and side with him. Greed, money, hatred, and fear were the ways this US President had governed for the past three years, and he had no intention of letting his power wane now. His thoughts moved away from his speech and on to his plans.

These people would be easy to smear and undermine. They have turned up to the United Nations in these robes, looking for all the world like a religious cult. They will be looked at through my eyes by the people that follow me. They will be seen as a threat to capitalism. They will be seen as a threat to normal life. They will be seen as a threat to the institutions that govern the way people live. Although there are many people that are suspicious of the ruling elite, they know no other way. They might want to overthrow us, but they are equally scared of what might replace us. I will bring these people to their knees and make the world believe that they are only here for their own ends.

The President was ready. He had rehearsed his speech and knew all the major points that he wanted to make. It was going to be short and straight to the point. In many ways, he didn't want to give them the publicity, but he could see that this might be a threat to his dominance. Already in different parts of the world, people were reacting to the earlier news with violence. He had taught them well. His strategy had been borrowed from the Romans—divide and conquer. As people were split in their lives, they made room for the devil. He got in between families, communities, and the people of different countries, so they lived in fear of each other. The barricades on the streets of Sydney were testament to that. The fights between the rival Roman soccer fans were testimony to that. The demonic President felt that he could rely on this level of fear and division to keep the planet under his control and stop this group of messengers from undermining him. He was determined to win this fight, even if he had to play dirty—especially if he had to play dirty.

Just like the earlier speech in the United Nations, the word had spread virally about the fact that another speech was going to be beamed across the world. People from every corner of the planet again gathered around television sets. Many hadn't slept since the first speech earlier, even though their body clocks were crying out to them that it was three or four in the morning and they needed some rest. The events of the day and the worry that it caused deprived billions of people of their precious sleep. Televisions were tuned in and turned up loud for the words that were about to be delivered.

Back in the White House Oval Office, they were ready. It was time to face the cameras and deliver the message that would grasp control of the world again and stop the evacuation in its tracks. The President was going to spread his message of evil again.

The head of the White House recording staff walked across and said, "Mr. President, you are on in ten seconds."

He slowly took a deep breath and swallowed. Then he began.

"Americans and people of the world, what you have been hearing is fake news from a few people at the United Nations. It all seems like fairy tales to me and anyone with a brain. You call me the leader of the Free World, why was I not at this event that they claim happened? Have I not fought the good fight since you elected me three years ago? Have I not brought peace around the world with our strength? Have I not given Israel peace and allowed them to rebuild their temple? As I have been saying, global warming is false. I claim, therefore, this wild tale of emanate danger to the Earth is also a falsity. I alone should be considered savior of this world."

As with the speech in the United Nations, this sent a shock wave around the world. Those that had already gotten into their cars and were headed away from the cities were listening on their radios. Those that were still near a television set were watching intently. This was a message of status quo. It was a message that everything that was will always be. It was a message that the world was not ending and that they would be all right. So why had the United Nations, a venerable institution, allowed people to spread a message of panic earlier in the day? People all over the planet were confused. They needed some time to take it all in.

The President gave them only a few seconds before he started to speak again. "We have had to deal with those that said the Earth was dying from global warming. I have led the calls to say that this is a lie. We are now supposed to believe that these people who have turned up here in robes like some religious cult have had an audience with Jesus? They say that they have been chosen as messengers. Wouldn't I have been chosen as a messenger seeing as my words carry more weight than anyone else on this planet? We need to stop this now before it becomes a real problem."

The President continued with a few more self-congratulations. He told the world what a great job he had been doing and that he was going to continue doing this great job. Never before in history had a man patted himself on the back so many times on live television. He also used the short time he had to undermine the messengers. He mocked the way they looked. He told the audience that their message was the ramblings that would have most people locked up in an asylum. He told the people of the world to ignore what they had been told earlier in the day.

His message was received with confusion. People had reacted to the news that the planet was in mortal danger with panic, fear, and sometimes violence. They reacted to this message that the world was just fine with a state of confusion. They had seen politicians argue over things in the past, and the world had grown tired of politics. The normal reaction to a disagreement in the Senate about a tax matter was one of apathy. People just didn't care. The reaction to this speech from the President of the United States was one of "We will have to wait and see." Maybe the world needed to sleep and then wake up the next morning and work it all out then. It was just too much to take in.

No matter what the people decided when they slept on it, the President and his allies were in no mood to wait. They had to wrestle back the initiative that the messengers had gained. They had to act quickly and maintain the steely grip that he had over the planet. He had to make the next move.

The message came through to the military base. It read that all personnel were to report for duty. The base commander had received a call from the Secretary of State saying that they were to be deployed in three units to protect the major cities that were closest to them. They were to use all of their troops and all of their equipment to ensure that calm was established and maintained on the streets. They were told that tanks were necessary. As the troops assembled in their units on the floor of the main hangar in the military base, the base commander gave the word to his three deputies. They were to take a third of the men each to a city and take control of the streets. All four of the men in that briefing felt that it had really come to something when they had to do this in their own country but were trained to carry out their orders. The authority of the President was paramount, and the word had come directly from the commander in chief that the country needed to be made secure. The three deputies then passed this briefing to the unit commanders, and then this message was delivered to the men. All of the base would be emptied, which had never happened before. Every member of the base was needed to help restore calm to the people of the nearby cities after the events of that day.

After the instructions, the troops were given fifteen minutes to get all of their things in order to leave the base for a prolonged period. They were asked to get all the personal effects they needed for a long stint in the field. They were then to report back to their units to prepare all the equipment they needed for this campaign. The cooks gathered as many meals as they could make to feed their team for as long as they could. The medics got together all the supplies they might take on a battleship bound for the gulf in case they needed to treat the people in the cities as well as their own soldiers. Everywhere the base was being prepared to be emptied of people and equipment. All the vehicles were filled with gas, as nobody knew how long they would be away for. It was as if they were preparing for war.

Across the cities of the world, Martial Law is being put into effect. The demonic President started his master plan to regain control of the world. With the panic and confusion that had spread across the planet in the wake of the announcement in the United Nations, he had the perfect opportunity to use the might of the militaries under his control to keep the people in check. His reach into the upper echelons of power in every country of the world enabled the President to influence every military to take to the streets with the expressed purpose of keeping control, keeping law and order. Tanks rolled on to the streets of Beijing, Paris, London, Roma, and New York all at the same time. This was a display of power from the people of the current world order that things were not going to change. They wanted the people of the earth to know who was in power.

On the floor of the House of Commons in London, England, a debate was raging about the different speeches given by the people in robes and the American President. There were some members of Parliament that had been present on the Star Craft, and they began the debate by confirming what they had seen. One MP began, "I was there on the same craft as the senator who spoke so eloquently in the United Nations yesterday. I have seen the fate of our planet if we do not act. The scientists in the room confirmed that we could be in grave danger. The fact is that we need to evacuate the planet if we are all to be saved. We were spoken to by a great man."

An opposition MP stood up immediately to speak. "Are we supposed to believe this man just because he turns up here in robes and professes to have seen Jesus? Why was he chosen? What makes him different? This sounds like a conspiracy to me. And you know what they say? If it looks like a conspiracy, sounds like a conspiracy, and smells like a conspiracy, then it *is* a conspiracy." He sat down to roars from the benches of the House. The speaker tried to calm them down with repeated cries of "Order!" but this had no effect for two minutes. It was a chaotic scene that the Houses of Parliament had absorbed over the years. It was an old institution that was officially known as the Palace of Westminster. An official building had stood on the site since the early eleventh century, and the building that was housing the debate was built in the 1830s. It had received little in the way of extensive repair since then and was at that point in need of major renovation work. The estimated bill of six billion pounds sterling was too painful to bring in front of the taxpayers, so the debates continued in an old and decaying relic. The debate on that day continued again after the noise had died down and the speaker had restored something that resembled order. He didn't know how long it would last. The whole site was visible from many parts of London due to the large clock tower known as Big Ben. It stood 315 feet into the London air. As the noise bellowed out from the chamber below, the hands on the clock face slowly moved to show the time: 2:11 p.m.

Another MP dressed in the flowing robe that marked him out as someone who had been on the Star Craft saw this as an opportunity to support his friend who had spoken earlier. "Thank you, Mr. Speaker. My right honorable friends, this is not a matter of party politics. This is a matter of salvation. My honorable friend and I have produced a white paper that outlines all the scientific arguments so you can all see that what we speak about is real," he said calmly.

He had barely sat down when someone stood up from the benches behind him and continued the attack on the calm people in robes. He started to speak loudly. "We have listened to all the nonsense about global warming over the years. We have listened as we were told that we're residing on a dying planet. We have been told to recycle, to cut down our carbon footprint, and to drive our cars, our own cars, less and less. What has the result been? Well, the so-called experts have changed their view. The phrase 'global warming' has disappeared from our lexicon to now be replaced by 'climate change.' The experts cannot be believed on global warming, they cannot be believed on climate change, and I see no reason to believe them on this new story. We don't need your white paper. We need you to leave."

The two members of Parliament that had spoken looked at each other across the floor of the House of Commons. They knew that they were in for a tough ride. The debate continued.

In the United States Congress two other men dressed in long robes were having a similarly tough time. House of Common rules dictate that no matter what else is said in the chambers, no member can call another a liar or refer to what they have said as a lie. That etiquette didn't hold true over the pond, and an influential member of congress spoke her mind when dealing with the men in robes who were about to speak. She tore into them. "I don't know why you have turned up here to speak. We have heard what you have to say from your leader in the United Nations yesterday. We have heard the lies that your people have told the world. The leader of the Free World has given his response. I consider the matter closed."

But of course, the messengers were not going to give up that easily. They had been given a task by Jesus and had to carry it out no matter what barbs and arrows were slung in their direction. As they listened to the attack from the member of congress, they looked serenely around the rest of the room. It was a calm that would serve them well in the debate they were having and the future that was forming in front of them. After being called a liar, one of them stood up to speak. "We are bringing a message of peace and hope. We are bringing grave news that we understand is distressing to hear. All of the people of the earth need some time to take it all in before we all take the road to salvation."

This was met with a great deal of noise from all corners of Congress. The power of Congress was formalized in the United States Constitution and as such has been at the forefront of US political power for centuries. It made laws, debated key issues, and passed judgment. Today it felt like the people that had turned up to Congress in flowing robes were being debated and being judged, even though they were elected members of Congress.

The panic that had spread on the streets after the speech in the United Nations had quelled. It began to burn itself out after the violent clashes and wanton destruction in the immediate aftermath of the announcement. It had further slowed with the speech from the President of the United States, and then the army had moved in to shut any lingering panic down completely. But where the panic had once been, it was now replaced with confusion. People did not know what to believe. They were told that the earth would be destroyed and that they had to evacuate. Then they were told that this was all a lie. But if the world had not changed, then why the tanks and military on the streets? Why were the world stock exchanges all closed for business? Why were the banks all closed and guarded? Why were all the stores closed? People had some very real questions, and they had little in the way of answers.

In the streets, people were talking to each other about the confusion that reigned over them at that moment in time. They wanted to know what was going on. As people began to talk, more joined them, and pretty soon groups of a hundred or more got together. They turned into multitudes that went from asking questions to demanding answers. In cities all over the earth, these throngs of citizens formed and started to assemble outside of banks and large stores. They didn't take on the might of the military for fear of their lives, but they did gather together, chant slogans, and ask questions. The people were starting to become restless with the void in information and guidance that the leaders of the world had created. In any vacuum, the void will be filled by gossip, speculation, and rumor. The crowds gained a life of their own, and quickly gossip spread among each group like wildfire. A common rumor was the one that all of these actions were aimed at, driving up prices and keeping people poor. Outside one grocery store, a group of people began to chant, "Keep our prices down! Keep the common man in charge! Keep our streets free! Keep our people safe!"

The President and his followers needed to take a firm grip on the world and make sure that these small crowds didn't get together and start a rebellion. Over the course of the next few days, a secret army started to emerge. The President and the demonic leaders that he had put into power in other countries tightened their grip on the people. This army was dressed in a way that spread fear throughout the population of the planet and caused the masses to disperse and move underground. They wore no army helmets, which immediately set them apart. They wore instead a black cap that was reminiscent of a general's peaked hat in the Second World War. They were dressed in a black uniform that consisted of black roll neck jumpers and black jeans. But the parts of their uniforms that instilled fear into anyone that encountered this secret army were the long black coats and black jackboots that reminded everyone over a certain age of the SS uniform that the Nazis wore in World War II, and for everyone under a certain age, it was like a phalanx of Stormtroopers had infiltrated the earth but dressed in black rather than white. It was a terrifying sight to see a unit of these black-clad troops approaching your neighborhood because the citizens that lived there knew that they were looking to intimidate and control the people.

This army was reviled by all the people of the earth. It was as though they had been invaded. They became known as the Dark Army by the good people of the earth that wanted to avoid confrontation and violence. Nobody knew where the Dark Army had sprung up from. Some speculated that they were always there in the shadows, waiting for an opportunity to seize power. Others said that they were merely the existing military just out to a different use by the President and his cronies. In a time of mass confusion, others still thought that these were not people at all but an alien race sent to conquer and colonize us. Whatever the true origin of the Dark Army, the truth was that they were brutal to anyone that stood in their way. When the Dark Army first started to rule the streets of the Earth, after the US President's speech, there were some that stood up to them. Some believed that the power of truth would win through and approached the Dark Army soldiers to make them leave or change their beliefs and rebel. Their faith was shaken as the troops beat these people to within an inch of their lives and left their bodies in the street for all others with such lofty ideas to see. They thought that the more brutal they were, the less chance there was of anyone else trying to question their authority. The people of the earth were living in a military state now with every aspect of their lives controlled by the Dark Army and whoever was controlling them from behind the scenes.

RASHURE CODEX

In a stark contrast to the chaos of certain parts of the world, there were places that saw calmness and people coming together as one. Across the holy sites where Jesus had spent his life, there were vigils of thousands of people who were praying in a spirit of oneness. Candles were lit, stories were shared, and faith grew stronger in these places as the devotion to Christ developed for those that had believed in him all their life and had now known that he was there to save them. For many, it was exactly what they had prayed for all of their life—the salvation of Christ. Christian churches in many parts of the world had delivered their sermons in one of two ways over the preceding years. They had either preached a message of unconditional love for everyone and everything on the planet or taught their followers to look with a suspicious eye at some parts of modern society. Business, television, money, capitalism, and gambling were all considered to be things to look at with a careful eye by some parts of Christianity. The people that followed this message had always wanted Christ to lead them away from the planet Earth and all the ills that were present there. This was their time. No matter what side of this small divide people were on, they all came together in the places that had the mark of Jesus from his short life. The message that was on the ground was one of hope and positivity.

At the Sea of Galilee, people of peace were gathered at many different sites to come together and wait for rescue and salvation. Some had travelled from great distances, even on foot, to be there where Jesus had walked and take it all in. A group of around four hundred or so had set up a camp at the site believed to be where Jesus had walked on the water. It was a site steeped in history and religion and was, thus, the perfect place for a camp of peace and hope. The group that had decided to live there had gone back to the days of Jesus in many ways by fishing for their meals and sitting around campfires at night. They all shared stories of their faith and devotion as well as rumors about what had happened on the spacecraft that the messengers in the United Nations had mentioned.

Laurell spoke about her journey to the Sea of Galilee. "I was working on a kibbutz in Israel with many of my fellow Americans when the owner called us all over. He said that something was about to happen and that we needed to see what was going on. We all huddled around a small television set in what smelled like a cow shed and heard the words from the senator. After hearing his words, some of us decided that we just had to be here. We are not all Christians, but we all believe in peace, the God-given rights of life, and we all want to be rescued."

Another told of their life and how it had been changed by Jesus. He spoke as though he were entranced. "I used to be a fighter. I was a boxer, but out of the ring, I caused trouble for my parents. I got into fights in the street, in school, and even with my teachers. When I was around thirteen, I started to drink, and this was soon followed by drugs. My promising boxing career fell apart as I did nothing to look after my body. I lived off the streets and only returned home when things got really desperate or I wanted to steal from my own family. I blamed God for my troubles and ask him why he did not help me. I was lying half-conscious in an alley one day when I saw the light. In my drugged state, I thought that an angel had lifted me from the gutter and taken me to a place of safety. My angel was the preacher's wife, and my place of safety was a shelter run by the church. The kindness and patience that were shown to me by those people changed my life. They taught me the Word of God from the Bible. They taught me that God did not cause my troubles. The devil was at work to see me fail so I would blame God. I have devoted my life in turn to Jesus. From that day, I have always had a strong belief that I would meet Jesus one day. I kept it to myself because I thought it was irrational, but now I know it to be true. I can say it out loud: "I will meet Jesus!"

On an early morning outside the Church of the Holy Sepulchre, people of Christian faith and non-Christians were standing together in a circle around the site where Christ's crucifixion, burial, and resurrection once occurred. They sang hymns and rejoiced that the earth was to be saved. Every one of them stood there with a smile on their face and looked to the heavens where their salvation would come from. The sun beat down on them hard for such an early hour of the day, but the bright light from the Star Craft was ever present in the sky as the Star of David was leading the way to the baby Jesus. It felt to every one of them that the earth and the heavens were as one for those few hours that they sang and talked and prayed together. It was as though this was a celebration of the life of Christ, a kind of party to thank him for his life, his death, and the salvation to come.

One of the revelers was called Stu. He didn't have a Christian upbringing but had always had some faith. He had come here to the area with Laurell, but they had split up when they neared the Sea of Galilee. He stood there surrounded by people of all shapes, sizes, and religions and smiled the biggest smile that had ever crossed his face. He thought, *If only the people of the cities could see how the news should be taken. If only they could make the journey to this site and join with us. I am surrounded by people who know what peace means, they know what life on our new planet should feel like. Emotions spread across people, across countries, and across continents. As our emotion spreads from the Holy Land across the world, at some point it will meet the emotion of fear and panic that is spreading throughout the cities of the world. I just hope that our message of love wins out over the message of fear. But I just don't know what will win out.'*

It was a thought that Stu was not alone in having. Many people were positive about the people they met in the Holy Land but concerned about the ability of people elsewhere on the planet to accept the news and believe in the rescue to come.

But by now, most of the world was a little aware of the impending doom. However, everyone was curious about the details. This is why so many religious centers around the world were welcoming so many new people to come get information.

It had only been two days since Simon and all the messengers had returned from the Star Craft. In the Cowboy Church near Lake Palestine, the congregation was gathered inside the church to hear what Simon, Daniel, and Sierra were to say about their experience. The church had been built in the 1970s from local timber and looked as though it had grown out of the forest floor rather than being built by man. Unlike many 1970s buildings, it had a certain sympathy to the landscape, and Simon was proud to be the preacher of this pretty little church. If they all crammed in tightly, it could hold around four hundred and seventy-five people, and they were certainly crammed in tightly that day. It was as though a celebrity had come to town to get married, and everyone was invited. People longed to hear what the three people standing at the front of the church had to say. Some hadn't slept a wink after the events of the last days and the excitement of hearing firsthand from their own friends. All of the congregation and visitors to the church that day wanted to hear what happened on the strange spacecraft that had been described at the United Nations.

Simon had installed a speaker system in the church when he was made preacher, and today it was playing a selection of music that Daniel had put together. They had been through a rotation of John Denver and Willie Nelson. The mischievous side of Daniel wanted to play a song like "Starman" by David Bowie, but he couldn't bring himself to undermine their message for the sake of a little humor.

The truth was that Daniel still hadn't come back down to earth himself. He was certainly ready for the day and would do everything in his power to spread the word and save the people, but he wasn't quite there. The meeting with Jesus and the healing of his leg had sent him into a euphoria that he was still riding. Simon wasn't sure if Daniel had gotten any sleep in the time since they last met. Not that Simon had found sleep easy himself, but he was sure that he had found some time to rest and close his eyes.

Sierra was something different altogether. Whether it was her tender years or whether she was just content that she had found her calling at such a young age, she had no problem at all in sleeping. Maybe she was just catching up on the lost sleep that she missed that night in the Star Craft. Whatever it was, she slept by night and spread happiness and joy by day, so many children are the light of their family's life. The energy and joy that they bring gives everyone else a new lease of life. And so it was with Sierra since she had returned to the house with her father. Her relatives were stunned to see her take the news of the destruction of the Earth in her stride like this. It was as though nothing had happened. What was really happening inside her head was the thought that nothing had really changed. She was still a ten-year-old girl with the world in front of her. It may not be the same planet that she thought she was living on, but Sierra knew that she could make the future her own. She knew that the actions she took over the next few years would determine the rest of her life. She had known that when speaking to her teachers at school. She had known that from speaking to her parents. She now knew that from speaking with Jesus. In Sierra's eyes, the actions she would have to take were still the actions that shaped her life. Nothing had changed.

As everyone was gathering into the Cowboy Church, Simon started leading everyone in a song. Simon and the usual church members that sang and played music every Sunday were joining in. Simon invited everyone to join in singing "Hallelujah." And joining Simon on stage were Sierra, her mom, and their friends from the singing group, Pentatonix.

I heard there was a secret chord
That David played and it pleased the Lord
But you don't really care for music, do you?

Well, it goes like this, the fourth, the fifth
The minor fall and the major lift
The baffled King composing Hallelujah
Hallelujah, Hallelujah, Hallelujah, Hallelujah

Well, your faith was strong but you needed proof
You saw her bathing on the roof
Her beauty and the moonlight overthrew you

She tied you to her kitchen chair
She broke your throne and she cut your hair
And from your lips she drew the Hallelujah
Hallelujah, Hallelujah, Hallelujah, Hallelujah

Baby, I've been here before
I've seen this room and I've walked this floor
I used to live alone before I knew you
I've seen your flag on the marble arch
But love is not a victory march
It's a cold and it's a broken Hallelujah
Hallelujah, Hallelujah, Hallelujah, Hallelujah

Well, there was a time when you let me know
What's really going on below
But now you never show that to me, do you?
But remember when I moved in you
And the holy dove was moving too
And every breath we drew was Hallelujah
Hallelujah, Hallelujah, Hallelujah, Hallelujah

Well, maybe there's a god above
But all I've ever learned from love
Was how to shoot somebody who outdrew you

It's not a cry that you hear at night
It's not somebody who's seen the light
It's a cold and it's a broken Hallelujah
Hallelujah, Hallelujah, Hallelujah, Hallelujah.

But for everyone else, the world had changed. The President in the Oval Office knew that his absolute authority was at risk. The Dark Army had gone from a group that nobody knew about to the people who kept law and order on the streets of the world. The people in the cities were now subject to checks whenever they wanted to go anywhere and lived in constant fear of the Dark Army.

The people who were in the places that Jesus had lived, walked, and died were living a happy and carefree existence safe in the knowledge that their world would change and that they would be saved. They could start their life anew. After finishing the song, "Hallelujah," Simon and Daniel gathered at the front of the church. They both felt that their lives had changed beyond recognition, and they were metamorphosing from a period of stability to one of massive change. They had both loved their current way of living. They were happy people, who were able to spend their time helping others, going fishing, and spending quality time with the people they loved. At that point, their wives both walked to the front of the church and stood next to Daniel and Simon. It was time to speak.

Daniel knew how to work a crowd. The first thing that they all expected to hear from him was the story of their journey into space to meet Jesus and back again. They were going to have to wait. Daniel spoke. "Let us pray . . ." Then they all bowed their heads in prayer. The next item on Daniels's agenda was a hymn, so the congregation all joined him in singing. He wasn't being nasty, just playing with people a little and making sure that they were in the right place to receive the news. Praying to God and singing to Him too were the best ways to get the heads of the people in the Cowboy Church ready to listen with open ears. Daniel needed a receptive audience after the words of the President had undermined the good work that the senator and astrophysicists had done.

Daniel began, "Thank you for being here today. We have gathered together to give thanks to God for protecting us. But as you all know, there is another step of protection that we need to go through in order to be safe. Simon, Sierra, and I will tell you now what happened to us over the last few days. We can confirm that the words of the senator in the United Nations were true. The three of us were levitated way up into the sky. When we were so high that it was difficult to make out any details on the ground, we were changed into these robes and ushered to a room in what we now know to be called the Star Craft."

At this point, Simon took over. "As we entered this room, we saw influential people from all over the world. There were politicians, religious leaders, people of business, and celebrities. We were told that the Earth is in great danger and that we must evacuate all of the people or at least as many people that want to be rescued. We have been chosen with the others to deliver this message of hope. Who chose us?"

"Jesus did," interjected Sierra. She didn't want to interrupt her father, but she wanted to be the first to say the words to the people gathered around her. Simon did not mind at all. He smiled at his daughter and thought again how calmly and maturely she had handled all of this. He was the proudest father in the world. Sierra continued, "Jesus and the other people on the Star Craft told us that this was not the first time 'man' had to be relocated from a different planet. That this has happened before and they had enacted an evacuation of another planet. They gave us hope that we can be saved, but we must act quickly and pull together."

A voice from the back of the church shouted, "But how are we to believe all of this? Why isn't Jesus here on earth to tell us himself?" Simon looked to the back of the hall. It was a man that he recognized but not from the church. He was the brother of one of the regular church members, and Simon had seen him in bars at all times of the day. He wasn't a man of faith and obviously saw this as an opportunity to put across his own view. Simon stepped forward and spoke. "The earth is ruled by the devil. Sin fills the earth, and Jesus is without sin. Jesus is not safe here. The Bible actually says that when Jesus first comes back, we would meet him above the earth. This is coming to pass in my lifetime. He will lead us to salvation, but that salvation has to be on another planet. The Earth is in danger of a gamma burst that will destroy us. The scientists at the United Nations are the most esteemed on Earth. They were there in the Star Craft with us, and they understood exactly which part of the solar system that the threat was coming from. This is going to happen." Simon said this firmly.

The man at the back stood up again; he had more to say. Either he didn't believe what he was being told or he had decided to play devil's advocate—quite literally. He piped up, "Jesus is a man of miracles, isn't he? If he was present on this spaceship you were supposed to be on, then why didn't he give us a sign? Any sign would do just so we had *something* to believe in."

"He did." At this point, Daniel stood forward to the middle of the church where everyone could see him. Daniel had been a part of the community for as long as anyone could remember, so they all knew him personally. Each and every person in the room also knew Daniel's story and how he had lost his leg. Playing to the crowd, Daniel did his best to walk with the slight hobble that his false leg had given him. He made his way slowly to the middle of the church, and then he spoke. "Everyone that knows me knows of my injury from the war, right? For those that do not know, I lost my leg over fifty years ago." He slowly lifted the white robe to show everyone that he had two "real" legs now. The room gasped and then applauded as they saw his false leg had been dispensed of and replaced by what looked to all of them like a real leg. The people in the room looked at each other with faces of amazement. Their friend, Daniel, had been cured. He had his leg back. This was a miracle. Even the man who had objected to everything that had been said up until that point stared in astonishment at the change to Daniel. Even he seemed to be turned around on the matter.

As the applause died down, Daniel spoke again. "I entered the Star Craft, and my leg was healed. It has a powerful property that cures people. There were people there that no longer needed their wheelchairs. These are signs that we are telling the truth. Come and touch my leg if you need any proof that it is real. I have walked miles on it. I am so happy." Nobody took him up on the offer to touch his leg, but as Daniel walked back to the front of the church, he was showered with congratulations and pats on the back. Daniel was a pillar of the community, and every one of them was genuinely pleased that he was whole again. Daniel couldn't wipe the massive smile from his face, even if he had tried. He felt so good to be part of this community. He loved the people that surrounded him.

Simon then pulled out one of his meteorites from a bag on the stage. Simon lifted it up over the crowd. "Everyone here knows I find meteorites as a hobby. I found this one over ten years ago in the desert near the Holy Land. It has just recently been analyzed and studied at Texas A&M University by Dr. Godfrey Hammond, a famous scientist in the study of meteorites," Simon stated. "He verified its age and composition to be old and authentic. Further, you can see what he discovered embedded in the iron." Only partly uncovered was a ring of gold with a band of symbols inside the ring. The symbols strangely were ancient Hebrew letters. Simon spoke distinctly. "These symbols say, according to the university linguist, YESHUA." Those in the audience that knew their Bible scripture gasped. Simon reminded everyone to read Matthew 1:21.

People in the audience asked Simon what this finding meant, and Simon said, "It means to me that God is real, Jesus is real, and this was the calling card sent to Earth."

"But there seem to be dark forces at play," said Simon in a tone that stopped the rejoicing in its tracks. He hadn't wanted to put a downer on their meeting, but he had to prepare the people in front of him for the tough times that may lie ahead. He looked around the room to make sure that he had the attention of every man, woman, and child before continuing. "Jesus told us that the earth is ruled by the devil, that people will stand in our way and try to undermine what we are doing. The tone from the President in his televised speech is a worrying development. He has made us realize that his people, who stand in our way, can be very powerful indeed. The streets are in lockdown, and there is a sinister army patrolling large parts of the planet. We have to stay united, and we have to stay strong. This finding I am showing you will become a target of the dark forces, I am sure of it."

There were many questions from people who wanted to know the experiences that the three had been through firsthand. Simon, Daniel, and Sierra spoke to people for some time afterwards and reassured people that wanted to know what to do and how it would affect them. The three people that had been on the Star Craft could not give specific answers, but they told everyone they spoke to that everything would be fine and that the people of the Earth would be saved. Simon and Daniel also asked everyone they spoke to for help. They would be in touch in the coming days to mobilize their messengers and spread the message to as many people as they could. Simon added, "We have not heard of a timetable for the evacuation yet. I am expecting it would be sooner rather than later."

The man who had been so negative from the back of the room came over and apologized to Simon. "I am so sorry. I don't know what came over me. My sister has told me that you are a good man many times in the past, and I have had my ears closed to the truth. I wanted to undermine you and mock you because it felt easier than listening to an uncomfortable truth. This man here has helped me see the light," he said as he put his arm around Daniel and drew him into the conversation. It was the most satisfying part of the evening for Daniel and Simon. They knew that there was going to be many more who would not believe them. Many more people who would need to be converted. He was the first, but there was no doubt that he wasn't going to be the last.

As the three of them spoke, Simon looked to his left to see his beautiful daughter talking to her friends. She was the center of attention, and he could see how she was keeping them all full of hope. It can be a lot for a ten-year-old to hear, and Sierra had the benefit of hearing it, seeing it, and taking it all in some time. She had been through all of this before any other ten-year-old present. She was using this experience and the maturity that was growing in her by the minute to reassure those that might not have her self-confidence. It was the second time that evening he felt flushed with pride. As he looked to his right, he saw his wife watching their daughter as well. They both felt the same way about her.

Simon's wife had been busy, as had the wife of Daniel. While Simon, Daniel, and Sierra were talking to people, the two wives of the men in robes had brought out the food that they had prepared for the evening. It wasn't quite on the same scale as the fish supper of a few days earlier (there was no time for a fishing trip on that day), but it was welcomed by everyone. In the same way as the gathering a few days earlier in and around, the same church people sat and talked, ate together, and were generally having a good time. Sierra wondered if this was what it would be like on their new planet. She really hoped that it would be. People shared their stories of hope for the future with each other. The message of positivism and salvation that Simon, Daniel, and Sierra had given in church was one that seemed to have gotten through. People were happy to be in the company of others that shared their faith. They had faith in Simon. They had faith in Daniel. They were starting to develop a faith in the ten-year-old Sierra because of the mature way she was handling all of this. They had faith in the church that they were a part of. They had faith in the teachings of Christ that Simon and Daniel spoke about each week. They had faith in the Bible, their community, and each other. They had faith in Jesus and the fact that he was here to save mankind.

The evening went well. The people of the church were able to put the events that were happening around the world to one side for a few hours. It was always there like a small itch at the back of their head, but if they ignored it for a while, then they could get on with being around like-minded people for a while without distractions.

The church all sat together outside and watched the sunset. As it left the Texas sky, there was a spirit of togetherness among the group. Each and every one of them had spent a few hours in each other's company and were now sitting together, watching a day disappear. None of them knew what the next day would bring. As the sun leaves the sky for the day, it commits the events of that day to history. It becomes part of the past and is indelibly written in the journals of peoples' lives forever. But what it also does is wipe the slate clean for the next day. The past is written in stone, but the future is a blank slate. The people around the church that night had a choice of what to do with that slate. They could either write their own stories on it through their actions or allow others to write the story for them. Seeing as one of the potential authors of their fate was the demonic President, none were willing to give up control of what would happen to them. As a group of people from the eldest to the youngest, they were all determined to spread the message and save the people that they could reach. The will was there, but it was such a daunting task that it was difficult to know where to start. Perhaps one of the preachers could help?

As the last of the sun drained away from the day and left the group shrouded in only the streetlight, someone from the back of the group asked, "Simon and Daniel, what should we do?"

Simon replied, "Pray and be prepared to leave for a new home."

Chapter 8

Beginning Rashure

Deep under the mountain range, the commander of the base had seen nothing like it. Even as a veteran of both Gulf Wars, he hadn't been a part of anything on this scale in all his life. The military operations that were going on at the surface of the Earth were like nothing that the entire planet had seen since World War II. There were not many left alive that had been through the Second World War. Every year the nations that fought in the war held ceremonies to honor their heroes, those that had fallen and those that had come out of the other side to tell the tale. Every year there were fewer and fewer soldiers left from the major war of 1939 to 1945 that spread its fingers to almost every part of the planet. As a result, the days that were being played out on planet Earth at that point were something that only a few eyes had seen before and that nobody had envisioned would ever return to planet Earth. It was as though the clock had turned back over seventy years and the world had returned to the dark days of suspicion and anger.

There were not as many battles on the face of the earth as there was during World War II but the fear and suspicion reached every corner of every home. Nobody knew what was going to happen next. The Dark Army had large parts of the planet in lockdown, and those that wanted to spread a message of hope and salvation were often afraid to speak out because of the fear of recriminations. The commander harbored doubts in his thoughts.

I don't know what the world is coming to. I have been trained to follow orders, respect the absolute authority of the President, and keep the peace, but I can't help feeling that there is a better way. The President has reacted to this news with a harsh solution. The news from the United Nations has sparked a backlash from him that hasn't been seen since George W. Bush and the aftermath of the attacks of 9-11. I will follow orders because I know nothing else, but I hope that this situation can be resolved peacefully. I do not want my soldiers killing other humans that offer nothing but a message of hope. Why has the President reacted so harshly? Where will this end? What does the future hold? I can't help but think that we should be able to work this out together rather than attack each other by words and actions . . .

As he drifted away with his thoughts, the commander was unaware that he was being approached by one of his deputies. He looked into the distance as though there was a fixed point in the base that would provide him with all the answers. From his left came a voice that stopped his thoughts, stopped his search for answers, and returned him to the classified military base deep under the mountains in the heart of the United States of America.

"Sir, we have been monitoring the skies around our planet and the moon. There is something that we have to tell you. We have identified something in the sky that we can't quite explain. We have never seen anything of this size before. We have no idea what this is. It is near the moon and moving towards us. We don't have records on anything like this. It is not another planet, and we don't have things in our universe that move at this speed. What do we do?" said the voice from the left that sounded full of trepidation.

The base commander absorbed the words of this deputy. He wanted to make all the right decisions since the ramifications would be huge. It was the ultimate ripple effect. Whatever he did would mean a lot of movement, a lot of change, and potentially others coming to harm.

"What do we *think* it is?" asked the base commander sternly. He wanted everyone in the room to know that he wasn't going to take a lack of information lightly. He had absolute control of the base and all the men and women in it. He had been given this position from years of service and by battling others to take his place at the top table of the military. His decisions were respected because they were always made based on having the right information. Even in the extreme circumstances that they were facing, he wasn't going to change the tactics that had gotten him to this position.

"Sir, we wouldn't like to hazard a guess. It feels as though it isn't from this planet or this universe. It doesn't show up on our scanners as anything organic. It's not a satellite or a planet or a moon," replied the deputy. He knew he had to give as much information as he could, but in reality, there was nothing to give. It wasn't anything that the crew could identify. He waited with baited breath for the base commander to speak, hoping he had given enough to keep him happy.

"Well, we know exactly what it isn't. I suppose this is a start," said the base commander. The deputy breathed a sigh of relief but knew that he wasn't off the hook yet. He knew that the base commander wanted as much detail as possible. The two of them had risen up through the ranks together. The deputy was always a step or two behind the commander, but by working together, they built a relationship that worked on trust and communication. He knew that the communication being offered about this strange object wasn't enough. But he also knew that he had nothing else to offer.

"Let me think about this," came the response from the base commander. He didn't want to make a decision based on little or no evidence, so he stalled. He stopped the chain of command right there so that he could decide what to do next. The deputy was off the hook because he had done his job—passing on the information to his superior. What happened next was entirely down to the base commander. He mulled over his options, not really wanting to make any decision at all. He wished that he had someone else to talk to.

He wished in situations like this that he could just pick up the phone and call his dad. But that was never going to be an option.

But no matter what he decided on, there was one man who he had to keep in the loop.

"Get me the President on the line. He will want to hear about this."

The phone rang in the Oval Office of the White House. It was a phone that sat on the desk unused for the vast majority of its life. The phone was reserved as a special line between the top military commanders and the commander in chief. In the days of modern government where most decisions were made by committee over a period of weeks, there seemed little use for the phone line straight from a military commander to the President. The Chief of Staff and the Vice President had spoken to him on more than one occasion about having the line removed. They didn't understand the reason for the line. They reasoned that any communications would come up through the chain of command and reach the President via the Secretary of Defense rather than directly from the operations. But the President had always known that there would be potential threats to his dominance. He had always reckoned on the ability to reach the field directly and have the field reach him in the same manner. He had been wary of threats from different avenues from before he was inaugurated. His prescience was being rewarded now. He was able to reach the Dark Army without the interference of other parts of the government machine getting in the way or watering down his orders. He was in full command.

As the phone rang, all of the other occupants of the room looked at each other in confusion. They had never seen this phone ring and, apart from the Vice President and Chief of Staff, hadn't been aware that it even existed. Well, now they were aware, and they were made aware of the importance of the phone when all were ushered out of the room with the brush of the President's right hand. They could smell the anticipation that the President had for this call. He exuded a strong sense of importance to the phone and secrecy by his actions. It made the rest of the room bristle with excitement, even though they were not to be present when the conversation happened.

This was another sign of why this presidency was different. Even if ushered out of the room by past Presidents, the rumor mill would always run, and the reason for the call would work its way back to the people in power. Although they were unable to acknowledge the information that had gleaned to the President, they were always "in the know." With this President, there was no rumor mill. Instead, there was a vacuum of silence that sucked away any chance of people finding out what the President wanted to be kept secret. This was another in a long line of secret conversations that stayed with the single man of President rather than the office of President that constituted all his aides and officials.

Once the room was clear, the President answered the phone. Those with access to the other end of the phone were always told to be patient when they rang. It could be that the President had to clear a whole room full of officials before answering. The base commander waited. He guessed from the pause that there were others present in the Oval Office, and he was prepared to wait as long as necessary. His mission was surrounded with instructions to keep the President informed of what was going on. It was a mission he dared not fail. He waited and waited, knowing that he had no option but to hold the line for as long as it took. He had also cleared the room of people so that he could speak freely. And still he waited. After what seemed like a full hour but was probably only a couple of minutes, the ringing stopped. The receiver had been picked up at the other end.

"This is the President."

The base commander felt a shiver work its way up and down his spine. He had never been so uncomfortable to hear the voice of anyone in his life. It shook him to the core. He couldn't decide whether it was the gravity of the news he was about to deliver or the person he was delivering it, to but something didn't feel right to him. It felt as though the next words he spoke could condemn many people to their death. He felt as though he had the fate of a large part of humanity in the palm of his hand.

"Hello. This is the President," the voice repeated. But this time, rather than a tone of anticipation, it was a tone of irritation. As a suspicious man, the President wondered if his secure line had been infiltrated in some way. He wondered if the forces that plotted against him were trying to contact him directly.

At the other end of the line, the base commander had reached a point of resignation. He knew that he had to speak, and he had to speak now. He began, "Mr. President, there has been a development. A large unidentified object has been seen approaching the Earth from the moon. It appears the stories of an evacuation might have been true. I have to inform you that we don't recognize this object, but my suspicions are that it is the spacecraft that the senator spoke about in the United Nations."

"Thank you," replied the President. "I will ensure that your loyalty is rewarded in the long run. Those that have supported me in this hour of need will see their rewards in eternity." The President hung up the phone and sat back in his chair. He would have to move forward his plans if he was going to defeat his enemies.

The base commander stood motionless. A tear ran down his cheek. He was unable to move, unable to think and completely terrified. He had divided loyalties that he could just not reconcile in his mind. He had worked his way up in the United States military, and all he ever wanted from his career was to be a commander. When he was a raw recruit full of energy and hope, the plan was to stay in the military for life and work his way as far up the ranks as he could. It was only when he had served in the second Gulf War that he identified base commander as his true calling. He loved being in charge of a complex station. He wanted the power of being able to make the decisions that protected people. The military was his life. But he wanted the power so he could use it for good and protect the people of America.

When he was only five years old, his parents died in a car accident. With no other relatives, he went into the care system. But unlike many other stories from the care system, he had a story that revolved around the kindness of strangers. He found that everyone he was in contact with tried to help him on his life journey. He saw the very best of people as they took pity on the orphaned child and gave him all they could to make his life better again. He wanted to repay this kindness back. The base commander loved his country and had sworn to protect the people in it. But the moves of the previous few days had shaken him to his core. He had to follow the orders of his commander in chief, but the orders made him feel uneasy.

And now speaking directly to that commander in chief, he felt sick to his stomach. He had conflicted feelings about even telling the President, and now he had been told that he was going to be rewarded for his loyalty. Rewarded by a man whose very voice froze the base commander in terror. He had to compose himself before he let the rest of the people back in the room. It was not going to be easy.

Over at the White House, the President was enraged. He was deep in his thoughts about this development and how it would affect everything. He had to speak to one of his followers. He opened the door to the Oval Office and called out a name. The man who was attached to that name strode into the office. He looked up and down the others waiting outside of the room. He knew that he had just been elevated to the President's right-hand man. He knew that this was a time to make his mark in the battle for the planet Earth. As he walked past the Vice President, he gave a smirk. He had usurped the Vice President and become second in command. He was going to enjoy that moment. He stood toe to toe with the Vice President, but he didn't have long. The door was closing, and after a few seconds, he scuttled off into the room. There was only time for the President to shout, "And the rest of you stand down," before the door slammed shut and the area was cleared.

No sooner had the man entered the room the President began shouting. He was enraged and wanted someone to sound off to. He hollered, "How dare they? It is one thing sounding off in the United Nations, but this is an act of war. They are coming to take over our planet. Forget stories of Jesus and salvation. This is an invasion. We are under attack as the people of Earth, and I will do everything in my power to stop them. You have access to millions of people through your media empire. Get the words out there that we are not going to stand by and let this happen."

There were vast similarities between the two men that were sitting on either side of the Presidential desk. Both stood around six feet tall with lean, muscular upper bodies, but both had signs of a little middle-aged spread around the middle. They both had hair that was leaving their head for good. As was the way of many men in their fifties, the thick hair that they had enjoyed in their youth had been a thing of the past, a distant memory, and was being replaced with an ever-growing area of bare skin. They had both tried different ways of covering this up, but neither had managed at that point to accept fate and go with it. Their hairdressers told them that "less is more," but it was an easier concept to fully embrace from behind the barber's chair than sit in it. Both wore impeccable suits, the type that big money gave you access to. Neither had chosen the suits themselves, as they didn't have time to go out shopping, but they had been measured by the best tailors in Washington, and then a range of suits were delivered. As it happened, both men were dressed by the same tailor. One was told that it would make them more trustworthy with the electorate, and the other had been told that it would exude power in the boardroom. Both ended up wearing the same suits for different reasons. And now the suits were joined again in the Oval Office, plotting to stop the evacuation of the earth.

There was a flurry of secret and careful activity going on outside of the Oval Office all over the White House. Some of the staff knew the senator who spoke in the United Nations very well and had been in touch with him over the prior few days. They had listened to him and put their faith in him. Many of the members of staff were secretly packing up documents and personal effects. They were going to leave the White House at the first opportunity and join those who would be saved on the Star Craft. They had no intention of staying with the President. He had struck fear in many members of the White House staff from his very first visit. It was as though he could read their minds. He looked intently at people for a few seconds, and they felt the fear. His way with people and his high degree of suspicion in every situation put the whole room, the whole White House, the whole government, the whole of Washington, and sometimes the whole county on edge. He trusted no one and always seemed to be looking for plots against him that were not there. Many of the White House team had been there for decades and served many presidents, but none like this one.

As documents were packed up, loved ones were called, and plans were made to leave; there was this feeling of mistrust again among the staff members. Everything was carried out in secret because they didn't know who else was looking to leave and who were allied to the President. People closed the blinds in their private offices and locked doors and filing cabinets wherever they could. Documents were packed into sealed "Top Secret" envelopes so that they could be secreted from the building without others prying. It was a difficult time, but if people were going to make it out of the building undetected, then their best bet was to do this alone.

As the base commander contemplated his role in the downfall or salvation of the Earth, the Star Craft continued its journey towards the Earth. As the President and media mogul plotted the next move in undermining the evacuation, the Star Craft headed towards the Earth to enact the salvation of the people. As the staff members of the White House made their preparations to leave the place they thought was the safest in the world, the Star Craft came ever closer to bringing them to another world that would protect them from threats that the White House denied. The Star Craft was so close now that radar was able to pick it up. It was confirmed. The process of evacuation was about to start.

Back in the United Nations, there was activity in every room. The ambassadors from every country represented by the United Nations were preparing for what was to be another monumental announcement. They had no idea what was going to be said, but the fact that the senator dressed in robes was here again and was preparing to speak to the assembly and the world via television link had the place in frenzy. It had been a few days since the first speech, but those few days had been filled with counter accusations from the President of the United States, something akin to martial law on the streets and reports the world over of a strange craft approaching the planet Earth. If you had looked closely enough, you would have seen reports of strange craft approaching the Earth on a daily basis throughout the preceding twenty years. They were always labeled as hoaxes, and the people who reported them were called crackpots. Now every mention of a spacecraft in the sky or an alien landing was seen as the truth. There was no more or less truth in the reports. They were just given much more prominence and authority in the light of the events that had happened in the few days before.

The senator paced up and down the room while he prepared his speech. He knew that the forces of evil would try to stop him. He had chosen the television company owned by one of the others that was on the Star Craft to supply the cameras and broadcast equipment for his speech. He knew that the President would try to stop him from reaching the world audience by any means, so he turned to people that he knew he could trust. The fact was that he was going to speak only a few minutes after he arrived in the United Nations. If he had announced his intentions much earlier, then the President might have had time to pull the plug. But with only a few minutes' notice, it was going to be nigh on impossible for the President to stand in his way. He had also arranged for the utility company owned by another fellow Star Craft messenger to cut communications from the media company owned by the biggest media mogul in America to the TV stations he owned. He was a suspicious character, and the senator had received reports that he was in the White House. It had to be more than a coincidence that this powerful media mogul was in the President's home when he was not a part of the government. He had the power to derail the message by pulling the broadcast from his many channels in different parts of the world. They could not afford to let this happen. His station managers would automatically assume that he wanted to show the biggest news event in the world that day live on every station in the world. Cutting his lines of communication would ensure that as many people as possible would see what the senator had to say.

The senator looked out to the main assembly area of the United Nations. He knew that he had to speak. He thought that there might be an attempt on his life. He thought that the evil forces that tried to stop the message of peace and salvation would stop at nothing to keep the devil in charge on the Earth and condemn the people of the planet to oblivion. He thought back to John F Kennedy and the legacy that he left behind after his death. He thought back to the extinguished hope in the country after his brother, Robert, was killed when he looked like becoming the second Kennedy to the presidency. He thought of the hope and change that Martin Luther King had brought to the world both before and after his death. The senator didn't want to be thought of in the same breath as these great Americans. He wasn't trying to covet glory, but he wanted to reassure himself that even if he were to be killed for his beliefs, it didn't mean that his beliefs died with him. He had a message to deliver. It was time.

    The senator walked towards the same place he had given his first speech. He now wasn't flanked by scientists and astrophysicists to back up his words. This was not a message of science but simple instructions that the time was now here. As he walked to the main stage, he could see the members of the United Nations taking their seats as they had done in this building for over fifty years. They were settling in their seats with their headphones on as the translators took the senator's words from English to their own native tongue. The imposing building in a city of imposing buildings was starting to quiet in anticipation of the senator. It was sure to be the most far-reaching speech in the history of the United Nations, or indeed the history of the world. With the advent of twenty-four-hour news channels, social media, smartphones, and SMS messaging, it was sure that this message would hit billions of people in a matter of minutes. It would be poured over by news stations for a hundred times the length of the speech and more. It would be trending on every social media platform in every country of the world. It would send the cell phone systems into meltdown, sealing with the sheer number of text messages. People would upload their own clips, their reactions, their memes, and anything else related to the speech on YouTube and on their blogs. The senator would speak, the media would relay his message, and the world would react. In fact, the senator was relying on the fact that the media would get this message to as many people as possible in as short a time as possible. It was the best way of getting the message out there. The time had come.

The senator looked up at the huge clock face that adorned the wall to his right. It was 11:11 a.m. He went through his breathing exercises for twenty seconds, and he was ready to address the world.

"My fellow United Nations members, people of the world, the time is now. I spoke to you all a few days ago about the danger we all face. The planet is under threat. We are all in grave danger. I gave you the scientists that confirmed what we had been told on the Star Craft. The message is still clear. We need to evacuate the Earth in order to save humankind," he said in a slow, steady, and decisive tone. He was a natural speaker. Many of his fellow senators had taken classes in public speaking, but he had never needed them. His voice carried well whether it was in a one-on-one situation, a crowded room, or in a large hall such as this. Of course, he was wearing a microphone to amplify his voice and carry it to the translators, but he could have carried the room without it should circumstances have required it. He continued, "There has been talk from others that we are here not to save you but to harm you. I am here again to reassure you that we only have the salvation of the people in our hearts. I urge you to look beyond those that seek to undermine us. I urge you to look beyond those that have put the streets into lockdown. I urge you to look towards the light and away from the darkness that threatens to engulf us. This is not an easy message to listen to. These are not easy instructions to take. I understand your concerns."

As with his first speech at the United Nations, the senator wanted to do two things with the way he spoke. He wanted to keep it short so that people listened to the message, and he wanted to pause at times so that those watching and listening were able to take it all in. This was one such place that he knew a pause would have maximum effect. It wasn't just for the information they had already received but for the information he was about to deliver next. *Thirty seconds should do it*, the senator thought. Those thirty seconds felt like an age, but the senator had counted them out in his head. *One Mississippi, two Mississippi, three Mississippi . . .'*

At the end of the thirty seconds, he could see that everyone was ready. The translators had stopped talking and typing. All heads were in his direction. He could also feel the same attention from the world through the television camera that was pointed directly into his face. With many speeches read from teleprompts, the modern politicians usually concentrated so much of their energy on reading the words that they lost all awareness of their surroundings. On this occasion, the words of the senator were not scripted. They came from the heart. This meant that he was aware of every movement in the gallery above him, every twitch of the camera operator, and it seemed as though he could feel the mood of the planet Earth around him. The thirty seconds were up. It was time to address the world again.

"The craft to lead us to safety is well on the way to the planet Earth. We will be in a position to evacuate very soon. I need you all to stay calm and prepare to leave this world. We will be led to safety by Jesus. He will be our guide to our new planet. I don't have details on how the evacuation will take place, this will be revealed when they are ready. At this time, I can only tell you that there is room for everyone, so we will leave in an orderly fashion. Remain calm. Thank you for your patience, and we can do this if we all stick together."

And then the senator stepped down from the podium. He had lost all energy and was barely able to make it back to his room. The hope and positivism of his message was uplifting to the people of the earth, but it sapped the strength from the senator. The weight of expectation of his speech and then the reactions that it might cause were heavy burdens for the senator, and he sat down to rest.

The senator reflected on the week he had been through. It had started normally with debates in the house and meetings with union delegates. From there, he had expected more of the same, but he was surrounded by a bright light when walking from the senate to a meeting with a colleague, and then everything changed. He had been awed by the Star Craft, and then this awe had been cranked up a notch when Hozai and Marta began to speak. The arrival of Jesus nearly knocked him off his feet. As a senator for nearly thirty-five years, he thought he had seen it all. His political life had given him access to sights that others don't know about. He had seen top secret files that were only distributed among the higher echelons of government. He had visited other countries and seen how their world was different from his. The abject poverty he saw in parts of India and Africa made him an advocate of foreign aid where many of his fellow senators opposed it. He had been privileged to see the US military operations both in peace time and wartime. He was proud that these guys and girls were there working hard to look after the country he loved. But all of this seemed irrelevant now. It was time to start afresh on a new planet, one where he hoped there would be no need for foreign aid and no need for a military. A place where he hoped poverty and war were eliminated by love and peace.

On the journey back from the Star Craft, he had been one of the reconciliatory voices. He listened and spoke in much the same way that Daniel had. He knew that all of the people on board had been selected because they could work together to build an evacuation that was safe and effective. Because of his reconciliatory tone and his penchant for public speaking, he had been put forward as the person of choice to speak to the United Nations. Not anyone could just address the United Nations assembly, so it had to be a top-ranking official, and the senator fit the bill. He spoke eloquently on the spacecraft and was expected to speak eloquently in the United Nations. Everyone who listened felt that he had spoken with passion and delivered the message in a positive way. Adding the evidence from the astrophysicists was the idea of the senator, and it added that extra layer of authority that made the speech effective. But perhaps it had been too effective. The senator had seen the reports of panic and violence on the streets of different parts of the world. He had heard the speech from the President telling the world that these strange people dressed in robes were here to undermine normal everyday life. He had seen firsthand the debates in the senate where he and his fellow messengers were branded liars. He had read similar reports from government debates the world over. He had seen the Dark Army take over the streets in an attempt to control the people.

He sat in his room at the United Nations, wondering what his latest speech would mean to the people of the world. Would they be further punished by the Dark Army? Would the President attack the

Star Craft? Would the people react with violence and panic again? Would chaos reign? He could not know at that time. He had a role to play, and that role was to get the message out there. By addressing the United Nations and ensuring that it was broadcast across the world, he reached billions in a matter of seconds. It was the best way to start the evacuation. It was the best way to start the salvation of the human race.

His part was delivered, and it was now down to those in the Star Craft to enact their role and get the spacecraft ready to take the people to safety. He looked upwards. The senator looked towards the ceiling. He knew the next move would happen up there.

On the Star Craft, Marta and Hozai were in the control room. They had spent enough time there to know how to direct the crew of the craft in a mission as this. It was intuitive to control, and the two of them gave orders in a systematic way that sounded more like two conductors of an orchestra while they were directing it towards the earth. They both knew by now that they could be seen by radars and telescopes all over the world. There was no hiding the fact that there was a spaceship coming towards the Earth, even though the Star Craft lights had been illuminated for days over the Earth next to the moon. There was no denying the facts anymore by the demonic President and the followers. Although they had no idea how things were going on the surface of the planet, the assumption was that the people they had brought on board a few days earlier were letting people know that salvation was on the way—and the reason that salvation was needed. They had the same faith that Jesus had shown in the messengers; in fact, Hozai and Marta had helped to choose them. All they could do from this distance was hope that it had been done and then send the spacecraft to save the people.

If the demonic President and his followers had tried to argue that the messengers in long robes were telling a lie or spouting a conspiracy theory, then the presence of the Star Craft would do two things. Firstly, it would show the world that the demonic President was wrong and a liar. It would show that there is a craft headed for earth that would provide a route out of the path of danger. But secondly, it would also up the ante. The demonic President would have to find a new tactic to counter the threat to his world dominance. This could easily be violence or oppression. Hozai and Marta were confident in the ability of the messengers to speak to the people but also knew that the demonic one was a dangerous foe. He had access to nuclear weapons as well as having the entire force of the military at his fingertips. This was going to be a critical time in the evacuation of the Earth. They were approaching to save the people, but they were also aware that their actions could put people in harm's way.

"I hope that we are approaching a planet that is ready for our arrival," said Marta. She always spoke first in conversations with Hozai. It wasn't that he didn't want to talk, but he wasn't very good at starting conversations.

"I'm sure that the messengers have carried out their role. I'm sure that they have warned as many people as possible," replied Hozai. He knew what Marta was getting at. The demonic one was indeed a tough enemy, and he would stop at nothing to maintain his tight grip on the planet and the people that lived there. "We just need to do our part and have faith that the rest of the necessary actions have been taken care of."

"I am sure that you are right. These people were chosen for their skills, their faith, and their reach. There are seven billion people on the planet. A mass evacuation of this scale has never been enacted before. We will be ready." Marta spoke again. She was more confident this time, her faith restored by Hozai's calm words. He had always made her feel confident in the actions they were taking out. He had a quiet dedication to the task in hand, and this instilled confidence in her as well.

The control room where the two stood was filled with touch screens and monitors. It allowed them to see all that was going on in every part of the Star Craft. As a ship with many parts and covering a vast area, the Star Craft took a long time to navigate by foot, so there were systems in place to ensure that whoever was in the control room could see what was going on. The room was as plain as the rest of the Star Craft. Everything there was for function and comfort rather than show. It was set out in white from bottom to top. The only differences were the different shades of light colors that denoted a button, switch, or dial. Despite the apparent lack of color and life in the control room, it was the place that Marta and Hozai liked the most on the Star Craft. It gave them a sense of purpose about their mission. In the control room, they were just that—in control. They could see the future and know that it would contain the salvation of the people of Earth. It was their role alongside Jesus to look after the people of planet Earth.

The time was upon them. All of the work that had been put in to get here was now going to bear fruit, or so they hoped. The two looked at each other. The time for talk was over, and the time for action was seconds away. Both Hozai and Marta felt a rush of adrenaline at that very point. The next few seconds would set in motion a series of events that could never be undone. The spacecraft would be heading out to different parts of the planet beneath them and would soon arrive. What reception they got when they arrived was still to be seen.

Everything was in place.

It was time.

Marta gave the order. "Begin Rashure."

Back underground, the base commander had put the whole station on red alert. The tone from the President meant that he had to be on top of the entire situation, and even the smallest development was something to be analyzed and reported back. It wasn't that he wanted to earn the rewards that the President had spoken about; it was the fact that he was petrified that if he missed anything, the punishments would far outweigh the rewards. The voice of the President made him shudder. Whenever he replayed that conversation back in his head, the base commander felt the tears well up in his eyes. He had to stay vigilant or face the consequences. He was sure that both he and his family would be in trouble if he missed something or failed to report.

As a consequence, the tension in the base was ramped up. All breaks were cancelled, and the entire team was expected to work until this situation resolved itself. Tired people watching strange events were a weird mix. The crew watched intently because they had all heard the announcement from the United Nations one way or another, and they all had their own opinions on what that meant for the world. The fact that the most interesting events ever to have occurred to the planet were happening right now kept their alertness levels high. From deep within the mountain, there was a lot of rock between them and the surface of the Earth. There was then a lot of sky between the surface of the Earth and the edge of the Earth's atmosphere. From the edge of the atmosphere, there was a lot of space until you reached the Star Craft, but it bore down on the planet as though it was just above their heads. The expectation of what might happen next made the Star Craft bigger and closer than it would if it were any other object. Every time a politician spoke about the situation, the Star Craft grew bigger in the imagination of the people in the base. Every time the President countered their claims, it grew a little smaller again. This game of growth and shrink had gone on for a few days now. The military and civilian officers in the base had been focused on the sky since the first announcement by the senator in the United Nations. Now the empty sky that they had been watching was filled. It was filled with something that none of them had ever seen before.

There were fourteen radars in the underground base. Some were there to look at different parts of the sky, while others were used only as a backup if the main ones failed. On this occasion, all fourteen were trained on the same part of the sky all at the same time. The radars were all picking up the same object, but the base commander wanted to be absolutely sure that he was tracking the right object and that he could be right on top of things if there were any changes. The fact was that the object was still making its way towards the Earth, but the speed of movement had slowed, if only a little. Was this enough of a development to relay to the President? Would he be thanked for keeping in touch? Would he be admonished for wasting valuable time? He decided that this wasn't a development at all. Little did the base commander know that he wasn't far from the next development, and this would definitely be something to speak to the President about.

The radar operators were all sitting with their eyes glued to their screens. The pressure and fear that the base commander had felt from the President had worked its way through the entire base. People were on high alert as they walked through doors or grabbed a drink. The tension was in every movement. For every member of the team, it felt like there were a thousand eyes watching their every move, all topped off by the all-seeing eyes of the President. The crew had all seen parts of the news conferences over the last few days. They all knew that there was a lockdown on the streets in large parts of the world. They knew that the President was behind it all. As a group, they were not going to get on the wrong side of that man.

The most pressure thus fell on the shoulders of the radar operators. They were the ones with their eyes on the sky. They were the ones with all of their senses trained on the large object moving towards the Earth. One of the radar operators was Sandra Smith. She had studied physics at university and had joined the military not long after graduation. She was staring at radar screen number 5 where she had been stationed for several hours without moving. She had reached the point with the screen that she used to reach with the television. After several hours of binge watching the screen, it was just there in front of her. It was emitting lights and sounds and a little movement, but she just wasn't taking it all in. She knew that there were thirteen other radar operators, and if something happened, one of them would pick it up. She could then shake herself out of her slumber and check the screen before confirming what was going on. Sandra was losing the concentration level that was required, but she was going to rely on the others there. But then she had a thought. What if all the other radar operators felt the same? What if they all switched off and left it to each other? All the radar operators had been working nonstop for, at least, as long as she had. They were all tired, and all had been focusing solely on a small screen for hours. If they missed something, there would be a problem.

The base commander was obviously scared by the potential consequences because he had put everyone on high alert. He would probably see to it that they were court marshaled. The President would probably see to it that they were all punished. In the current climate, she could only imagine what that punishment might be. She had to stay awake. She pinched herself on the arm. The pain was sharp but short. She felt it move up her arm and towards the receptors in the brain that would keep her awake. It worked. Sandra decided that she needed to do this every minute or so until the feeling of tiredness passed or the situation was resolved. She reached into the drawer under the desk. She shared the desk with two other radar operators. There was three of everything in the base. This meant that they could all work eight-hour shifts and be rested for when the next shift started. Sandra had no idea where the other two radar operators for radar number 5 were, but she could say that she hadn't seen them that day. There was a lot of activity in the base, that was for sure, and the other operators may well have been working away at the lower levels preparing whatever it was the base commander, probably on the orders of the President, had directed them to.

In the desk, there was a four-pack of energy drinks. Sandra had never even tasted one of these. The pungent smell had always left her reeling from them. She knew colleagues that swore by them. She knew of people that had one as soon as they got up in the morning. She had heard of people downing six or eight during a shift. She knew that some people took them with alcohol so that they could party harder and longer. Sandra had none of these experiences, but she had the need to stay awake and alert, so she broke off one of the cans, clicked the top, and lifted it to her mouth. The smell was there again—a smell of sugar and caffeine. Sandra held her nose and took a swig. Sandra could feel the drink coarse through her body. It was like a thousand pinches across the top of her torso, arms, and head all at the same time. She resisted the urge to put her fingers down her throat and bring it all back up again. Sandra felt a buzz of sugar racing through her body. She knew that this was the high and had no idea how long it would last. She gave up on pinching and took another swig. She was sure to stay awake for quite some time now.

She looked across the room and saw all the other radar operators trying some technique or other to stay awake. They stopped short of matchsticks to keep their eyes open but tried pretty much everything else. They were pinching themselves as Sandra had done, stretching their arms and legs simultaneously, rotating their heads, crunching their shoulders, and slapping themselves on the face. The struggle to stay alert had hit the whole team. Sandra felt a step ahead of them with her first taste of an energy drink. If she felt like she didn't need to have the other three safely tucked away in her drawer, then she would have offered them around. She didn't want to share the feeling that they had given her. She wanted access to more if she had to sit there for hours more.

As it happened, she didn't have to wait that long for something to occur. It was only a few minutes after she had perked up from the effects of the energy drink that the object on her radar started to change. It was growing. The object on the screen of all the radar operators was doing the same thing. On the screens, it started to increase in size, at first by a little, and then gradually over time it went from a big object in the sky to something massive, something that the radar operators had difficulty grasping.

"Sir, you have to see this," said Sandra to the base commander. She was the first to react and the first to speak. While all the others were sitting open mouthed at the radar screen in front of them, Sandra had seen what was going on and called the base commander over. That was the power of the first ever energy drink, Sandra told herself. She thought it was a shame that she could never have that first again.

The base commander didn't speak. He lifted his head from where he was sitting and looked across the room at Sandra. She was sitting bolt upright with one eye on the screen in front of her and one on the base commander himself. As he looked down the line of radar operators, he could see the expressions on their faces. He knew that this was the development that they had all held their breath for. He knew that this was going to be something he did have to see. He knew that he was perhaps only minutes away from another awkward and frightening telephone conversation with the President. He strode slowly over to the radar operator number 5 to see what was happening. He thought that his slow purposeful stride would do two things. Firstly, it would instill a sense of calm in the room. He knew from the faces of his radar operators that something major was happening in the sky above their heads. He had seen over the last few days what panic can do to people, so with a calm demeanor, he could keep the others in the room calm. Secondly, he also walked slowly because he hoped that by the time he reached radar operator number 5 and looked at her screen, the thing would have gone away. He didn't want to deal with the consequences, so he hoped that his slow walk would give whatever it was the time to undo itself and restore everything back to how it was. He knew it was a vain hope, but it would make his life so much easier.

During the slow walk across the room, only Sandra looked in his direction. She wasn't sure if he had seen from that distance away which of the operators had called him, and she wanted to make sure that he knew it was her.

They both looked together at the screen. Sandra knew that the room would soon be cleared again. She knew that the base commander had to tell his boss.

The Star Craft was preparing for the evacuation of the Earth. The spherical surface of the Star Craft contained thousands of docking points for all of the smaller triangular transport craft. So, as each of these became detached from the main craft to head for earth and the people, it appeared from way below that the Star Craft was actually getting bigger and bigger. The radar screen could only pick up the fact that the object in front of them was growing. What it could not see was the fact that all of the extra growth was parts of the original craft that had been spotted far earlier. The movement of the triangular transport craft away from the Star Craft was noiseless. Sound has no way to travel in space, so the sound of thousands of craft leaving their docking and heading away from the mother ship was eerily silent. But the noise that they made back on Earth when they hovered and started the evacuation would shake the White House. By now, the base commander would have emptied the room. By now, he would have picked up that secure line and spoken to the President. By now, the base commander would have been congratulated again. By now, the terror would have been audible in his voice. By now, the

President would have been in a rage over the movement of the transport craft. By now, the world would be one step closer to salvation, while the President would be one step closer to drastic action.

But the transport craft were programmed to carry out their task. They were not fueled by human emotion. They were there to carry out their mission and deliver the people back to the Star Craft and safety. As each detached from the Star Craft, it moved into position. Each would spread further from the Star Craft than the last. The transport craft would eventually be positioned all around the Earth. They were positioned so that every part of the Earth had a corresponding triangular transport craft above it, miles into the sky. When the full set of craft was positioned, it looked as though it might be a scene from a movie. The craft could have been viewed by anyone with a sinister mind or who hadn't heard the words of the messengers as an invasion of the planet. Science fiction had taught people that this was the way the planet was going to be invaded. But this was not an invasion; this was an evacuation.

Over the years since the launch of Sputnik 1 on 4th October 1957, mankind had launched thousands of satellites into space. If you add to this all the debris left behind from space missions, then the orbit of space can be a dangerous place to fly. Space junk, as it is known, was becoming quite a problem for the commercial companies that wanted to sell space flights for tens of thousands of dollars. Most of it would leave dents in their craft, but some of the bigger ones would wipe out a small commercial spacecraft and kill all of those on board. It was a problem that was being considered. On the Star Craft, they were also aware of the number of objects that could stand in their way on the journey to and from the Earth. The atmosphere of the Earth posed some pretty serious problems, especially seeing as they were flying billions of people on thousands of transport craft.

Before the journey into the Earth's atmosphere, Hozai pressed a button on the white control panel of the Star Craft. At once, the triangular transport craft all aligned with the Earth. In a simultaneous action, the three corners of the craft ends glowed a low red light for around fifteen seconds, and then this light grew in intensity before leaving the craft towards the Earth. This collective blast vaporized all the metal satellites and debris orbiting the Earth. This was a safety measure for the transport craft to land on the Earth. The people of the planet were going to be saved, not put in danger from all the debris that might take out a transport craft and cause damage. This action didn't only cause the atmosphere of the Earth to be safe to enter, but it also wiped out all the satellites and other equipment used by the military and the Dark Army. Almost at once, the capabilities of the President to see what was going on and command a large army were neutered.

In the underground base, the base commander and Sandra were still huddled around radar screen number 5. They had watched the strange object appear to grow bigger and bigger as it approached the Earth. After a brief period where the room was cleared and the President was informed, the study of the radar screens continued. The base commander had taken up the same position around Sandra's desk as he was before. As the two of them sat together, they watched in confusion as the now bigger object appeared to break off again into smaller pieces that were positioning themselves around the globe. The radar picked up the movement, and the whole row of radar operators looked in a confused state at the proceedings. Nobody had any idea what was happening.

Sandra was just about to speak to the base commander. Just as the words reached her lips, all the screens went blank. From where she was sitting, she could see the screens immediately to her left and right, and all of those were blank as well. As Sandra and the base commander, both now standing up, looked around the room, they could see blank faces to match the blank screens. There was not a radar in the entire building that was working. The base commander ran along the line of screens, checking each one to see if there was any sign of life. As he moved up and down the line, each radar screen operator looked up at him from their seat. The glances were a mix of fear and confusion. They wanted to know what was going on. They wanted the base commander to help. They wanted to know how he was going to react. The base commander had no idea how he was going to react either. This was a most strange development and one that he had not foreseen. They must have taken out the satellites. They must have begun the evacuation plan.

J.R. PHILLIPS

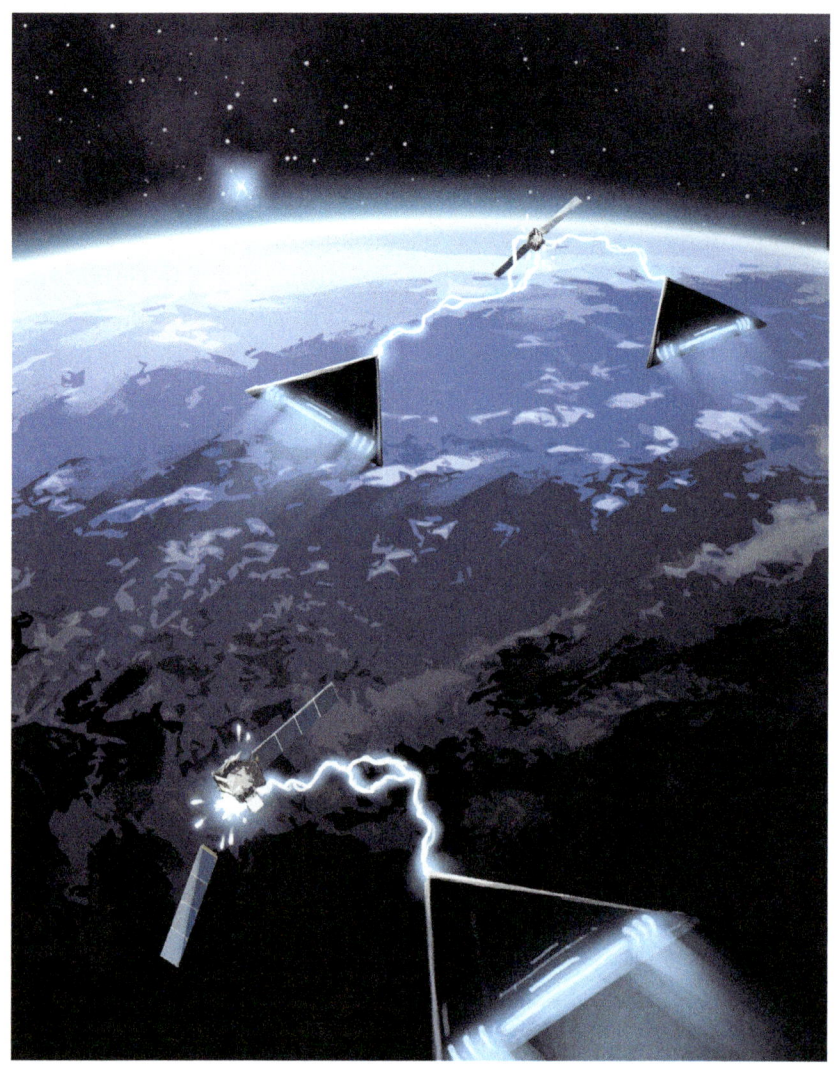

It was the same scene the world over. The communication systems that so many people relied on were switched from on to off in an instant. It meant that the world lost the ability to communicate through technology. GPS shut down straight away, as did the cell phone network. People who were on their phone and suddenly had it cut off looked to the sky. The social media and cell phone network that had helped to deliver the message that the planet was to be evacuated had also signaled the beginning of that evacuation—by being shut down. Many people rejoiced and threw away their technology. They were ready to be saved and start a new life.

There was a different reaction in the military bases of the world. The screens went blank in the bases of every army and every part of the Dark Army. It caused a sense of disbelief in every military base, in the same way as the underground mountain base where Sandra and the base commander were sitting. The blank screens and blank looks of the underground base were repeated all over the world. With a lack of information, the military were rendered motionless for a short time. The military all over the world were blind and powerless for that moment. Without access to data on what was going on at the surface of the Earth and the skies above it, the military had no idea what to do next. There was a vacuum of activity that engulfed the military and Dark Army. Each individual base commander, each battalion leader, each group commander on the streets were in a state of confusion. But like any vacuum, it had to be filled.

The base commanders of the world started to think about their situations. Each had been charged with protecting the Earth and repelling the advance of these strange craft that were heading their way. Each base commander had been given explicit instructions by the President or one of his loyal followers that they must do everything in their power to stop the craft from entering the earth's atmosphere and causing an invasion. There was no option left to them but to follow orders. There was no course of action but to fight back, and fight back with everything they had.

Tanks rolled onto the streets. War ships left their docks and headed out to open seas where they could launch their missiles at the sky. All of the air forces of the world were deployed to head to the skies and patrol the area. They were told that there was going to be an attack from above, and it was their job to stop these strange craft from entering the sovereign air space of the Earth and to stop them from hovering or landing. There were scenes of chaotic action in every military installation of the planet. People ran from their rooms and prepared their equipment. The troops on the streets were to be reinforced with guns and armor. The tanks that were not needed to secure the streets were to be taken out to isolated areas with their guns trained on the sky. Naval personnel were called back from shore leave to board their vessels and prepare for war. The seas were filled with battleships from different nations. Usually, battleships, submarines, and other naval craft in this close proximity to each other would cause a standoff and a diplomatic storm that shook the world in the same way as the Cuban Missile Crisis. But they were all united in the same task—to clear the skies of the spacecraft that they had been told were here to invade the Earth. The President and his followers had made it clear. This was a fight to save the planet. This would be a fight to the death.

Sirens wailed at air bases all over the world. Planes were filled with fuel, ammunition, and missiles for the battle that lay ahead. The activity was a blur to most. They had all seen the television news reports of the previous few days. They had all seen the senator speak in the United Nations to the people of the Earth. They had all then seen the President speak and state that all the senator said was a lie. They had seen the chaos on the streets, they had seen the order restored, and they had heard now of all their radars and communications being wiped out by these alien craft. It was time to fight back.

Two pilots were waiting for their planes to be loaded and fueled before they took off on their mission. "We are going to have to fly without radar, without communications. What will we do?" he said.

The fellow pilot responded with a simplicity that cut through the tension. He said, "Just point at the strange things flying through the air and shoot. You don't need radar for that!" His colleague was shocked at the clarity the second pilot showed in such a tense situation. He knew that there was no other way. Thinking too deeply about the matter or trying something new wouldn't work. Just fly, point, and shoot. That was all they could do to save against the invasion that was now imminent. As their planes were finally loaded, the two pilots wished each other luck and entered their cockpits. They were ready to fight the invasion that their President had warned against. They were about to fly off into the sky and repel the invaders that they were told were here to conquer.

Air bases all over the world prepared to fight. Pilots had conversations with each other about what to do without radars. Support teams got them ready. The Dark Army was taking further control of the streets, the seas, and the skies. The President was tightening his grip on the planet Earth.

It was as though the Dark Army went through a similar growth pattern to the one the radar operators thought the Star Craft was going through. The army on the surface was only a small percentage of the overall power of the Dark Army. They had been waiting for the messengers to up the ante before they moved *en masse*. Even though it had only been a few days since the speech in the United Nations, the Dark Army had also been busy recruiting new members. Those that did not believe the messengers and supported the President were easy to find. The Dark Army recruiters looked in bars for those that said too much when they were full of liquor. The business world that looked to the dollar for their faith, love, and inspiration were another rich source of new recruits for the Dark Army. They also looked in brothels, in drug dens, and in certain areas of politics for people that wanted the world to stay the way it was. The Dark Army had added recruits, promised them the Earth (literally), and then given them the incentive to support the troops that were already starting to emerge from their underground caves, military facilities, and secret hideouts. The Dark Army grew and grew until it was a fearsome force that could reach out across the whole planet. In the first few days, it was obvious that they could control the streets of the major cities. Then it was obvious that they had friends in high places that were willing to support the Dark Army with supplies and equipment. By this point, it was quite obvious that the Dark Army were going to try to stop the evacuation of the people on Earth wholesale. They were going to try to wipe the spacecraft from the sky and stop the evacuation form even starting. The skies filled with war planes.

In many parts of the world, the attention that had been focused on the words of the senator and President moved upwards. People took to the streets where it was safe and the fields in rural areas to crane their necks, tilt their heads backwards, and stare at the sky. The world acted almost at one on many occasions over the previous few days. First, the world acted as one when they tuned into the broadcast from the senator in the United Nations building in New York. They acted as one with the panic and chaos that spread around the globe in the few hours after that. For some, the fear caused them to stay indoors; for others, they took to the streets and spread violence. Others refused to believe what they had seen and waited for someone to tell them it wasn't true and that it was going to be all right. This didn't happen for a few hours, and the world sat in terror. Then the world sat as one for the counter broadcast from the President. If television companies were looking at their viewing figures and contemplating the advertising revenue, then these massive television events within a few hours of each other would have made them rub their hands together in glee. The money created would have been massive. As it was, nobody was even the slightest bit interested in viewing figures, focusing groups, and advertising revenue. The concentration of everyone in the media was the same as the rest of the world—survival. But then this was the point that the world split. It split between believers and nonbelievers. It split between the peaceful and the aggressive. It split between those that believed the senator and those that believed the President. The split was going to have grave consequences because at that time, the nonbelievers were prepared to go to war to stop the salvation of the believers. And the nonbelievers started to grow in number.

As people decided what side they were on in a conflict situation, there were two things at play. On one hand, they sided with the argument that they believed in. They looked at what they considered to be right and wrong and chose right. But as time progressed, they had another consideration to make. On the other hand, they had the likely outcome. Even if people believed that they were on the side of right, the consequences of being found on the losing side after the battle was won was a heavy price to pay. People who believed in the message from the senator were concerned about their future under the Dark Army. They believed in Jesus but also believed that there was a fair chance that Jesus would lose against the combined militaries of the world. If they sided with the winner, then their life would be more bearable after the war had been fought, won, and lost. As a consequence, more people started to side with the President and the Dark Army. The might of the army that the people could see on the streets and in the air was always going to feel more powerful than the peaceful army that was so far into the sky that they couldn't be seen.

Those that believed were looking to the sky for salvation. Those that doubted were looking to the sky to see the battle take place. It was going to be a tremendous sight whichever way it happened. There was going to be the focus of the world on those skies.

People looked up in anticipation of leaving the earth. They had in their mind an image of the God that they would meet. Different religions had different views of what would happen at the end of the Earth. They all had their own deities to meet, they all had their own stories of what would be waiting for them as the Earth met its end. In truth, there is only one God. The son of God, Jesus Christ, returned to earth to rescue all of the children of God, all of those who believed. Those that chose to be rescued showed faith and belief and deserved to be rescued. God gave us all the ability to choose, and that choice determined a life of salvation on a new planet or the plight of the planet. People have to choose wisely. The heads turned to the sky were in expectation of something happening. Churches all over the world taught two views when thinking about God. The bowed head in prayer signified the deference to God, but the fact that God was omnipresent and omnipotent meant that he was viewed as someone in the sky. He was imagined to be above us all the time, looking down on all that we do. So, at that point of salvation, people were looking intently at the sky for the signs of salvation. But the sign was there among them.

The fact that thousands, tens of thousands, hundreds of thousands, maybe even millions of people, had gone out to look into the sky for help and salvation was the biggest sign that humanity was worth saving. The hope that this brought the people was amazing. They looked around and saw others with the same hope and expectation in their eyes. They smelled the planet as though it was the last time they would smell. They breathed in the air through their nostrils as though the sense of smell wouldn't be needed on their new planet. It was a smell that none of them had taken in this way before. The people as one smelled the grass, the rain, the trees and plants, the smell of humanity, the fumes from aircraft, and the slightest tinge of fear. The sense of smell conveys many things. This was the smell that people would take with them. This was the smell of the last day of planet Earth.

The senses bring many things to a human body. As well as the sight of the planet preparing for war and evacuation at the same time and the smell that would live with the believers forever, there were the sounds of the planet. The fact that there were noises from aircraft and tanks was overlooked by the small sounds that made their way between the large rumbles of war. The birds still sang. The wind still rustled the remaining leaves on the trees of late fall. The sound of people talking to each other started to be the background noise to all the other events that were happening. Even though the Dark Army were intent on controlling the streets and stopping the invasion, the people still had hope, and hope spoken about was hope multiplied. Every time a believer spoke to another, they believed even more. The people that had faith bred faith in the others they spoke to. The human spirit was alive and well; it just needed an outlet.

But as groups of believers formed in quiet parts of cities and the countryside, there was a more sinister gathering of people in the busier parts of the cities. The believers had chosen their places to gather carefully to avoid detection from the Dark Army. They had found quieter neighborhoods and places where the Dark Army didn't need to patrol. Places with no banks, no military installations, and no stores and places of political significance—these were quiet and peaceful places where people could talk and listen to the sounds of the planet with only the occasional interruption of a war plane flying overhead.

But the streets where there were places of significance told a very different story. The demonic President talked a good fight. As the leader of the Free World, he automatically spoke to certain people. He was believed wholesale by parts of society that did not look past the lies they were told by their leaders and seek the truth. Many in society worshipped money and greed. Many worshipped alcohol and narcotics. It fueled their life. The way that the Earth had worked for these people up to that point was under threat. They saw this as an opportunity to grab whatever they could in whatever way they could.

The plushest shopping streets on New York surrounded Upper Fifth Avenue in Manhattan. In this location, the top designer stores sold their clothing for thousands of dollars at a time. The top technology companies had their stores stocked with thousands of gadgets at a time. The department stores were full of gifts and goods for the preholiday season rush. This was a scene of retail delight only a few days earlier, but on that night, it was the scene of carnage. Gangs of nonbelievers rampaged through the streets. They were smashing everything in sight and breaking into these stores to leave with armfuls of goods. They would smash up the displays of anything they could not carry so that it was destroyed. This was destruction for the sake of destruction. The people were smashing everything in sight. This played out in the shopping districts of the biggest cities on the planet. The Causeway Bay in Hong Kong, the Avenue de Champs Elysees in Paris, New Bond Street in London, and the Pitt Street Mall in Sydney were all going through the same terrifying events. People were listening to the voice of evil and committing acts of terror. Some were caught up in the group mentality and moving along for fear of being hurt. They wanted to believe but lacked the strength to resist the wages of sin.

In Japan, there were people running amok on the streets with homemade weapons. They were fighting anyone they met for no other reason that they wanted to fight. This nation had been submissive since the end of the Second World War and was a nation of people that seemed to live solely to work. The Japanese culture of working hard and then retreating to their own home had disappeared over the course of the last few days. It had become an aggressive nation again in many ways, and the people on the central streets of Tokyo were ready to act on those aggressive feelings and fight whoever they came across. It was as though the samurai traditions of the country had come back to the surface again and come out to all the people standing on those streets. Although they did not have swords, many people carried baseball bats, pieces of wood, or makeshift sticks to protect themselves but mainly to attack. People would form short alliances and pledge to help each other before seeking the first opportunity to hit their newfound colleague on the back of the head and move on to another fight—or another betrayal. The people on the streets were looking for a fight from all the pent-up anger that modern Japanese life had brought them. Being beaten into submission after World War II had obviously hit them hard. The years since the war where the people had to behave in a dignified manner had been released after being kept bottled up for so long. The release was bloody and violent for some, but still some of the people on the streets wanted to believe. They wanted salvation and a peaceful life, but they lacked the willpower to act in any other way.

Another nation that had thrived economically but struggled morally since the Second World War was Germany. On the streets of Berlin, there was a disturbing rise of neo-Nazis. They had always been a tiny part of German society that the people tried to morally punish and the press tried to ignore. They fielded candidates in many local elections but without success. The party still ran on similar themes to those of the 1930s but tried to put a modern face on it. Their candidates were not skinheads with swastika tattoos but businessmen and women dressed in suits, looking to the entire world like any other politician. While the political classes of the neo-Nazis were aligned with the demonic President and the higher echelons in touch with him directly, the lower parts of the neo-Nazi groups were left to rule the streets of certain parts of Germany. In the areas of Berlin where Hitler and his cronies were most active, the neo-Nazis ruled. They had taken over the Olympic Stadium with all the echoes of 1936, the Reichstag where the Nazis plotted their rule, and the corridors of power on Wilhelmstrasse where the government war machine kept up the propaganda and planned their next invasion. These were all now sites of neo-Nazi groups, and they put up banners, shouted slogans, and abused anyone who dared to walk nearby. The Jewish memorial to all those killed in the war had been destroyed by the neo-Nazis. The good people of Berlin feared that history was repeating itself.

They had gone back to the concentration camps and staffed them as though they were ready to start taking prisoners again. The neo-Nazis knew that this action would strike fear across the world. The terrors of a war that had ended over seventy years prior came rushing back to the people of the world. Fear and panic spread among the towns and villages near to the concentration camps, and people fled without taking any of their possessions. The stories of what happened there had been passed down from generation to generation, and the potential of those atrocities happening again was too much for the people to bear. Wherever in Germany and the surrounding countries, the believers gathered and made sure that it was away from any sites connected with the Nazi regime of the Second World War.

In Brazil, there were scenes of chaos. The people of the favelas had made their way down on to the streets and beaches of Rio de Janeiro after the news from the United Nations had reached them. The small number of television sets in these slums were the focal point of hundreds of eyes at a time as the world watched the senator speak. After this speech, the people moved *en masse* to rejoice in the carnival capital of the world. The famous beaches of the Copacabana and the Maracaña, which had been the scene of much celebration and togetherness in the 2014 Soccer World Cup and the 2016 Summer Olympic Games, were once again the place where tens of thousands of people met to be together. The speech of the President was missed by many, as they were partying on the beach, celebrating the return of Jesus together. Over the next few days, the beaches turned from areas of celebration to the center point of the lockdown the state police had enacted. As a main ally of the American President, the Brazilian Premier had been swift to turn the attention of the people of the country to fear. The Dark Army was strong here. The Brazilian Premier wanted to keep the strong ties to the American President and protect the trade deal that he had worked long and hard to forge with the United States.

Although the country of Brazil was highly religious and full of regular churchgoers, the Brazilian Premier wanted to have his nation lead the solidarity with the American President and his view of the world. He had a strong army as the major country in South America and used this military power to suppress the rejoicing of the people and turn them back to where they lived. People cowered in their homes for fear of being outed as an enemy of the state and dealt with by the Brazilian military. As the grip of martial law on the streets of Rio de Janeiro tightened, the people found small enclaves of peace to spend their time. The favelas that many middle-class residents of Rio, known colloquially as carioca, would not ever contemplate going to under normal circumstances were seen as the safest places in the city. The favelas were seen by many in Brazil as a spot on the face of their country. Some administrations had tried to pull them down, others had tried to shut them off from the cities with poor transport links and walls. But now, they were the perfect place to hide, congregate, and wait for salvation. The Brazilian favelas were too difficult for the military to monitor. The streets were too narrow and maze-like for the Dark Army to effectively shut down. The believers of Brazil found a new haven away from the oppression of the streets and fled to the place that they once feared the most.

Down on the beach, the nonbelievers were out in force. As the streets had been controlled, the Dark Army started to move away from beach area. As this stranglehold loosened, the beach became the domain of the street gangs. Usually, they specialized in handbag thefts and selling drugs, but with the good people of Rio elsewhere, they had to look at other ways of using up their spare time. The nonbelievers in Rio de Janeiro set fire to anything they could find. Bins, cars, stores, animals, and anything else in or around the beach area was alight. In and around these fires, people gathered to stare into the fire as though in a trance. As each fire went out, a fight erupted among the people that were standing there. It was as though the fire had made the gangs forget that they used to fight each other. The fire kept them together. As soon as that fire was extinguished, then hostilities resumed, and the separate gangs of Rio were separate again. These fights were bloody and brutal but without any implements. Everything that might have been a weapon was burned on the beach. The gangs saw fighting with their fists and feet as a kind of honorable way to do battle. The fights lasted around ten to twenty minutes each and then fizzled out. People became distracted by another fire and would go and stand there to start the whole process of "fire and fight" again. There were some on the beach that stood on the periphery. They didn't burn anything of community value and shied away when the fights started. They wanted to believe, but they were not strong enough to stand up to the others. They didn't have the willpower to walk away. Some were disgusted by the thought of spending time in the favelas. Others just drifted along with the crowd and offered no resistance to the horrors that were being carried out.

The streets of India were awash with people. As a country that is filled with believers of many faiths, it was a part of the world that had seen atrocities carried out in the name of religion before. The streets of Mumbai were filled with people of the many faiths of the world: Christian, Hindu, Sikh, Muslims, Buddhist, and followers of Jainism. The people stood side by side, looking up at the sky. They were waiting for what would happen next. The belief systems of these disparate religions had been fractious when placed side by side in the past. The way that people reacted now was going to be a test of faith for all concerned.

The first few hours after the speech in the United Nations were quiet. People had no idea what to do. In many ways, life just carried on as normal but at a slower pace. But the fear and panic that had hit other parts of the world blew up in isolated parts of the city. The Indian Prime Minister had spoken to his people and told them to be strong and calm. This had mainly worked, but now it appeared that the world was at war. People had to choose a side. Would they join with the believers and put their trust in these strange craft that were coming to take them away from their home planet? Would they side with the American President who had told them this was threat and that the spacecraft were invaders, not rescuers?

The choice was stark. The choice was simple. The people of India had a decision to make. The Christians rejoiced in the fact that it was their God who had sent help. They were eternally happy that Jesus had been seen and was coming to lead them to salvation. The followers of other religions were far more confused by the events of the previous few days. Many had spent their whole life following a belief that was shown to be false. They had to reconcile the fact that they felt let down by their religious leaders with the fact that they wanted to be saved from the imminent extinction of planet Earth. The gangs started in the outer suburbs of Mumbai. Groups assembled in their religious meeting places and then took it upon themselves to go out onto the streets. They were looking for Christian imagery to desecrate and destroy. The groups of other religions felt hate and anger towards the Christian faith. It was a reaction to the shock of the situation.

Churches were ransacked, and crucifixes were smashed to pieces. The work of the demonic President was being carried out in the name of other religions. All Christian imagery was being destroyed. Those that were quick enough got into their church and saved what they could. But not much was saved. Makeshift churches were made underground or in secure locations where Christians could gather and worship without fear of recrimination.

The gangs roamed the streets, looking for someone to blame for the situation that the planet faced. It was easy to blame the messengers because they brought the news to their attention. It was like the much-used phrase, "Don't shoot me, I'm the messenger." Messengers were not being shot. They were working hard to spread the word to the believers. But the believers were being attacked, vilified, and driven underground by the gangs of angry mobs who wanted to smash the reality away from in front of their eyes. Those who had followed another religion forgot the teachings of their faith and turned to aggression in order to confront their fears. They attacked religious iconography of the faith that was trying to lead them all to salvation. They threw rocks, lit fires, smashed buildings, and generally caused mayhem. Those caught in the crossfire were either caused to run for their lives or injured by flying debris. In the gangs, there were some that wanted to believe. They felt let down by their own religion and felt angry. But they wanted to be saved. They lacked the moral strength to break away from their group and become a part of the people who were to be saved.

From the sky, the evacuation was being put into force. Hozai and Marta were busy at their control panels in the Star Craft. Both were now pressing furiously away at switches and dials that gave them some power over all the triangular transport craft that were heading towards the earth. Although they could not navigate each one separately (there were far too many), they were giving commands that all of the craft would follow at once. It was a sequencing event that slowed down the transport craft as they entered the Earth's atmosphere. The craft were all in position across the face of the Earth and were now moving towards the surface of the planet at a slow speed, so they did not cause a disturbance in the atmosphere of the planet. That many craft all entering the atmosphere at once at speed could have shock waves that might have upset the tides and caused mass floods. They had to be careful at this point. Hozai and Marta knew that the arrival of the transportation craft must be seen as peaceful and in the spirit of salvation rather than causing catastrophe. That would be just what the demonic President wanted. It would give the devil more ammunition for his lies. He could point to the fact that the craft the people of the Earth were told was here to save them was actually causing death and destruction. But no, Hozai and Marta ramped down the speed of the craft on their dials and made sure that they entered the atmosphere of the Earth at the pace of a snail. It was essential to keep the trust of the believers and convert the nonbelievers to understand how grave the situation was for planet Earth.

Hozai turned to Marta. They had set the speed of the craft, and all were on the right path to the planet. He said, "The final stage of entry is upon us." But at a point above the orbiting satellites, the transport craft will sequence a pulse to disintegrate all the metal-orbiting objects. This will create safety for all the transport craft and eliminate the "eyes and ears" of the demonic ones. The craft were in position around the Earth to take out the orbiting objects. Marta, spoke the command. "וישכע קפודה" (translation: "Pulse now").

Hozai stated, "The transportation craft are all entering the Earth's atmosphere in ten, nine, eight . . ."

The two of them held their breath. They were sure from all their calculations that the entry of thousands of craft at the same time would not cause any problems if they chose the correct speed. They had checked and double-checked and were absolutely sure that the slow speed they had chosen would cause no problems.

"Seven, six, five . . ."

Marta looked in the direction of her screens. She wanted to know that there were no readings coming back that would indicate a problem. From where they stood, the two of them could see the planet and would be aware of any major tidal events happening from the movement in the oceans. It was a tense time for the two of them.

"Four, three, two . . ."

The time was almost upon them. Nothing had changed on the dials, and the planet seemed to be operating as it was before. The triangular transportation craft were heading towards the atmosphere of the Earth, and the fact was that the craft would be visible to the naked eye very soon. The time to see whether they would be met with terror or with open arms was about to become reality. Hozai and Marta still hadn't let their breath in or out as they watched fixedly the transportation craft leave space and enter the realms of the planet Earth. When they returned to space, the craft should be full of people. The craft should be ready to save those who believed and lead them to a new planet away from the danger that the Earth was now facing. The craft should be full of people who want to follow in the peaceful teachings of Jesus Christ.

"One, zero, we have entry."

Both let out the breath that they had been holding in. Marta thought that this was the longest ten seconds she had ever been through. Then there was silence. There was silence in the control room of the Star Craft as all on board waited to see what would happen. They were concerned that the entry of the transportation craft into the atmosphere of the Earth would be met with nuclear attacks or the aircraft of the world.

There was silence from the transportation craft. They were powered by a force found many galaxies away and as such did not rely on noisy or polluting fossil fuels. They moved around the atmosphere of the planet without any noise at all. If the demonic President and his followers were listening for the start of salvation, then they would not detect the transportation craft in this way.

There was silence in the church of Daniel and Simon as their congregation sat in quiet contemplation of the fate of the planet and their role in it. Each was sitting with their head bowed, and they all took a few minutes to think about the few days that had just passed and the journey they all had ahead of them. Some thought about relatives that they had in the big cities and the fact that they could not reach them. Some thought about the future of their children on a new planet and what their future prospects were like. Others thought about the healing of Daniel's leg and their own illnesses and afflictions that they hoped would be healed by the strange spacecraft that they had been told about. Others just sat silently, hoping that their brain would make sense of all the events of the last few days if only they could give it some time to be alone.

There was silence on the streets of the world. Although the transportation craft had not come into view yet, there was a sense that something was happening. People stopped in their tracks and contemplated their fate. The believers were silent in thought of how they would escape unscathed from the perilous cities they inhabited to the craft that would take them to safety. The gangs of marauders who had caused havoc on the streets paused to consider what they would destroy next. The Dark Army looked upwards to see the threat that they perceived from the sky.

In the Oval Office of the White House, the President and his close circle sat in absolute silence. Without communication from the Dark Army or the military bases, they were playing this game blind. The President was sure that the craft that had been promised were coming, but he wasn't sure when or how many of them. The others in the room were all waiting for the President to make the move. They were all high-ranking officials but were in awe of the power that the President had been able to display since the start of the crisis. They knew that he was in complete control of their actions and the actions of the military in response to the words of the senator in the United Nations. They had barely left the office over the last few days as it became the battle command center of the United States President as he led all those that would follow in a verbal attack against the words of Christ. He had put the streets in shutdown in many parts of the world and had been preparing an attack force to welcome the invaders with as much fire power as the combined militaries of his followers could put together. That was until the communications systems had been shut down. He had people working on this, but without satellites, there was little that could be done to get effective communication out there to those that would be assisting him.

The last few hours in the Oval Office had been unbearable for many. On their frequent trips outside of the office to grab a drink or visit the bathroom, they had become aware that the White House staff had drifted away in their droves. What had been a bustling office of the biggest administration on earth had dwindled away to a handful of people. Those that were loyal to the President had stayed, along with those that were too scared to leave. The rest had made a break for it when the door to the Oval Office was closed and the coast was clear. They were more scared of staying in the White House than they were of the President himself. These were people of faith that wanted to return to their families and escape the plight of the planet Earth. These were good people who wanted to follow their savior, Jesus Christ. These were people that were now at home, ready and waiting for their chance to be saved.

Apart from the movement of chairs and feet on the carpet of the Oval Office, the room was in silence. The mood of the President dictated the way that the rest of them reacted, and he was in a foul mood. He wasn't the type of person to go around screaming and shouting. He was plotting his next move and how he would see the demise of the messengers and the believers that followed them. He was desperate to keep control of the planet Earth. He was prepared to put everyone in danger to do so. The room sat there waiting for the cogs to turn and the President to speak. He had to put his faith in the military, which were put on high alert before the communications were cut. He had to think that all the plans he had relayed were going to be actioned to the letter. He had informed the leaders of the Dark Army units that they were to stop the craft from landing at all costs. The demonic President had to trust those that he had tasked with stopping the evacuation.

The silence continued.

Outside the Lincoln Elementary School on the outskirts of Seattle, Washington, a blonde mother was waiting for her daughter to come out of school. It was typical weather for that part of the world at that time of the year, and she had arrived at the school early. She decided that it was too early to get out of the car and wait near the school gates. As the rain lashed down on the car, she wondered how long it would be until it turned to sleet. It was always around the time of the school run that the weather turned for the worst. She had lived in Washington State all her life but had never gotten used to the weather. It was just something that she had to endure. The weather in Seattle could be bad at any time of the year, but it was almost guaranteed to be bad from October through April. The iconic Seattle Space Needle was either invisible or shrouded in rain and mist for a large part of the year. The weather fronts that battered Washington State came in off the Pacific Ocean and never seemed to leave. Once the wind and rain hit, they felt like they stayed for days on end. If it started to rain on a Tuesday, then it was going to still be the same rainstorm on the Wednesday without fail. This was a Thursday, still there was the rainstorm that started on the Tuesday, and there seemed to be no end in sight of the weather that engulfed the area.

The blonde mother sat still in her car. She listened to the rain pound on the roof of her MPV, which had been bought three years previously. They had only just finished paying off the finance for the car, and it was already showing signs of aging. The dash looked dated, and some of the dials didn't always work. A few taps usually brought the dials back into life but not always. The left rear side of the car was showing the first signs of rust. The blonde mother thought that there was little wonder that anything metal rusted with the amount of moisture it had to endure in the state of Washington. She was surprised that the Space Needle itself wasn't starting to rust in places after being left out in the rain for year after year. She was sure that it must cost the city's taxpayers millions of pounds a year in maintenance, and a lot of this was due to the fact that they built it in the wrong city. They built a partly metal monument into the sky in a place that the sky was covered for large parts of the year and where metal rusted away. But it had stood there as the symbol of the city since 1962, and was even the feature on the title sequence of the popular television program, *Frasier*. The blonde mother wondered whether the maintenance was offset by the tourist income the tower derived.

Washington State was largely untouched by the events of the previous few days. With only a couple of military installations in the state, the focus was on protecting the border with the ocean rather than any focus on the cities that lay within the state's boundaries. With the effects of the poor weather and the isolated nature of Washington State, there were no people on the streets in the aftermath of the speech in the United Nations. With the time difference too, it was still fairly early in the morning when the senator spoke in the United Nations, and many people in the state of Washington were either just getting up or going about their normal morning routine. Children were getting ready for school. Workers were on their morning commute in the car or on public transport. The city of Seattle was experiencing a fairly normal day in November when the news hit the rest of the world. It was conditions outside that many would see as terrible, but those who had lived and worked in Seattle would consider it a standard Seattle winter's day. So, with the howling wind and driving rain that intermittently turned to sleet, there was no appetite for destruction. The people didn't go out onto the streets to fight each other or destroy buildings. They pretty much went on as normal. The people were still shrouded in the fear that the rest of the planet felt but without the conditions for it to manifest into violence and panic. Even later in the day when the President responded, the reaction wasn't one of panic but of the people of the state and city taking in the news and weighing it up against all else they had been told and seen.

While the blonde mother sat in the car waiting, in those last few minutes before she just had to get out and walk to the school gates, she looked up at the sky. After three days of a weather system, it often passed and left behind a short lull before the next one came in off the Pacific Ocean and took hold. She looked up in the vain hope that this would be the end of that weather system and a lull that lasted long enough for her to collect her daughter from school and get back home without having to get soaked to the skin. The blonde mother looked up, expecting to see the same dark, gray sky that had surrounded the area for the prior days. She had noticed that the light in the car was a little brighter than before as she sat with her eyes half-closed a few minutes earlier. But it wasn't until she craned her neck forward and looked up to the sky that she saw a change. It wasn't something that she had been expecting. It wasn't something that she was used to in a Seattle November. Different clouds. She saw that the regulation gray uniform Seattle sky had changed. The cloud formations were white. The clouds were puffy. The clouds in the sky were churning.

It might have been the change in weather systems that she had been looking for, but they had never happened quite like this before—certainly not when she had been looking. The clouds moved constantly as though growing in size and then receding. The ebb and flow of the clouds were mesmerizing, and the mother sat and stared up at the sky without blinking for several minutes. She fixed her stare on the area of the sky where the clouds seemed to be emanating from. It was as though there was a cloud-making machine in the center of the sky that was pushing away the gray clouds that formed a blanket over the area and replacing them with churning white clouds that were far more interesting to look at. The blonde mother only broke her stare every few minutes to see what the time was and if she had to get out of the car to pick her daughter up. She finished school on that day at three fifteen in the afternoon, and the blonde mother had gotten a great parking space so it would only take five minutes or so to make the walk to the school gates. She was going to leave it as long as she could.

She quickly glanced over to the other parked cars along the same street. They were all covered in rain as was hers but what she could see through the rain-soaked windscreens looked as though every occupant in every car was looking up at the sky in the same transfixed way as she was. She looked back up to the sky again. She was sure that something was going to happen, and she was determined not to miss it. Even if she was a couple of minutes late to the school gates, her daughter would be safe. The teacher wouldn't let her go out of the schoolyard on her own. They would keep her under the shelter until someone was there to collect her safely. The blonde mother also knew that she wouldn't be the only parent that was running a minute or two late that day. Nobody else had left their car on the street she was parked on. They were all too busy with the sky. They were all transfixed on what might happen next.

The blonde mother watched the sky intently, her gaze still focused solely on the center of the sky where it appeared the clouds were being generated. The area had produced nonstop white fluffy clouds for minutes and showed no sign of stopping. The blonde mother wondered whether something significant would happen or if she was just seeing a weather anomaly. She had seen many programs on television that had shown how freak weather events were happening all over the world. They put it down to climate change and the fact that the people of the Earth were polluting the planet at a faster rate than ever. But then a few days after the series finished, the President pulled out of the climate change talks with the rest of the world and declared that climate change and global warming were myths. He wheeled out some scientific experts that backed up his assertions and told the people of the world to carry on as normal. There was no cause for a change in behavior, the American people was told. The blonde mother couldn't help but think while she was watching that the scientists were speaking, but there was no conviction in their words. It drew parallels for her with the airmen shot down over Baghdad in the first Gulf War, which were wheeled out on television by Saddam Hussein and spoke of the peaceful nature of the Iraqi leader. It was as though the scientists had been captured by the President and forced to speak out. The blonde mother had kept an open mind on the subject, and this news conference had left her with uneasy feelings about the President. She wouldn't be voting for him at the next election. She felt that he wasn't to be trusted.

The blonde mother was giving up. She had little time left to collect her daughter, and the sky was still as fascinating as it was when she first looked up, but it didn't appear to be showing her anything different. She reached across to the backseat and picked up her coat. The blonde mother took the keys from the ignition and placed her hand on the door handle, ready to open the door and leave her car. She checked the wing mirror and rearview mirror before leaving to ensure that there were no cars coming along the road. She had seen a child hit by a car when getting out of her father's car on the school run one day, and it had occupied her thoughts when getting in and out of the car ever since. There was nothing coming, so she was ready to leave. As the blonde mother went to leave, she checked the clock. It was one of the dials that hadn't been affected by the aging of the car and clearly showed the time. It was 3.11 p.m.

Before the blonde mother could leave the car, something caught her eye. In the part of the sky where she had trained her eyes for several minutes, there was a movement. She pulled the car door back closed and again craned her neck, so she had the fullest view of the sky that she could manage from inside the vehicle. Through the clouds, she saw a black point moving slowly through the clouds and towards her. At first, it was just the black tip of something that she knew was going to get bigger and bigger. After a while, the tip became closer, and what was behind it was becoming broader. It looked triangular in shape, and the blonde mother put her hand up over her mouth. She knew that she might say something to herself over the next few moments and didn't want anyone else to be able to lip-read what she might say. She was a Christian, and many of the other parents at the school went to the same church. She didn't want them to see her mouthing anything blasphemous at this point. She was shocked to her core and had no idea how she might react.

As the seconds ticked away, the triangular transportation craft became more visible to the blonde mother. She couldn't help but think that these clouds would help the Space Needle to be more visible and perhaps attract more tourists to the area. After a quick mental journey across the city, she raced back to the situation she was in at that very time. She hadn't taken her eyes off the sky, and the black craft in the sky was almost fully visible now. It looked to begin with like a stealth bomber that she had seen on the news several times when the United States was at war with other countries. The stealth bomber was seen as complete affirmation that the United States was at the forefront of military capability and could not be beaten by any foe. But after only a few moments, it was obvious that this was not a stealth bomber and that United States military had something much bigger to deal with than their usual foes on Earth.

The blonde mother watched the craft move its way through the sky towards where she was parked. It was difficult to see exactly how large the craft was and how far away it was because of the constant movement and the fact that the sky was still full of churning clouds, but the blonde mother knew it was large and knew it wasn't that far away. She watched intently as the craft made its way closer to the ground and closer to where she was sitting. At that moment, the blonde mother quickly remembered what she was sitting there for and jumped out of her car to go and fetch her daughter from school. She looked in both her mirrors again as the realities of life took over from the very unreal visage she saw in the sky. As the blonde mother got out of the car, she noticed that it had stopped raining. She instinctively put her hand up to the sky just to check that the lack of rain falling on her head wasn't just her imagination. She quickly stood for a moment as thoughts raced through her head.

I need to get to my daughter. I was so busy looking up that I forgot to look down. I wonder how close that thing actually is. It was moving slowly, and now it doesn't appear to be moving at all. I need to rush to the school. I'm not sure if my daughter has seen it. I'm not sure if the school will have let the kids out. How do I explain this to her? How do I explain it to myself?

"I guess this is what everyone has been talking about."

The blonde mother's thoughts were interrupted by a voice. Had she heard someone speak? Where had it come from?

"I guess this is what everyone has been talking about." There was the voice again. The blonde mother looked across the street and saw another mom that she recognized from the school gates. She was a redhead, typical of the people of Washington State that were the descendants of immigrants from Scotland and Ireland in the nineteenth century. The Irish had fled famine to start a new life. The Scots had joined them. Washington State had similar weather conditions to these two countries, and the people of Scotland and Ireland made themselves at home in this windswept part of the new country they inhabited. She walked over and joined the other redhead mom on her side of the street, not without looking both ways four times to make sure that it was safe to cross. She joined her fellow mom as the two of them stood looking up at the sky. The mother was speechless.

The other redhead mom again spoke the same words. "I guess this is what everyone has been talking about."

This time, the blonde mother broke away from her trance and spoke in return. She said, "I know. I must admit that I had my doubts, but here it is. What do you plan on doing?" The blonde mother knew the other redhead mom from school but hadn't seen her at church, and she was unsure whether she was speaking to a believer or not. In fact, the other redhead mom lived a little further away from the school. She had moved there from the other side of Seattle and was so embedded in the church in her former neighborhood that she travelled the ten miles every Sunday to worship there.

"Oh, we will be saved," the other redhead mom said with a huge smile on her face. "As I'm sure you will be as well. Shall we walk to school?" As she said that, the two women started out on the walk towards the school, which was also the walk towards the triangular craft that they had both watched appear slowly from the clouds and head their way. They walked together in near-silence. Both women were expecting the craft to make a loud noise as they approached it, so they put their conversations to one side. But the strange craft made no noise at all. The women were confused. How could something so large and obviously being powered by large engines make no noise at all? In fact, not only was there no noise, but it was as if the large craft wasn't there at all. There was no noise, no wind turbulence, and there was no movement of the clouds around the craft. It just sat there. They both wondered whether or not it was a figment of their collective imagination. They wondered whether they were the only ones that could see this massive craft in the sky that appeared but gave no other sign of its presence. As they looked around, they could see that others were able to see the craft, as all eyes were on the sky.

When the women had figured out the fact that the craft wasn't going to make a noise, they started to talk again. The blonde mother said, "Where were you when the senator made his speech?" It was the "Where were you when JFK was shot?" moment for this generation. It was the point where the world would reference their existence. Pre-senator speech and post-senator speech were the only time sequences that mattered to most people now. The time before the speech was now seen as the carefree world. Although people had stresses and many lived in dejection, it was a much easier time to look back on with fondness. It was before people were told that the world was going to end. It was before the President tightened his grip on the world. It was before the Dark Army. It was before the decision on whether to believe the senator and his message of salvation or the President and his message that the status quo remained. The two women knew already that this was the first defining line of this significance that their life had seen. The second was to arrive soon with the evacuation of the planet.

"I was in the gym. I had dropped my sons off at school," replied the other redhead mom. She looked a little younger than the blonde mother and obviously worked out. It was something that the blonde mother had planned to do ever since her daughter started school but never got around to. It wasn't as though she was particularly overweight or unfit, but she wanted to be a little fitter and carry a little less weight, even if it was just to keep up with some of the other moms who were obviously quite competitive about it.

"How about you?"

"I was at home. I had dropped my daughter off at school, and I was just killing some time watching trashy daytime TV. I know it rots the brain, but it was just on in the background when I was cleaning up, having a coffee, and catching up on some reading," the blonde mother replied. She knew by now that the other redhead mom was a believer too, so she felt comfortable about opening up to her. She spoke as the two of them still walked towards the school, still with one eye on the craft hovering above. "I wish I'd never voted for that creep. He makes me uneasy."

"Me too," replied the other redhead mom. She looked as though they had just been given a second chance after making a mistake. "I guess he won't be joining us in leaving the Earth for a safer place," she added.

"Ha, no!" the blonde mother blurted out. She hadn't meant to laugh in such a serious setting, but it came naturally. She was happy that others saw the same things in the President. To her, he seemed untrustworthy and not the type of man that should be in charge of a nation in which her daughter was going to grow up in. She wished that she had been able to see it sooner. She wished that the rest of the population of America had been able to see it sooner. He was an outsider that wasn't even expected to get the nomination, but somehow he managed to pull the strings behind the scenes. He went from strength to strength in the presidential election and won comfortably in the end, even if the media was still calling it for his opponent up until the voting was closed.

"We can move on to better things without the likes of him. I am willing to forgive anyone, but there seems to be many people in this world that just don't want to believe. I guess they just have too much to lose if they walk away from things as they are now," said the other redhead mom. They were nearing the school now, and the sight of the black triangular craft above their heads was starting to feel normal. They had been under this craft for only a matter of minutes, but it felt as though it had always been there.

"I want a better place for my daughter." The blonde mom began to speak. "I have always hoped for something better. She is a bright girl and deserves every opportunity that she didn't have. I just want the best for her. Every parent wants the best for their children. I expect there to be many families in the evacuation. I think that our new world can be great again, especially if there are families . . ." The blonde mother stopped midsentence. She felt herself welling up. She had lost her parents when she was young and never felt part of a family until she had her daughter. Not long after that, it all felt real for her. She became part of a family and never wanted to let it go. She felt a huge hope for the future when it was filled with families, the type of which she missed out on in her younger days.

By the time that two women reached the school, they were joined by scores of other mothers and fathers who had arrived at the same time to pick up their little ones from school. The school gates were always the place where people met and exchanged gossip. This was where the parents caught up on all the things they missed from their own kids. This was where they made plans to meet up with other parents, including the kids at weekends or without the kids during the week. But that day was devoid of all the chatter and gossip that usually filled the air. People were not interested in how much homework was given out the day before, who the teacher had told off, or what happened on the playground that week. There was a void that was usually filled with voices. In its place was tension.

The parents were tense at the black triangular craft that was above them in the sky. They were anxious that their children would be out in the schoolyard looking up at the craft in the same way that they all had when it first appeared. They were concerned that the children in classrooms on the south side of the school would have already seen the craft and have been asking questions of their teacher and each other. The parents looked up. The craft was still there, and now they wanted their children by their side. They wanted to be in a position to put their arm around their children and answer any questions that their kids had. This was a time for family in all parts of the world. This was especially a time for family in a Christian part of Seattle where parents were waiting outside for their children. The parents looked up. They saw a huge spacecraft in a lot more detail when they were standing still. It covered a huge part of the sky. Although it hovered around twenty thousand feet above the ground, it was clearly a craft that was of the size where everyone watching could tell it was not made on Earth.

In all, the black triangular craft was three miles wide and three miles long. The parents still looked up. The blonde mother gulped. The other redhead mom scratched her head. They were all waiting for the craft to make the next move. Little did they know that the craft had finished moving for some time, and little did they know that the craft wasn't the only one that was positioned close to the surface of the planet. Around thirty miles to the east, there was another craft hovering over a field near a town. Around thirty miles to the north, there was a craft hovering over a highway next to a shopping mall. Thirty miles further north of that, another craft hovered over an interstate road that had slow-moving traffic crawling along as all eyes were on the sky. Around every thirty miles along the inhabited surface of the Earth were more of these craft.

In the Sears Tower in Chicago, there were office workers huddled together around a northern facing window looking out towards Lake Michigan. They were looking out towards a huge black triangular object that had first come to their attention a few minutes earlier. Until that time, they were all huddled around the window, sitting at their desks and mulling over recent events. Their communication with the outside world was severely impaired due to all the satellites being knocked out, but the owner of the company had insisted they come into work. The team mainly sat around talking to each other and only tried to look busy if the boss or one of his supervisors passed through the office. They knew that the boss of the company had gone to school with the President, and many in the company still felt that he had contact with the President. One thing that was for sure was the fact that the owner of the company shared a worldview with the President. He was happy with his lot and wanted nothing to change. Those with the most to lose in the new world were often those that closed their eyes to the truth. They were the ones that turned a deaf ear to the words of the enlightened. They spoke only of the lies spread by the President and his followers and ignored all that was said by the messengers in long-flowing robes.

As the craft appeared, it was spotted first by those in the higher floors of the Sears Tower. The 103rd floor of the tower contained an observation deck that saw a million visitors a year to look out over the greater Chicago area and out across the Great Lakes. Most of the rest of the building was occupied by various companies that wanted to say that they had offices in the tallest building in the world. Although the Sears Tower lost that accolade to the Petronas Twin Towers of Kuala Lumpur in Malaysia in 1998, by then many companies had signed thirty-, forty-, or fifty-year leases and had made the Chicago tower their home. But by that point, nobody truly knew what or where home was going to be.

The group of workers stood looking at the spacecraft. Although it was hovering thousands of feet higher than the tower, all the occupants of that office felt as though they were eye to eye with the craft. It looked as though it had been sent just for them. As was the same scene in many different parts of the world, the group stood together motionless just staring at the craft. Each kept their thoughts to themselves. Each wondered what they would do next.

As the group all stood together, there was movement at the office door. None of them had noticed, but the keypad was operated, the door was opened, and another person entered the room. The person moved towards the group at the window. The person spoke. "I need all of you on your hand. The President may get all of the communications up and running at any moment, and I want you guys ready to get our operation back into swing. If I do pay you this month, then I want to do so in the knowledge that you've earned it."

It was the business owner, no doubt fresh from doing absolutely nothing himself. You see, with no telephone network and no Internet, most companies just shut their doors. Even most of those who believed in the President were waiting for it all to blow over before they started their business again. They just had to put their faith in the fact that the President would stop the invasion and make sure that none of their workers were able to leave. It was only truly diehard business owners like this one that insisted their team turn up and be there "just in case." It didn't inspire any confidence. The team trudged back to their desks and looked at their blank screens.

In London, one of the transportation craft was hovering directly above the River Thames. As a major river through a major city, the Thames was a large part of the life of the average Londoner.

It was crisscrossed by no less than thirty-three bridges in the Greater London area. It was the way that many of the people who lived and worked in London got around. There were foot bridges, rail bridges, road bridges, bridges over locks, and bridges for the underground system known locally as The Tube. And above all of these bridges was a three-mile-wide, three-mile-long triangular transportation craft that dominated the London skyline. Until that moment, the skyline was dominated by a building known officially as 30 St Mary Axe but colloquially as The Gherkin. It derived its unusual name from the shape of the building. It bulged out in the middle and looked like a gherkin to most.

It contained office buildings and, in the style of modern buildings, was clad mainly in glass. This meant that the people who occupied the office building on the top floor had a front row seat for the appearance of the transportation craft. Much of the center of London remained open for business. Although the city was a sprawling metropolis that housed over eight and a half million people and this number swelled by another million commuters during the daytime, the city of London was small. The part where all the banking and other business was carried out was known to many as the Square Mile. And the British government had come up with their own way of keeping business moving in some ways. The Square Mile became a protected area like the Green Zone had become in the middle of Baghdad during the second Gulf War and subsequent years of brokering something that resembled peace. There were army posts stationed along the barricades assembled along the Square Mile, and staff members were given special passes so that they could enter the area. While in the area, people walked around freely and carried out their business by word of mouth rather than technology. The group that were standing at the top of the Gherkin, watching the spacecraft, had done well from this new state of affairs. They were all now looking at the craft and wondering what it meant for their business, their country, and their planet.

"I wonder if we are the only ones that have got a giant spaceship above their city," said one of the workers.

"I suspect we are not alone," replied a colleague. They were right.

In Miami, there was much excitement at the arrival of the transportation craft. It was a party city most of the time. As a city right on the beach with great weather most of the year, Miami knew better than most cities how to celebrate. Although the city was associated with hedonism and free spirit, a lot of this was rooted in the Christian beliefs of the people of Latin America that resided in the city. When the transportation craft arrived over Ocean Drive in South Beach Miami, since the speeches in the United Nations, the makeup of the city of Miami changed. The holidaymakers all made their way back home by plane, by car, by coach, and by train wherever they could. They took with them the people that worked in the hospitality industry. The people that were left behind were those that lived and worked in the rest of the city. They were the bank workers, the office workers, those that worked for the city, and those that helped the wheels of the city keep running.

It was a little-known fact that many hotels gave up whole floors to business. This happened all over the world. You may have booked into a hotel feeling that you were surrounded by other vacationers, but for a large degree of the time, your fellow hotel residents were people who worked around the clock for a company. Some hotels had entire floors given over and converted for the needs of a company. They had rooms used as bedrooms for people to get their eight hours' sleep before passing that up for someone else as they prepared to get back to work again. Some rooms were converted to offices so that those who had been refreshed in their bedroom had somewhere to go earn some money. Boiler rooms, share dealers, venture capitalists, and marketing companies were all companies that sometimes operated in this way.

In the Four Seasons Hotel, the tallest building in Miami, a group of these office workers were looking out at the triangular transportation craft. The group had woken up the rest of the team, and they were all watching intently from the window of one of their offices. They had been able to keep up some level of trade despite the communication issues that plagued the world. But business was the last thing on the mind of the people that were standing at the window of the highest occupied floor of the Four Seasons Hotel. They were all looking out at the craft and thinking about the party that would be going on along the streets and beaches of Miami later that day. In short, they were all desperate to finish their work for the day and get out to the beach for a few drinks, to meet with friends, and to have a party in anticipation of the salvation. Even those that were due to work later that day were sure that work would take a backburner when the evacuation of the planet was imminent.

One of the bosses walked away from the window for a few seconds. He had to make a decision on what the rest of the day would involve. In fact, he had to make a decision on the future of the company. If he and his team were going to move to a new planet, then there would be little need to push the work forward. He decided to let them all walk away now. He wanted them to see their families and prepare for a new life. He spoke. "Ladies and gentlemen, the company exists no longer. Go home and see your family. If the new world is going to save us, then I will see you all there." And they were gone.

The triangular spacecraft stayed motionless at twenty thousand feet above the ground in locations across the globe. As they arrived near cities and towns, the craft just came to a standstill. The people of the Earth stood and looked up at the craft for hours on end, as they were enormous and took up much of the sky. It could have looked like an invasion if the people were not already told by the messengers that the craft were on the way and the reason for their arrival. Instead of the fear of invasion, the believers of the Earth were so happy to see the craft. It marked the next step on their journey to safety, to another planet, and to Jesus. Many were told all their life that if they had faith in Jesus, then this was the path to enlightenment and salvation, and so it came to be. The people of the planet Earth that believed in Jesus, believed in the messengers, and believed in the truth now believed that they were going to be saved. It was a happy occasion on the planet as those who believed gathered together to be close to others with the same belief. The small enclaves that had formed of believers grew in number as the Dark Army patrolled the parts of cities that were important to the demonic President. They protected military installations. They protected the cash reserves of the banks. They protected electricity stations to keep power lines moving electricity to the homes, offices, and other buildings of the world. It was as though the President needed to feel power at all times. But in truth, his power over the believers had gone.

In the areas of the world such as Seattle, the Holy Land, and the countryside, the people were able to gather freely and spend time with each other. It was like one big party where everyone was invited. Only those that chose not to come were not present. Those that had attended were partying with people like there was no tomorrow. Little or no alcohol was involved as people were drunk on the free spirit of their fellow humans and the thoughts of being saved from not only the fate of the planet Earth but the ills of it too. The ills of the planet were obvious for many to see. The events that had followed the speech in the United Nations had reminded many good people of the bad that can happen on planet Earth. The fights, the damage, and the destruction showed all too painfully what might happen if things were left to get out of control. But the response of "control" from the President was a reminder of the power that the leaders yielded and the ills that power brought. The good people of the Earth deserved a better place to start again and become a safe, happy, and prosperous place again—prosperity for all rather than placed in the hands of the few. These were the hopes of the good people as they partied long into the night. Across the globe, the evening, and into the night after the triangular spacecraft arrived, the people who believed stood and spoke together *en masse* in towns and cities in every country of the world.

At the cowboy church near Lake Palestine, there was another party. The people of the church had worked hard with Simon, Daniel, and Sierra over the prior few days to get the message out there to as many people as they could. They visited other local towns and spoke to as many people as they found. Throughout the congregation, there was a spirit of positivism, and the people had delivered the message in a personal way that meant far more than watching it on television. It brought home the truth, and the believers of the area listened intently to the words of the people of the cowboy church.

The day that the triangular transportation craft arrived in the area, at first, it appeared to be right over Lake Palestine. As it moved slowly towards the Earth, it became obvious that the craft was heading to a position that it had already been in once. It was over the top of the church where it had transported Daniel, Simon, and Sierra days earlier.

    The church was the scene of a party that night. People came together from far and wide to sit with Simon, Daniel, and Sierra and talk. The connections that were made by the congregation were passed on. So, if one congregation member had spoken to another church around thirty miles away, then they took the time to introduce the members of this church to the members of the cowboy church. All in all, this made for many, many introductions, but it made the conversation flow. Everybody wanted to meet the three messengers who had already been on the Star Craft. They had many questions about what it was like and what would happen. Simon and Daniel talked nonstop to new friends all evening and late into the night. But the center of attention was Sierra. She was handling the questions and the attention like she had been born for it. As the night wore on and people spoke, nobody noticed the churning clouds in the sky had started again. As time went on, the clouds churned more, and then a beam of light appeared. It moved across the sky towards the group of people that were talking together outside the church.

    All of a sudden, the good people of the cowboy church and their new friends were taken up on board the transportation craft. As they rose above the ground, Simon and Daniel spoke to keep them calm. But all eyes were still on Sierra, and she smiled. Her smile calmed down the whole group. This was what they had been waiting for.

    As night fell across the planet, the same scene unfolded. Daytime passed, people gathered in groups, and then the transportation craft sent out a beam of light that took the believers up to safety. People in every corner of the world were being lifted to the craft away from the Earth. Some reacted with happiness and others with a little fear, but most were silent throughout the movement from the Earth to the craft. The dark of night made the experience of travelling four thousand feet from the Earth to a spacecraft supported only by a beam of light less frightening. The fact that people travelled together also helped. As the believers looked around and saw other making the same movement, they felt comforted. They were not alone. They would be safe with their fellow believers.

Every believer floated onto the ships like Simon, Daniel, and many others were days before, but it happened again at night so that people would be less traumatized since they would not be able to perceive the danger in the dark as much.

The one thing that had confused many people when the triangular transportation craft arrived was the fact that they were not attacked. The President and his followers had made it clear that they saw these craft as an invasion force and would do whatever was necessary to remove them from the Earth's atmosphere. As the craft appeared in the sky, the rejoicing was tinged with a little concern that they might see the air forces of the world unleashed on the craft, or even a nuclear strike. But throughout that day and night, there was nothing. In fact, those that had been observing had seen little sign of the militaries of the world since the day they were first scrambled and seemed to take over the cities, the skies, and the seas. It was a development that nobody had anticipated. In the favelas of Rio de Janeiro, the talk was that the President had given up and decided to rule those that chose to stay behind. It was the talk in the minutes before the beam of light took them all up to their own transportation craft. In the Holy Land, the people told each other that the President would look only to his own country and try to stop the evacuation of Americans in the United States only. They were speculating about the fate of the United States as their transportation craft set out a beam of light to take them to safety.

But the people of the favelas and the people of the Holy Land were wrong. The President had been gathering his troops together, and they were waiting for the opportunity to strike. They had taken to the seas so that they could plot their next moves without the prying eyes of any believers. After the exodus from the White House, the President became even more suspicious and insular. He only wanted his own followers around him for fear that the believers were leaking information out to the messengers and to Jesus Christ himself. The military had been working on communication devices that had no need for a satellite, and although they hadn't been tested fully, it was time to put these into effect.

Through this system, the President had been able to tell his allies that the time to strike would be when the people had entered the craft. This would cause maximum devastation. This would send out a message to the rest of the people on Earth that his word was to be followed. Anyone who didn't listen would be killed in the way that the believers were in these spacecraft that had arrived. The first message on this new system was simple. "Move your people out to the seas and await further instructions. But be prepared for war." The message moved out across the channels. It hit the military commanders, the presidents and leaders of other allied countries, and the base commanders all over the world. It reached the Dark Army as they planned to take back control of the planet from those that were ready to desert the Earth for some religious message of doom. Aircraft carriers, submarines, troop carriers, and battleships were among the thousands of craft that had moved out to sea in preparation for the battle that the President had predicted.

As the people of the planet Earth were transported to these craft in order to evacuate the Earth, the order was put out by the President to begin the attack. Submarines moved to the surface and readied their missiles. Battle planes took off from their carriers and headed towards the triangular craft that they had been told were here to invade. Troops assembled on deck to assist in the imminent attack. Some made sure that the planes took off, while others manned the guns that would soon be trained on the black triangular objects that dominated the sky. As the people of the Dark Army looked up, they sensed victory. They could see no weapons on the craft and thought that this would be a chicken shoot. Large craft that would obviously be difficult to maneuver against the nimblest planes that the military could muster would be a one-sided fight in the eyes of her Dark Army. The commanders were already projecting an easy victory, and their minds moved forward to the next stage of the war. What would they be asked to do? How would they keep control of the inhabitants of the Earth? How would they be rewarded?

The triangular craft did nothing in response. As the threat gathered, they didn't move, didn't retaliate, and in fact didn't even seem to notice that the guns of the world were trained on them.

The Dark Army advanced. All guns on all battleships were trained on the nearest black triangular object. The missiles of the submarines were loaded and ready to fire. Their target coordinates had been set. Their warheads were primed and ready to explode on impact. The planes were all lining up to unleash their weapons on the craft that were well within range at only four thousand feet from the surface of the planet. The Dark Army was set. The message went back to the President. "Sir, we are ready. On your order, we will take down these invaders."

The President sat in his Oval Office surrounded by the family and followers that he felt he could trust. Some of the nonbelievers had left the building at one stage or another, and the people that were left were either loyal or too frightened to leave. Either way, the President had them under his control. He spoke. "They are ready. We are about the see the Earth saved and these invaders destroyed. Look out of the windows. We can see one of these craft eliminated from the comfort of the White House. This is a scene that will be replayed the world over. The craft, the messengers, and their believers will be no more."

As the people moved towards the window and looked up at the triangular transportation craft, the President picked up his communication device. He spoke slowly and clearly. "It is time. Finish them."

By this time, there was a little of the communication networks of old left. Cable television relied on the network of underground wires to deliver their programming, so it had dominated the airwaves since the satellites had been destroyed. Some basic cell phone networks still hadn't moved over to advanced satellite technology and beamed their signals from mast to mast across nations. The landline phone network survived largely unscathed from the events of the few days before. There were ways of keeping in touch. People had seen others taken up to the spacecraft and told their friends and family.

The people of the Earth were still in touch with each other in small ways that could spread the word.

After the order from the President, the military moved into attack mode. They prepared to fire on all fronts all at the same time.

A gunner on a battleship that was close to the Eastern seaboard had his gun trained on the craft hovering over the Washington, D.C. area. He had received the order to fire in ten seconds. As he looked at his watch, the time was 6.11 a.m. He noted this as the time that the world would be put right again.

Nine, eight, seven . . .

He took a deep breath. He hadn't fired the gun in battle before. He was ready to take out the enemy.

Six, five, four . . .

He looked again at the instruments in front of him. He wanted to be absolutely sure that the gun would hit the immobile target. This would be easy.

Three, two . . .

He thought, *I know this is the right thing. I know that the Earth must be protected from these invaders.*

One.

He pulled the trigger. Nothing happened. He tried again—nothing. He looked across the rest of the ship thinking that he had a malfunction. He would be able to see the rest of the ship fire at the enemy and the destruction that followed. All he saw as he looked across the craft was more gunners with the same confused expression on their faces. What was happening?

The planes in the sky had the same issue. All of their missiles were trained on the craft, but when they pushed the button to launch missiles, nothing happened. The submarines had their warheads stuck in the torpedo tubes. No manner of button pushing or overriding would remove them in the direction of their targets. All of the military force had been stopped at once.

The Dark Army was so sure of their victory. They thought that all they had to do was turn up on the battlefield, and success would be theirs. But just like the transport craft eliminated the satellites around the world with a single blast, so did the smaller war craft become disabled by a percussion blast from the larger transport craft. The effect was a complete disablement of the military might that the President and his allies had assembled. In effect, the war was over before it had even begun. The believers on board the triangular transportation craft were safe.

When the news reached the President, he was furious. This was a development that he had not expected. He felt assured of victory and the message to go out to the rest of the people on Earth that he was not to be undermined. But the result of this battle would be seen in many parts of the world. He would lose his grip of terror in many places. He would see more people look to leave the planet and desert him. Even members of the Dark Army in places were having second thoughts on what side they should be on. This was the non-battle that would make the nonbelievers sit up and take notice. If the power of Jesus is to neuter the entire military force of the world in a stroke, and then perhaps he was someone worth following. If he could transform a war into peace in one second, then maybe he was right about the fate of the planet. The effect of this was not lost on the raging President. He threw the effects of his desk across the room one by one. It was the outlet of rage that he needed and suddenly allowed him to think clearly again. He picked up his communication device and ordered a full investigation to be reported back to him within the hour. He wanted the top engineers in the army to repair the weapons and have them operational as soon as possible. He was not going to give up. Little did he know that the weapons had been disabled forever. The percussion blast had rendered them useless.

The craft had carried out their first task. They had evacuated the believers from the face of the planet Earth. They had in one blast taken away all the power of the military. The people that wanted to be saved were safely on board, and the demonic President was rendered powerless. The people that were on the transportation craft were ecstatic. Through the large glass windows, they had been able to see some of what was happening below. To begin with, there was a small ripple of fear going across the transportation craft as people could see the might of the military line up to attack the place where they stood. In a conventional war, it is army against army, soldier against soldier. This means that the people being attacked are expecting it, have been trained for it, and are used to it. In this situation, these were ordinary people who had done nothing but believe. So, when they saw air force planes starting to approach, the feeling was one that they had never felt before. Although they believed in the words of Jesus through his messengers, it was still a frightening experience to have the might of the world's military pointed straight at the vehicle you stood in. When it transpired that the military was powerless, the feeling of joy spread out among the craft. People hugged each other, and everyone was happy. Although they did not know what had happened, they all knew that a divine force was involved. They knew that their faith had been repaid. Jesus had promised salvation, and now that promise was coming true. The triangular transportation craft were happy places to be.

For many, the face of the Earth was not a happy place to be. It was becoming more obvious to the members of the Dark Army that they were losing the battle. The reports were coming through thick and fast that the problems with military hardware were global. No member of the Dark Army had been able to fire their missiles, launch their torpedoes, or fire their guns. It was a disaster for the members of the forces that supported the President and his global domination. But he had just lost billions of people whom he had previously dominated. This loss was one that he felt down in the pit of his stomach. He wanted to stop the craft from reaching the Earth. He wanted to stop people from leaving. Now that both of these things were looking impossible, he just wanted to lash out. He cleared the Oval Office so he could spend some time on his own. Many of the people in the room took this as their opportunity to leave the White House. Many of them didn't stop to collect their belongings and didn't even look back. They knew that their time on Earth was coming to an end. They didn't know how, but they would do everything they could to get onto one of the transportation craft and leave for a new life. The courage that they needed to transform their beliefs into actions had come with the events of the previous hour. The time had come to take action.

On the streets, the gangs of people that were roaming the cities looking to destroy everything in their path had run out of steam. In the early few hours and days, it felt like they were creating their own empire. It felt like they were ruling over all the others that didn't have the same capacity for destruction and fighting as them. It felt as though they were taking over the cities, but it became obvious over the next few days that they had nobody to fight, nobody to dominate. The believers had just gone underground and found places to be together away from all the carnage and destruction. The nonbelievers had nobody to fight and nothing to burn. The people that really followed the President and were hell-bent on destruction started to fight with each other. The ones that wanted to believe but had to find the strength to follow their convictions started to move to the periphery.

As the black triangular spaceships arrived overhead, the fighting pretty much stopped completely. In the same way that the rest of the world stood and looked up at the craft, so did the nonbelievers. They wanted a front row seat to the attack that the President had promised. They wanted to see the believers suffer and see them wiped from the face of the planet. As they sat and watched the combined military force of the world rendered useless in a matter of seconds, the streets of the cities fell silent. The people that had stood there to watch their fellow humans perish had no answers in the face of the might of Jesus Christ. They sat without action for minutes that turned into hours. The world that was left on the face of planet Earth waited for a sign. The people who did not believe were waiting for some decisive action from the President. The people who wanted to believe were waiting for a sign that they would not be left behind.

The President stomped across his Oval Office without purpose. All he could do was wait on the work of the mechanics and engineers. All he could do was wait for a communication that told him they were ready to fire again. All he could do was wait for a communication that told him all the missiles were ready, all the torpedoes were ready, and all of the guns were trained on the craft in the sky. But even if he got that call, what was to say that the powerful craft wouldn't just wipe them all out in an instant again? He was resigned to military defeat, but he wanted to inspire his followers one last time. He called out of the office for the media mogul to join him. He wanted to go out on television across the world and spread his message of hate. He wanted to tell all of the remaining followers to stop anyone they suspected of trying to leave the planet. He called again for the media mogul. He was ready now. He may have lost the physical battle, but he hadn't given up on the mental war that he had raged with Jesus and his followers over the centuries. He called again for the media mogul. As he called the third time, a figure walked into the room. It wasn't the media mogul but the Vice President. He walked into the room with his head held low. He spoke, but his voice was barely audible. He had bad news and was afraid to say it. "He has gone. Most of them have gone. There are only a few of us left with you," said the Vice President. He knew that the game was over. He knew that the Earth was heading for its final days. The Vice President had made his choice. He had sided with the President. It was now time to accept his fate.

The use of the remaining communications systems of the world to connect with the people was a great idea. It wasn't just the President that had come up with this thought. Back up on the Star Craft, Marta and Hozai had watched the series of events carefully. As the transportation craft approached the Earth, they set the orders to stop at four thousand feet so that the craft could do their work. The two watched as the people of the planet rejoiced at their pending salvation. As the movement from the ground to four thousand feet involved floating people up, the two decided that this would be best done by night. Moving upwards is scary enough without seeing the entire world disappear beneath your feet. So, as each part of the world plunged into darkness, they instructed the relevant transportation craft to get their believers on board. It was also under the watch of Hozai and Marta that the percussion blast was emitted from the craft to disable the military power that had been assembled against them. The Star Craft had been built for missions such as this. It was developed with cutting edge technology over a long period of time, so it had all the facilities needed to evacuate a whole planet in an orderly fashion while potentially being under attack from a hostile force.

One of the other facilities that was on the Star Craft was the ability to communicate. With all of the satellites destroyed, the Star Craft was the only thing in the Earth's atmosphere that could transmit to the whole planet simultaneously. There were still television stations, some cell phone coverage, and a basic computer network functioning across the world. This would be the outlet for Marta to speak to the rest of the population of the planet. She would do this as soon as she received reports back from the transportation craft that all was well and that they had suffered no damage. Although there was little possibility of damage, Marta had to make sure that if she was going to put out a call for people to join them, then they had to be going to a safe place. The transportation craft were programmed to send back a signal once all the people were on board and once the automated checks had been carried out to assess damage. All came back one by one.

Washington—all is well
New York—all is well.
Baltimore—all is well.
Philadelphia—all is well.

And so it went on. The reports came back within seconds of each other from across the planet. Marta and Hozai listened intently. They were checking the status of all their craft. They were checking the well-being of all the believers.

When the word came through that all were safe, Marta then triggered the facility to take over the television sets, cell phones, and computers of the world. She spoke slowly and in clear tones. Throughout the evacuation, she had been speaking mainly to those that already believed. But now the message was going out to those that had doubts. She was speaking now to those that wanted to believe but might not have had the courage before to act on them. She had to get this communication right in order to speak to their hearts.

She spoke. "People of the world, by now you can see that we have come in peace and salvation. We are here to save people, not to harm them as the President of the United States and his allies tell you. Many people who believe us are now safely on board the transportation craft. They will be with us soon and moving towards a new life on a safe planet. We want you to join us. There is still time to be saved. The transportation craft will be sent back to the surface of your planet one more time. In two days, we will return to save all of those with goodness in their heart. If you want to be rescued, then start praying. We will hear you. We will come back for you."

Marta paused for a few seconds. She knew that like many of the communications that the people of Earth had received over the previous few days, this would take a little time to sink in. She knew that this was going to be the final opportunity to rescue people from a dying planet. She wanted to make sure that the message was received and understood. One more time, she spoke. "I repeat, we will come back for you. We will not leave behind anyone who believes. Pray and we will hear you. Pray and we will find you. Pray and we will save you. Thank you."

Marta closed the communication. She had done all she could do. The fate of the rest of the people was in their own hands. The Star Craft could detect the bodies of those who prayed and believed. In two days' time, they would send back the transportation craft to collect those that were ready. The final days to evacuate had arrived. There was little time to spare. By the calculations that had been worked through, the gamma-ray burst could happen within the next thirty days. But that did not mean that they had thirty days to evacuate the planet. To survive the blast, the Start Craft had to be two light years away from the blast. The two days that Marta had given the other people on the planet was all that they could spare. Time was of the essence, and any delays would endanger the whole mission, the Star Craft, and all the people on board. There was urgency in the air with everything the crew did on the Star Craft. It wasn't a mad panic like the one that had engulfed large parts of the planet Earth in the days before. It was a sense of urgency with a purpose. The people all knew their roles and all knew that there was much to do to get the people on board the Star Craft and get away from the danger. People moved about in all directions first one way and then the next. Living quarters were prepared, the dials and switches were checked, and the whole Star Craft was made ready for the people that would soon arrive.

The two days passed quickly. The people who were on earth and wanted to be saved prayed. They found the communes and areas that the believers before them had settled in and grouped together. Praying as a group seemed like the best way to ensure that they would be detected and collected by the strange black triangular craft that had occupied the sky a couple of days earlier. Like any situation of panic, there were rumors running through what was left of communities. Those that wanted to spread lies and panic told that the triangular craft had disappeared without trace and would never return. They told tales that there was no movement of good people and that the craft had exterminated the people that had gathered before. Even in the final days of the Earth, when the belief of the good people had saved their lives, there were still those that wanted to do nothing but wrong. They tried through their words to undermine the salvation of the planet that the President and all of his military might couldn't do with guns and bombs.

But those with faith ignored the rumors and prayed. They gathered together and prayed. They slept, ate, and prayed. Prayer became a strong part of the lives of these people in the two days from missing out on the first transportation craft and waiting for the second. Their prayers were answered. Just like the first time the triangular transportation craft had arrived on the planet, they moved as one. The craft arrived in the same locations above towns and cities all over the face of the globe. They dropped slowly to four thousand feet again surrounded each by churning white fluffy clouds no matter the location and no matter the prevailing weather conditions before they arrived. They arrived above Seattle, above New York, above Sydney, above Paris, and above Roma. They arrived to the joy of the people who had prayed. Like the last visit of the transportation craft, people held parties to sing together, swap stories of their belief, and speculate on what life would be like from now on. The people were ready to be transported to a new life. Their belief had grown over the prior two days from something that was locked inside to something that was now out there for the entire world to see.

The transportation craft arrived at four thousand feet and stopped. Back up on the Star Craft, Marta was at the controls. The new residents of the Star Craft were all on board and finding their way around. It was the job of Marta to scan the areas below the transportation craft to see where the people were who believed and then effect their transition through the air to safety. All of the time, she was watching intently so that she could make sure that another attack was not imminent. Marta knew that any attack could be thwarted in the same way as the one before, but she always had to be prepared for the worst.

As night arrived and darkness fell in the cities and towns of the world, the transportation craft worked their light beams and transported the people from the surface of the Earth to the safety of the craft. This was the final evacuation of people from the planet, and this was all the time they had. The next planet that these people would step foot on would be their new home. The journey from the face of the earth to the craft was one that many of the people were not ready for. Rising four thousand feet into the sky seemingly without any support is a sensation that most humans are never prepared for. There was much shouting and fear in the voices of the people. None of this turned into panic as the people could not see clearly due to the fact it was night, and they had been told before that the ships were there to save them.

As the people boarded the transportation craft, there were whoops of joy. The people were on their way to salvation. Those that were left behind were far from joyous. They were prepared for the worst.

Chapter 9

Departure of the Earth

On the Star Craft, the scene was one of mass activity. As you can imagine, moving billions of people was a big task. Moving billions of people to somewhere that they did not know was a huge task. Moving billions of people who had been traumatized by the events of the recent past to somewhere they did not know was a mammoth task. However, to overcome the potential overwhelming feeling of being on a massive Star Craft, every corridor, every room, and every section looked different in order that people could find their way throughout the massive Star Craft. So, what might have been a long walk for someone, the perception was that the distance was short and enjoyable. Not that anyone minded. As they moved about the Star Craft, they were faced with more and more people who were in the same situation. The people that they bumped into were also believers, they had also been through some pretty harrowing times over the prior few days, and they were also in a strange place. This furthered the spirit of togetherness. If someone was lost, then there was always someone else who was willing to help them find their way to where they were going.

Little groups formed of people that were heading in same direction but just didn't know exactly how to get there. The spirit of human togetherness was strong. Groups of crew members were tending plants all over the Star Craft. Plants were important to have on this long trip. They helped with cleaning the air, and visually they helped with the whole quality of life throughout the entire Star Craft. Large clusters of plants were located as people ventured along the pedestrian ways within the Star Craft. Other locations had vegetable gardens that many people were starting to help the crew members.

On a lower level of the Star Craft, a pair of camels stood calmly being tended by people from the Star Craft. They were joined by some of the people from the planet Earth who wanted to help. The Star Craft crew was handing over responsibility for looking after the camels to two bright young people who loved animals and were willing to be of assistance. The two young people listened intently as the Star Craft crew talked to them about the diet the camels would need, the grooming they required, and their temperament. They explained that if the humans were afraid of this strange place, then the animals would be too. Keeping them calm throughout the long flight would go a long way to making sure that these animals would be ready for the transition to the new world.

As the two bright young people looked up from their camels, they saw a similar scene about ten feet away with two donkeys. The people of the Earth were being shown by Star Craft crew how to look after the animals. Looking down the line, the two saw the same conversation happening next to a pair of elephants, two zebra, male and female wildebeest, and a couple of bison. There were elks, buffalo, antelopes of all varieties, tigers, hyena, dogs, cats large and small, and horses. All the animals of the Earth were protected in pairs to start again on the planet that they were all headed for. Some were in cages, some in tanks, but all had been saved to populate the new world. All across this immense level of the Star Craft, there were pairs of animals that had been rescued from the Earth to start their species again in the new world. It was as though the Ark had been reborn, and Noah himself was there to oversee the protection of all species on the planet. The two bright young things looked back to their camels and listened again to the instructions from the crew of the Star Craft. They would have to pass on these instructions so that the camels and all the other animals were looked after the entire day. This was going to be a job that took up a lot of their time. The animals were as precious to the new world as the people.

As the animals were kept in pairs, the people started to take over from the crew of the Star Craft. There was much to do on the craft, and the people were willing and able to lend a hand. As time wore on, the humans became more confident with their chosen animals. Experts from zoos and safari areas of the world were found and brought to look after the more dangerous or complicated animals, and it all worked well. The area was a happy place, and being at one with the animal kingdom was an experience that produced calm for all those involved. The animals of the world would be saved too. In all the hysteria about the human world, many people had forgotten the animals. Now they were in safe hands.

On another level of the Star Craft, Marta was looking for three people. She had looked around the outside of the level but was now moving her way towards the center. The device that she carried in her hand gave her the exact location of the people she searched for. Marta was ready to start revealing some of the secrets of the Star Craft to certain members of the human race. This would enable the people to understand what was going on and contribute to the new planet functioning just like the one they had left behind but without the demonic President, his followers, and the evil they brought.

Marta walked. She knew that with the size of the Star Craft and the sheer number of people on board, it might take a little time to find the three that she wanted to speak to. She walked some more, but at every turn, she saw people that had questions for her. It was part of her role, part of her calling to help people along the way. However, the crew members were also able to help the passengers. So, Marta directed all those people to the crew members standing nearby. She knew that there was plenty of time on the journey, so she helped everyone who asked when she could. The device in her hand would lead her to the people she wanted to find. It was just a matter of time.

"How many people do you think are here?" asked Sierra. She was excited by the activity on board the Star Craft and had heard stories already about the animals on the lower level. She was giddy, and it was up to Simon and Daniel to keep her entertained.

"I reckon you should try to count them all," Daniel replied. His sense of humor was still intact and was needed now more than ever. "If you can't count all the people, then why not count all the legs and divide this number by two," he continued. "Even I have two legs now." He smiled at Sierra, and at that moment, she worked out that he was joking. She had been trying to decide in her head whether he was serious or not. She could never tell whether Daniel was being serious or not. She pushed him lightly on the arm. He knew that he was keeping her entertained.

While these two were bantering, Simon was in thought. *I know that we have left the atmosphere of the Earth now, and we are headed for a better place. The people that chose not to believe are left behind, and the people that are on board will help us start a new life in a new world. This is the chance that humanity has needed for some time. Although as a preacher I have never given up on anyone, there were some who didn't want to be saved. I wish I had the chance to try to reach them. I wish I was able to speak to all of those that were left behind, if not to persuade them to come with us but to understand why they would not.*

"I have found you."

Simon's thoughts were stopped by a voice. He instinctively knew that it wasn't the voice of Daniel—too low—and not the voice of his darling daughter, Sierra—too adult—so he broke off from his thoughts and turned around; it was Marta. She was holding a strange device in her hand, and her face wore a huge smile. It was good for Marta to see the people that had been chosen. It was good to see that their hard work had gone to save the lives of billions of people. Every one of the messengers had played their part. Every one of the messengers had returned to the Star Craft. "Can you three follow me? I have something I need to show you," said Marta by way of an instruction and not a question.

"Hi, Marta, it is so good to see you again," said Sierra as she gave her a hug around her waist. She had used the same greeting with everyone she recognized on the Star Craft. She was so pleased to see everyone that she told them so. It was her way of spreading the joy she felt in her heart. The three of them looked at Marta, wondering whether this familiarity was acceptable.

"Hi, Sierra, it is good to see you too. Shall we walk?" replied Marta. The three followed Marta to the edge of the room and then to another level. As they walked along the corridor, there was no conversation. The way that Marta had approached them and her manner gave the impression that she was there on business rather than pleasure. They walked along a corridor and then stopped outside of a room. Marta told them to wait for a few seconds while she got the room ready for them. Simon felt that this was to increase their concentration and to mark this room as especially important.

Around thirty seconds passed before Marta opened the door again. "You can come in now." Marta motioned to the three of them. They were all intrigued and eager to get inside of the room. Only the etiquette of letting the young girl through the door first slowed Simon and Daniel from running into the room. They really wanted to know what was inside.

It felt as though they had been walking for a long time to get to this room, and it was in a remote part of the Star Craft. Nobody else was around, and the three humans stepped inside, ready to listen to what Marta had to say. She told them, "This is our room of souls. We have not only evacuated our living 'seeds' but also the souls of our dead seeds. We have here the souls of the people of the Earth that have gone before. All those who have lived their lives in the right way and believed in Jesus are here. They will be coming to the new planet with us. The life of our souls will also be saved."

Simon wept. He openly cried at this revelation. He had spoken in church many times about the way that people should live their lives and the rewards that they would receive, but he had no way of ever proving it. The march of science into the lives of ordinary people had started to erode the traditional beliefs of good and evil, of doing the right things, and of the importance of the soul. People believed more in the deeds of science than having faith in God. Simon's beliefs and faith were now there in front of him; the emotion of the situation was too much for him at that moment in time. The tears rolled down his cheeks and dropped onto the floor. His daughter comforted him. Simon knew that Sierra was strong, and he wasn't afraid to cry in front of her.

Marta explained that the souls were brought on to the Star Craft in much the same way as the people were. She explained that a happy new planet would need the souls of the believers present so they could watch over their descendants. It was a wonderful moment for the three of them. Marta had personally chosen Simon, Daniel, and Sierra to visit the room of souls. It would be their job to spread the word to all the other believers on the Star Craft.

Marta also brought up a different subject when she asked Simon if he still had his special finding. Simon's face was blank at first. Then his face expressed the realization that Marta was asking about the meteorite with the gold medallion. "Yes, I do. I keep it with me at all times." Marta continued, "If you remember when we told you, 'You are us and we are you,' this medallion was sent to Earth to enforce the faith you and all the people of Earth have that Jesus is real. And his covenant to return would come true. So, share this story and the medallion with all that you know."

On another remote level of the Star Craft, Hozai was leading a group of archaeologists through a doorway. Just behind Hozai were John-Paul Moreau and his wife Michelle. On the walk to the level, the couple were talking to other archaeologists about their work on earth and wondering what life might be like on a new planet. Would there be artifacts from this new world to discover? Would there be universities? Would there be a need for archaeologists? Hozai listened in but did not intervene because he knew that the level of the Star Craft that they would soon arrive at would give them all the answers they needed. The door opened slowly, and as they stepped inside, the Moreaus were the first to see what was inside.

John-Paul immediately spotted Puma Punku as he walked through the door. There was the site that he and his team had been working on so diligently and which now sat in the Star Craft right in front of his eyes. It was just as glorious as the first time he had laid eyes on it. He was so happy that he could complete his work on the site in the new world. He ran his eyes across the vast room, and there were other archaeological sites that he recognized straight away. Hozai looked along a large corridor that ran straight down the middle of the level, and the archeologists walked hurriedly along this corridor. What they saw was amazing.

To the left in the first section were the finest paintings from planet Earth. The Mona Lisa was suspended in midair at the eye level of Michelle Moreau. As a resident of Paris, she had seen the painting many times before, but this was by far the closest she had been. Even on the special evenings where the professors of the Sorbonne University were given exclusive access to the Louvre Museum, there were still restrictions on how close people could get to the most precious and valuable pieces of art. She looked the Mona Lisa in the eye and felt herself well up. Behind the Mona Lisa, suspended in the same way, were hundreds of other pieces of art that told the story of human culture. There was *The Scream* by Edvard Munch, Da Vinci's *The Last Supper*, *Girl with A Pearl Earring* by Vermeer, Picasso's harrowing *Guernica*, and the *Night Watch* by Rembrandt among the hundreds of works of art that had filled museums and galleries for centuries. The old masters were supplemented by modern works of art that were less old than these paintings but no less revered. The modern masters such as Dali, Warhol, de Kooning, Basquiat, and Rothko were well represented in these suspended paintings so that the culture of the Earth could be recreated in the new world.

Some of the archaeologists had walked a lot further than John-Paul and Michelle Moreau and were looking at other cultural aspects of life that had been rescued and were being transported to the new planet. The most beautiful cars were all lined up as through about to start a race in a section of this level of the Star Craft. There were vintage Bentley and Rolls Royce cars lined up along the most stunning cars from the 1950s and then modern supercars that would have cost hundreds of thousands of dollars to buy back on Earth.

There were other vehicles, sculptures, reams of books by Shakespeare, Dickens, Twain, Hemingway, Sartre, and hundreds of other authors who have described the rich history of the planet Earth. The archaeologists spent an hour just walking among the first section of artifacts that would give their new planet a culture that would inspire people to greater things. They knew that they could each spend weeks at a time in this space and still never be remotely close to seeing it all. It was like the museum of the Earth with all the best aspects of the planet brought together under one roof. John-Paul wondered what price the director of the Louvre would charge for people to enter here!

They all returned to the door where they entered. They were as giddy as school children, excited by all the wonders of the Earth that had been saved and were now exhibited here right in front of their eyes. They were all delighted that their new planet would have all of this beauty.

As the archeologists returned to the door near the front of the level, Hozai spoke. "This is our room of character. We have not only evacuated our living 'seeds' but also the art, culture, structures, inventions our seeds have created." Hozai looked across the group and could see the absolute delight on their faces. He smiled broadly and continued, "You have all been chosen to look after this culture when we arrive at the new planet. These are important parts of human culture, and as such, we could not leave them behind. We trust you, the most eminent scholars of your race, to help us look after these items and help to spread the word to the rest of the people. We want the new planet to have a culture and history that people feel comfortable with. The fact that we are moving light years away from home will be a big enough challenge for people. If we made that move to a place where the people found everything new, then it might be too much for them to take. This is the best of human culture. We entrust it to you."

The archeologists were overwhelmed by the words of Hozai. They knew that they were being given a great privilege with access to these beautiful objects. John-Paul looked at his wife. They both looked as proud as they were on their wedding day. Their work would continue on the new planet. They could be together while looking after the objects that defined the human race. They would not let Hozai down in any way.

As the people learned new things about the lengths that the crew of the Star Craft had gone to in order to make the transition to the new planet run smoothly, the scenes on planet Earth were something very different. The Star Craft was full of people who trusted each other, were dedicated to helping, and were looking after the best of humankind. The people left on Earth, however, were full of mistrust, dedicated to hurting each other, and were displaying the worst of humankind.

After finding that all of the weapons of the Earth were futile against the transportation craft, the President grew angrier and angrier. He had seen the broadcast by Marta that stated the craft would return and save the people. From there, he had told the Dark Army to seek out those that were looking for salvation at the second chance. But by the time the Dark Army warriors returned to the cities from the sea, the two days were almost over. The people had hidden well in the secret places used before by the believers and were not found at all. The President in his role as the leader of the dark forces could not stop people from leaving the planet. Now the whole place was out of his control. He was satisfied that those left on the planet were carrying out his evil work, but he knew that the days of the planet Earth were numbered.

Without functioning weapons, the nonbelievers attacked each other with whatever they could lay their hands on. People fought openly in the streets with each other. They had no reason to fight, but it happened anyway. As the fights raged on, people lay bleeding in the streets until they bled out and died. The stench of rotting human flesh filled the air as nonbelievers decided to just try their best to hurt each other. Battles raged on many levels from one against one to whole gangs of attackers. There was no mercy shown to women or children; all were fair game. The people that were left behind on the planet fell into all manners of depravity from harming animals to the destruction of all remaining works of art. All of those that had chosen not to believe were suffering for this choice. They left no room in their hearts for love and faith and filled their hearts with anger and destruction. The last days on Earth were going to be filled with pain for all left behind. Those that had chosen to believe the demonic President were now left bewildered and confused as a lack of leadership took over. The Earth may have been close to ending, but it was going to go out with horrors being enacted all over the face of this planet.

The demonic President received updates from the Dark Army commanders that were out in the field. He was told that the face of the Earth was being scorched with the rotting remains of the people and the fires that had been lit and were ravaging in forests in every corner of the Earth. He listened intently as the reports grew more and more about the atrocities that the people who followed him were enacting on each other. The people of the Earth were delivering the ultimate evils to each other in the name of the devil, but he could feel no pride in that fact. He had ruled the Earth for a long time, but now that rule was coming to an end. His face dropped as he could think of no way to change the future. His chance had passed. He resigned himself to his fate. The President looked at his watch. It was a Rolex that was gifted to him by the members of his party when he won the election and became President-elect. He had no idea how much it had cost, but he knew that it was well into the tens of thousands of dollars. He looked back to that time. It was the peak of his powers. The American people had just voted him in on the back of his negative rhetoric, and the people in his party were so indebted to him that they bought him lavish gifts. Either that or they were so afraid of him that they felt they needed to appease him. Whichever way it was, he didn't care. Respect and fear worked the same way for the demonic President. He was still able to get people to do what he wanted rather than what they felt was right in their heart. The watch said 4:11 p.m., but time was irrelevant now. He took off the watch and hurled it against the wall. It smashed into a thousand pieces. His influence over his fellow Americans was over.

It was as if the Earth felt the horrors that were being played out on the surface. As the people fought with each other, the planet went into its own spiral of destruction. First, the tides rose as never before, and large areas of coastal land flooded, leaving behind thousands of dead. All of the volcanoes of the Earth erupted on the same day, causing the atmosphere to be filled with noxious gases that affected the breathing of anyone within a hundred miles. The lava flows destroyed towns and villages. Like the ancient city of Pompeii, people were frozen on the spot by the baking hot volcanic ash and killed instantly. Earthquakes happened along the fault lines of the earth, and massive cracks appeared on the surface of the planet. Anyone and anything that was near fell in and perished. Tornadoes lit a path across the surface of the continents and tore into homes, schools, and other buildings, flattening them to the ground. Any people that were hiding inside for fear of being attacked were killed by the force of the tornado. Destruction and devastation reached every country. There was no part that wasn't affected by the floods, the volcanoes, the earthquakes, and the tornadoes. People and animals fled from the coast only to be faced with an earthquake. They moved away from earthquake areas only to find that a tornado was waiting for them. Every turn was fraught with danger. Stampedes of people and animals went in every direction, and thousands were killed underfoot. There was no hiding place. The last chance of salvation had passed. Those that were left had chosen not to believe. They had missed out on the first salvation. They had seen the power of the transportation craft in the face of every weapon on Earth. They had been given the chance to believe and pray, and they had missed all of these opportunities.

The earth was taking more lives than the fighting. The planet was weeping for all the evil that was being waged across the globe. It was a series of events that would have been called cataclysmic under any other circumstances, but after the events of the previous few days and the warnings for the immediate future, these events just passed by the people of the planet. By now, they knew what they had let themselves in for.

Armageddon type conditions had begun on Earth with all the remaining people.

From the Star Craft, the Earth could still be seen in the distance. From the way that events had unfolded since the senator's speech in the United Nations, the people on board the Star Craft would have a fair idea of how the remaining people on the planet were reacting to the fact that they had lost their chance for salvation. The way that the President had acted was something that had confused many of the people on board the Star Craft. Although they had been warned that the demonic President ruled the face of the Earth, none had really thought that the President was that demonic. Of course, they knew that he had strange ways and huge influence, but none was prepared to face a foe that would wage all the military power of the entire planet against a peaceful group of people who wanted nothing but salvation.

The large glass windows that surrounded the Star Craft gave the passengers on board a clear view of the solar system around them. The Earth was disappearing from view at a fast rate but was still there, center of the window as the collective scientists were sanding together in the room of character. As they stood with a view of the Earth, the Star Craft picked up speed. They passed the moon and then Mars with the Earth disappearing from something that looked the size of a quarter of the window to something that looked no bigger than a baseball.

The sad fact was that some of the people on board the Star Craft knew someone who was left behind. Their friends and family had greeted them with open arms and open ears. They had listened to what the messengers had to say and joined them on the Star Craft, but every messenger had thousands of friends, work colleagues, fellow club members and acquaintances that they were just unable to reach for one reason or another. The grip of the devil was strong with some. The amount of time that the messengers had between returning to the Earth to spread the word and leaving the Earth for safety was short. The fact was that not everyone had it in their heart to be saved. The plight of those left behind was only the stuff of imagination or speculation right now, but what was sure was that soon, possibly within the next thirty days, the Earth would receive a gamma-ray burst, and their fate would be sealed. Until then, there was bound to be much violence and panic on the face of the Earth. The new home that all were travelling to would see that eliminated from daily life.

The scientists all stood open-mouthed at the wonders of the universe. No matter what discipline of science they were involved with all harbored dreams of going into space. It was one of the final frontiers of human exploration, along with the deepest oceans, the center of the earth, and the human brain. It was the fact that so many of these scientists had been brought up on a television diet of *Star Trek* and a movie diet of *Star Wars* that space seemed so alluring. And these scientists had reached space. They stood as one looking out into the darkness and wondering what the future might hold.

At the front right of the group were John-Paul and Michelle Moreau. They hadn't left each other's side in days and were even more helplessly in love than when they first met. Their dreams for life were to work together as closely as possible. They both had a very strong faith that was strengthened further by the events since they were first on board the Star Craft and returned to Earth in long-flowing robes. They had returned to Paris and spoken to their friends and family about their experience and how it was vital to leave the planet for salvation. They had both done some research on WR 104 in the Sagittarius constellation to better understand the plight that the Earth was facing. They could not find a lot of detail about a constellation and planet so far from Earth, but they could see the warning signs about this constellation that was going to produce the gamma-ray burst that finished the Earth. They both spoke passionately to their families and persuaded the head of the church at Notre Dame de Paris to allow them to speak at the church service on the Sunday after they returned. This was to reach out to their friends in their congregation to listen to the words of the senator and be saved.

But now John-Paul was surrounded by people different from his friends and family. He was now surrounded by the scientists that would help build and understand the new world. But there were not enough scientists to go around. There were tens of thousands of treasures at least, John-Paul had estimated, and each was going to have to be transported to a specified location, kept in perfect condition, and then explained to the people of the new planet. Art galleries and museums would have to be constructed and maintained to house all of the artifacts that were brought on this huge level of the Star Craft to the new world. John-Paul had spoken to Hozai and explained the need for more people to help look after these treasures and understand them more both during the journey to the new planet and once they were on the ground. Hozai was one step ahead. He had seen the need for more assistance as they were loading the huge numbers of works of art, vehicles, sculptures, literature, and more onto the craft. He had instructed some of the Star Craft crew to work on a list of people that would be able to help. Many were university professors and science researchers or enthusiasts that were identified as the type of mind that would be able to understand and assist in this task.

As they all stood near the huge window of the Star Craft in the room of character, looking out into space, their focus would soon turn to the room that they were standing in. The people that had assembled were given two hours by John-Paul before walking the room and getting some idea of the scale of the task. All had returned with eyes wider than the Grand Canyon as they realized that it wasn't just the people of the Earth that had been rescued. The overwhelming feeling in the room was that this was on a scale that they could never have imagined before. None were aware that there was this much treasure on the Earth. None were aware that even half of this existed. As a scientist, you get lost in your own field of work. The number of possibilities in your own area of research becomes endless as you look deeper and deeper into it. So, when these scientists were faced with the work of every field of science and culture on the planet all at once in the same room, they felt a little nausea at first. They felt as though this was a task that was beyond them. It had taken mankind millennia to deliver this much art, literature, buildings, and other artifacts, and they were here to transport it all to a new world. It was a dizzying prospect, but after the initial shock subsided, they then realized that they were in a privileged position. They had access to all the wonders of the world and were charged with protecting them, understanding them, and showing them to all the other people of the planet when they arrived in a new world.

That was another dizzying prospect, and many had to sit down at several times during their two hours as the weight of expectation hit hard. But two hours was the right amount of time. John-Paul had figured that giving people two hours would be long enough for them to absorb the shocks and come back raring to help. It worked. The people that walked back towards that large window and took their last look at the Earth stood tall. John-Paul could see that they were each ready to take on the mammoth task that lay ahead and become the cultural champions of the new world.

John-Paul was deep in thought as the rest of the room said good-bye to their former home.

I have made it on to the Star Craft. There were times when I was back home in Paris when I thought that this might not happen. There were so many people to save, and I would have gladly given my life to save others. But thankfully, that was not necessary. My family is all safe here on the Star Craft, and we can be together again in our new home. I wonder what that home will be like. Will they try to recreate Paris? Will there be rivers and seas on our new planet? Will there be a new Seine? I miss all the parts of my wonderful home already. Will I ever be able to take a boat ride along the river again? Will I be able to eat croissants and drink coffee while watching the world go by? Will there be a university for my wife and me to teach in? Will the other people of the Sorbonne be happy? The world has changed, and we are saved but in many ways. I want things to stay the same. I want my city, my job, and my wife. I worked all my life to get there, but I also know that this is a brave new world. There will be much to learn, and that is what my life has been dedicated to—learning. That is a continuous process, and it isn't going to stop now. I am surrounded by brilliant minds, and I am going to lead them in the understanding of the culture that we have brought with us. I love to teach, and I love to learn. This is the perfect opportunity to do both in a way that I never have before. And I get to do all of this with my wife beside me.

At this point, John-Paul broke off from his thoughts and looked down towards his wife. He was sure that she would be watching the window intently with no thought for looking at him. They had looked at each other nonstop for many years, but now there was something fascinating out of the window that they had never seen before and would never see again. He looked down at his beautiful wife.

Michelle looked up at her husband. It was as though his thoughts had told her to look in the direction of her husband. She first glanced at her husband out of the corner of her eye. She had a strange feeling that she ought to look up but didn't know where it had come from. She didn't trust feelings like this all the time. As a scientist, she believed in cold hard facts, but as a wife, she lived by her feelings. Standing in that room of artifacts surrounded by scientists, she felt like a scientist, not a wife. As the glance confirmed that her husband was looking at her, she turned her head and met his gaze. They looked into each other's eyes. Michelle stepped closer to her husband. She wanted to feel his strength close to her as she knew that they would work tirelessly. She knew that the days, weeks, months, and years ahead would mean long working days side by side. This felt like her last chance to have a moment between them before the hard work began. As he held her, Michelle pulled his head lower. She positioned his ear close to her mouth and softly said, "I love you, John-Paul." A smile appeared across his face. It was the type of smile that could be seen in the eyes as well as the mouth. His eyes lit up, and his mouth spread as wide as it could. John-Paul was just about to reply with the words "I love you" when Michelle spoke again. "You are here for a purpose. You are here to lead these people to transfer the brilliant culture of the Earth to our new world. I need you, these people need you. It is time for you to lead the way. I am so proud of you, and we will listen to your every word. Hozai has trusted you to look after the room of character. You have a responsibility to him. You have a responsibility to all of the people on this craft. *Allez les obtenir!*"

Now was the time.

John-Paul said, "Ladies and gentlemen, school is in session." The people that were gathered around the window stopped their long stare into space and walked the few steps to where John-Paul was standing. They were all listening to him and all ready to build the culture of their new home.

On the other side of the Star Craft, Simon, Sierra, and her mother were all standing together, looking out of another massive glass window. The way that the Star Craft was constructed meant that views of the universe were able to be had from many parts of the craft. This meant that people of the Earth could see the planet that they had left behind disappear from view. It was an emotional moment for many. Some were now in their nineties and beyond, and moving home was always going to be a major event for them. It was a wrench to leave the sofa for the kitchen at times, so to leave their home for ninety plus years and move many light years away brought out emotions like sadness and fear. The crew of the Star Craft was ready for this and acted as personal guides for those of a certain age and disposition.

The three family members were surrounded by others who were in the same position, saying good-bye to their home. Simon just hoped that it didn't mean Sierra saying good-bye to all her dreams. She was a mature girl for a ten-year-old, and Simon often thought that she already had her life mapped out in her head. He knew that she studied hard and wanted to go on to university, but all of those dreams were dreams about her life on Earth. He wondered if the same opportunities would exist on the new planet. He wondered if the events of the last few days had shaken her dreams. He wondered if her ambitions were relevant to her new home. So much was known about the reasons why they had left the planet, but there was so much to know about exactly what was waiting for them. What would the planet look like? Where would they live? How would Sierra be taught? What would he and his wife do? But he had faith that Jesus had not only a plan to save people from the perils that the Earth was about to face but also a plan for life in the new world he had found for the good people.

Simon, Sierra, and her mother stood huddled together. Simon had his arms around both of them as he tried to protect them and show them love at the same time. If he had looked to his left or right, he would have seen fathers doing the same to their families all along the length of the window. If he could have seen the other levels, the other windows that the Star Craft had, then he would have been able to see what might look like a photocopy of his family replicated thousands upon thousands of times. No matter how different people are, they look for the comfort of their family. They want to feel the warmth of their family all around them. Simon stood with his family for what must have been over a half hour until the Earth disappeared from view. He was sure that even as the Earth dropped to the size of a baseball, he could see volcanoes erupting, the Earth splitting, and the tides washing over the land. He told himself that this was just his imagination when he thought of the plight of the people that followed the devil. He told himself that this was the teachings of the Bible that had turned his mind to imagine these events. He would never know because the Earth was now millions of miles away, but this was exactly what was happening. It wasn't his imagination at all. It was the reality for the nonbelievers of the Earth.

After the Earth had disappeared out of view, all Simon did was listen to the breathing and heartbeats of his two precious people. It was something he hadn't done since Sierra was young. When she was a baby and she slept, he used to sneak up to her room, lie in the floor near her crib, and just observe. He listened to her breathing. He watched her chest move up and down with the intake and expiration of air. He was so happy to be a father that he just wanted to see the tiny miracle that he and his wife had created. He wanted to be around his baby daughter. The three of them together reminded him of those days. He could listen to the breathing and heartbeat of his baby girl forever. They had come so close to losing everything, and only the intervention of Jesus and their faith had rescued them from the destruction of their home. Simon stood silently and listened. Sierra and her mother stood silently and prayed. Their prayers were for a safe passage through the universe to their new home. Their prayers were for the animals that they had learned were on board the Star Craft. Their prayers were for the souls that Sierra had seen with her father and Daniel. Their prayers were in thanks to Jesus and the crew of the Star Craft for saving their lives. And still Simon listened.

The three of them were so happy to be together and safe. All of their life as a family had been based around spending time together and keeping each other safe. The journey on the Star Craft to another planet was an extension of this. The fact that Simon and Sierra had been chosen as messengers was important. It meant that they could keep many others safe as well. All of those on board the Star Craft were now part of their extended family. These were people that had faith, that believed, and that could be trusted. Simon hoped that this would signify a change in the way that people acted towards each other. He hoped that people would rally together for the common good without the influence of the devil. Sierra knew that the new world would give the people a fresh start. She knew that the people of the old world had changed for the better and would begin a new life somewhere safe.

The three of them stood together and looked across the Star Craft. They saw smiling people in every direction. It was a pleasure to see people interact in this way. Simon held the hands of the two women in his life—Sierra in his right hand and her mother on his left. The two women joined hands so they formed a circle, looking in towards each other. Simon spoke. "All we have learned is coming to pass. We have lived a life of faith and respect to others. We can now see that there are many like us. The new world will be populated by people who believe. I hope that it stays this way." He looked his daughter in the eye. He had dedicated his life to her and was now worried that this change might affect her future. He addressed her, "Sierra, I know that you might be scared about the future. You are only young, and you can make of life what you want. There are so many possibilities for you."

Sierra said, "I feel so happy and a little sad at the same time." She had known nothing but the safety of the Cowboy Church, her home, and her school. These were the three places that Sierra spent her life in. She was at one or the other for the vast majority of her time, and all three were safe places for her. The church was already full of people that had looked out for Sierra from when she was born. After she had become a messenger, the people looked out for her even more. She became a beacon of hope as well as a messenger. Everyone wanted to see her; everyone wanted to spend time with her.

At school, she was with people whom she knew, liked, and could trust. Her friends were all the sons and daughters of others from the church, so they had kind of grown up together. Sierra was not afraid to speak about her feelings and her beliefs, as her mother had witnessed in the church the evening she had been first taken onto the Star Craft. She was a strong girl who led her friends away from the path of temptation. But it was at home where Sierra really shone. She was the apple of her father's eye. She took over the house with her singing and dancing and just loved to entertain her parents at any opportunity. With all three of these places now gone to Sierra, she had strange feelings about what was happening. Until that point, she was filled with joy about meeting Jesus and finding out that her beliefs were correct. She loved speaking to people about her experiences after being on the Star Craft for the first time and felt her mission to save people as something of paramount importance. But at this point, she realized that there were so many things she had to say good-bye to. The three places that had been the backdrop to her life story were the hardest to let go of. She saw the Earth disappear from view and thought that she had to now find new places to be the scenes of her life. The church was no more, the school was no more, her home was no more. She would have to find somewhere else to be free, happy, and full of life. Although she knew that there was no choice and that she had immense faith in the Word of Jesus, it was still a little sad to let go. At least, she had her family around her, along with her school friends and the people from church. They would all start a new life together on a strange faraway planet. Sierra thought about the animals that had been transported with them and had been told about the works of art and other artifacts that were being brought along. She wondered how different the new planet would feel. She knew that the nonbelievers and the demonic President were left behind, but from what she had heard, many of the brilliant things about life on Earth were coming with them.

Chapter 10

Beginning the Trip to a New Earth

The scale of the Star Craft was beyond comprehension for most people. The fact that it now comfortably housed billions of people was a fair indication to anyone that asked that it was well beyond any scale that man had built on before. People started to learn the layout of the Star Craft and where they needed to be at certain times. Those that tended the animals were able to quickly find their level and locate the animals that they were charged with looking after. Those that were helping John-Paul and Michelle Moreau with the room of character were able to get to where they needed to be by remembering the corridors and levels that they had to pass in order to be in the right place.

Hozai sat in the control room. He and Marta had led the people this far on the journey, and he had to admit that he was feeling quite pleased with himself. The salvation was well underway, the nonbelievers were left behind, and the power of the demonic President was destroyed. All the weapons of the Earth had been left behind, and the believers were behaving impeccably. He looked across to Marta. She was giving instructions to two crew members regarding the regulation of heat on the Star Craft. She had feared that with a long journey ahead, the animals needed to slowly acclimatize to outside temperatures again, so the heating on the level where the animals were housed was to be slowly turned down so that by the time they reached the new planet, it matched the temperature that they expected outside. It was all the little details like this that made Hozai respect Marta even more. She was an expert in her role, and Hozai couldn't imagine anyone else to do the job as well as her. It was a pleasure for him to work alongside Marta.

As Marta continued to speak to the crew members, Hozai looked at the screens that showed all the areas of the Star Craft. These were to ensure that safety was maintained at all times. Before the Star Craft was filled with people, Hozai used to imagine what it would look like. He looked at room after room of nothing and pictured in his mind the masses of people that were to be saved. Now he didn't have to imagine. He just looked at the monitors in front of him.

Hozai looked at the corridors. They were wide open corridors that were designed for high traffic. There were thousands of corridors on the Star Craft, and each one on the screens in front of Hozai were busy with people passing one way or another. At first, the people started to walk on the same side as they drove back on Earth. This did cause some confusion as the Australians and British walking on the left were approached by Americans walking on the right, but this was soon ironed out. Each corridor was marked with a number and a series of directional signs as you might find on an interstate road. This meant that the people could see that they were travelling in the right direction and roughly how long it would take to walk there. From the small screens in front of Hozai, it looked like ants working away near their hill, bringing food and building materials to their home. In reality, it was people moving around the Star Craft to help out, to get something to eat, or to meet friends. The corridors of the Star Craft were the arteries that kept the place full of life. Although nobody ever spent any time standing still in the corridors, they were the most populated part of the entire craft. Hozai was amazed at how many people filled the corridors. Even in his imagination, they were never this full of life and activity. He moved his head to another bank of screens.

Hozai looked at the windows. The huge glass windows were an integral part of the Star Craft. They were ground-to-ceiling windows that gave the most amazing views of space as the craft passed through. People gathered in their thousands by the windows to look at the wonders around them. But it was far more than that; it was about being together and sharing the experience. People were in groups, large and small, just talking to each other and enjoying their time around each other. Hozai could see groups get together and grow in size as people that just happened to be standing near to each other merged in a flurry of hugs, handshakes, and conversation. It was a delight to watch. Hozai looked to his right and found that Marta was still talking to the crew members. She had a fine attention to detail, and this was an important instruction. Hozai turned back to the screens and watched. He saw families spending a long time just staring out into space. The wonders of the universe were there for all to see. People had never seen anything like it, so they took it all in as often as they could. After the corridors, the windows were the place on the Star Craft that attracted the most people. Hozai watched the people as the people watched the universe. He was as transfixed as they were. He sat motionless with only people in his view.

Hozai was inspired by the people gathered around these large windows. He looked out of the window in front of him into space. He had spent so much time there that it wasn't something he ordinarily took notice of. The dials and switches he was familiar with. The star charts that told him which constellations to avoid and the direction of travel he could recite with his eyes closed. But the actual detail of space had passed him by. So, he followed the lead of the pope in front of the glass windows and looked out into space. They passed planets to the left and right, and asteroids whizzed past the Star Craft close enough to see but far enough away not to cause any alarm. The view was 99 percent darkness, but this only made the parts that were not dark look even brighter. The stars in the distance that signified distant suns sparkled. The space debris that they passed was clear to see, as it stood out so much against the darkness. The planets that they passed were of stunning colors. They were the deepest blues, the brightest reds, and the most luminous greens. He was awestruck by the beauty of the universe. But he knew that he could not look out of the window all day. He looked back to the screens.

Hozai looked at the restaurants. The task of feeding billions of people was a mammoth one. They had stocked up on enough food to last the people for the entire journey—that was not going to be an issue. However, getting this out to the people in an efficient way was a logistical nightmare. The way that people would respond to best was to set up restaurants that they were used to back on planet Earth. This would be far more sociable than delivering the meals to their living quarters and would mean that people could eat in a relaxed atmosphere surrounded by others. Hozai watched as people ate and talked. It was the way of life that people used to carry out every day. Before long work hours and the rise of the TV dinner people used to spend hours in each other's company at mealtimes. This made people comfortable with the journey, and the fact that it felt like they had a lot of time on their hands got people spending quality time with each other over meals again.

Hozai looked at the social areas. In addition to the vast windows that attracted groups of people, the crew of the Star Craft knew that they had to provide stimulation for the passengers on their vast journey. The social areas were comprised of a large area of seats that people could sit around and arrange in many different ways. Sometimes one or more of the entertainers from Earth that were on board would have the seats arranged as though they were on stage and give a performance to keep people happy. Singers, comedians, public speakers, and others would keep people entertained for a few hours at a time. This helped to pass the time and gave people renewed hope for their journey to the new planet. There were thousands of copies of classic books available in the social areas so people could sit and read surrounded by like-minded people. The Bible was a popular choice, as many people had read excerpts when they were young but never really read the whole Bible from cover to cover. The words in the Bible seemed so relevant at this point that people would read and then sit in groups to discuss what they had just read. The relevance of these words now that they were headed to a new world, travelling with Jesus and moving away from the clutches of the demonic President, was immense. People would sit for hours in silence before forming large groups to talk about how they would use the teachings of the Bible in their new life.

Hozai looked at the classrooms. He knew that he would soon be in one of the classrooms teaching people himself, but as he sat in the control room he could see the faces of concentration from the people of the Earth as they looked on. The crew of the Star Craft all had special skills that they were passing on to the passengers on board. He watched the classroom be filled with life and activity as the crew showed something new and interesting. There was much bad work to be undone by the crew before they could teach people to be free. It was important that the people on board the Star Craft were ready for the new world in all ways. Just to put the people back down on another planet and hope that they would behave differently was not the right way to go about things. To teach them to love each other and work in a different way would change the ways of the world at the same time as changing the world itself. The new planet would need people to work together. Teaching them the way to cooperate and become one was a highly important part of the mission that the crew of the Star Craft had been set. The most important part of this was teaching the children. Many had been disrupted in their school life with the events of the last few days on Earth. The crew of the Star Craft had gotten them back on track with their learning and made sure that they understood where they were going and where they came from.

The living quarters did not have surveillance, as the people needed some privacy to be alone and spend time building their family bonds. The living areas were off the corridors on many levels of the Star Craft. People needed to be close to where they would help out, learn, and eat, so the living quarters were sectioned into distinct areas. For example, so that the people who tended the animals did not have to travel great distances, their living quarters were on the level directly above the level where the animals were kept. It worked like this so that billions of people could inhabit one craft and not have to travel for hours each day. It worked really well for the people.

Each living quarter housed a family unit. In many ways, they functioned in a comparable manner to the homes that people lived in on Earth. Because all of the food was provided, there was no kitchen, but all the other features of a home were present, just on a smaller scale. In order to house billions of people, the Star Craft could not accommodate the vast living spaces that some were used to occupying on the planet Earth. Each living quarter had bedrooms, a bathroom, and a small communal area for spending time with each other and relaxing. This was the most important room in the living quarter. All of the other areas were functional—the bedrooms for sleeping and the bathroom for getting clean—but the communal area was where people spoke about their hopes and fears for the future. The communal area was where family bonds were strengthened or repaired after years of working hard and living life at a fast pace. The fact that people were now able to live their life together as slowly as they liked gave them the time to get to know each other all over again. Families where both parents worked had become fractured on Earth with people being tired all the time and not having any quality time to spend with each other. The Star Craft gave them all the time they needed.

Hozai got up from his desk. He looked at the monitor that recorded their travel. They had been away from the Earth for eleven days. He took Marta by the arm. They had both reached a point where they had to leave. Hozai had finished his scan of the monitors, and Marta had given the crew her instructions. The two of them walked from the control room towards the main part of the Star Craft. They walked along several corridors before they split. Hozai walked to the left and Marta to the right. Only a few hundred yards later, they both stopped outside the door of a room. Inside people were waiting for them. They paused, took a deep breath, and entered their respective rooms. A light ripple of applause went across the room as they entered. Both flushed a little with embarrassment. They were there to help, but they both knew that they were only carrying out the Word of Jesus. The rooms hushed. The two walked to the front of their rooms and began to speak.

Hozai stepped into a small classroom that was laid out in the style of an amphitheater and looked around the room. He saw some faces he recognized. From the first time the Star Craft had picked up the messengers, Hozai recognized the faces of Dr. St. John and his colleagues, Dr. Kalas and Dr. Nucci. They were eminent astrophysicists that had good background knowledge of the universe. He looked across and saw John-Paul Moreau who was leading the scientific team sitting next to his wife, Michelle. In the row behind them was Dr. Liu Xiang and PhD student, Shu Yi Chang, sitting with Dr. Kadir whom they had met on the expedition to Puma Punku.

As he looked around the room, Hozai knew that this was the cream of the crop with regards to the scientists on Earth. There was very little he could teach them about their own fields of science. They would be able to tell him about the archaeological sites of Earth or the finer details about the DNA of man. But that was not what Hozai was there for; he was there as a guide to the universe that they were passing through, the home that they would make, and how all of this came to be in God's universe. The disciplines of science and religion had been pitted against each other for centuries. The church saw a threat from science when it first started to uncover details about the origins of life on Earth, the universe around us, and the way that things interacted with each other. Scientists were persecuted in the Middle Ages and beyond as heretics. The church and science had both moved forward to a time where they coexisted, but the relationship was frosty, to say the least. Scientists mocked people of religion at times, but the truth of the matter was that they just didn't have the same level of faith that people of religion were able to display. A new breed of scientists that had strong religious beliefs were starting to make progress with their research, and the fact that there were so many people of faith in the room comforted Hozai that the two disciplines of science and religion could be reconciled.

Hozai's words were about new knowledge of the universe but making the relationship between science and God's grace. He explained that science must be a power for good in the new world that they would soon inhabit. The science of cloning and of DNA manipulation were a thing of the past. Even at the time these were happening, the media would call it "playing God," and this was not the direction that science should be headed in the new world. Thankfully, the people that had practiced this branch of science had lost all faith in God and were still back on the planet Earth, facing whatever fate the devil and the gamma-ray burst had in store.

Hozai knew that the scientists he had in front of him were strong characters that would listen to his words and make sure this was happening on their new planet. Each was bringing special skills with them that would enhance the new planet. Hozai had faith in the people that he spoke to. Hozai spoke for around an hour and took questions both during and at the end of his talk. He wanted the scientists to know that all of the beauty and splendor of the universe and of their new home was of God. His Son was leading them to safety on a new planet where the believers could start again.

Along the corridor in a similar room was Marta. She looked up and saw a small amphitheater-style classroom with rows of seats above her. She knew that the style of the room would carry her voice to the back without having to use a microphone or raise her voice. This was the style of building that the Romans had perfected to give plays and speeches. They had understood acoustics centuries ago, and this design could be found all over the places of the Earth that had been under Roman rule. But the theater design that was on board the Star Craft was not being used for works of fiction. Marta was there to talk to the business and political leaders about the new world.

She looked up and saw some faces that would have seen the biggest political and financial events on Earth over the past twenty years firsthand. They would have been there at stock market crashes as wars were declared and were major players in the events from the speech at the United Nations through to the evacuation. These were hardened men and women that on Earth would have let nothing surprise them. Yet here they were huddled together looking like children on the first day at a new school. Their eyes were wide and their mouths open. They were ready to absorb every word that Marta was about to deliver.

Marta began to speak. "Ladies and gentlemen, we will be at our new home soon. Although it is a long journey, it will pass quickly, and we need to be ready for the new world. Things have to change . . ."

Marta remembered the speech she gave to the messengers when they were first brought on board the Star Craft. She remembered how they listened in absolute silence, but she could feel the mood of the room change. She remembered that she had given the information in short bursts with a pause in between so it could all be absorbed by the audience. Marta used the same technique here with the political and business leaders. She was determined for every word to have the maximum impact.

She resumed, "The way that business was carried out on Earth brought problems. The way that politics worked did not resolve these problems. The reliance on money as the sign of status made people greedy. It made people suspicious of others. It made people want to tread on others to get up in the world. The teachings of God were ignored by the business world as the top executives tried to squeeze an extra dollar from the poor to line their pockets and look after their wealthy shareholders. As a way of promoting equity among the people of the Earth, the system of money was an abject failure. Money and power lay in the hands of the few. We need this to change in our new world. All men were created equal."

Marta stopped again. She looked around the room and saw many faces from the original messengers that had been brought on to the Star Craft. She saw the Chinese Premier sitting, listening intently to her words. She saw the senator who had taken the lead on Earth and spoken to the people via the stage of the United Nations and the broadcast media of the world. She saw business and political leaders from all corners of the Earth. She saw business leaders that had great intentions when entering the business world but had been caught up in the way that corporate society worked. It became all about the balance sheets and the shareholders rather than about the people. But change had happened. These were the people who were going to start afresh the system of governance and industry on the new planet in a way that benefitted all of mankind, not just the privileged few.

Marta delivered to them a new knowledge of self-governance and freedom from monetary means but making the relationship between surviving and God's laws. She spoke for over an hour and felt that every word was taken in by the people sitting in front of her. Marta knew that this would be more than one session with the people she had gathered, but she had made great progress in the classroom on that day. There would be more talks to come both as a group and on a one-to-one basis. Marta knew that the believers that were on board the Star Craft would see the equity in working this way rather than the way it had been played out on Earth. The influence of the devil was gone, and the greed of big business would disappear with it.

The Star Craft flew through space. It needed to be two light years away from the Earth before the gamma-ray burst struck, and it was making good progress. As it passed unknown planets and systems, the Star Craft monitored the nearby areas to ensure that there were no obstructions in the way or dangers to the craft. Although it was a large craft that was solidly made and could withstand an impact, it was advisable to steer clear of any asteroid fields so that the people on board were not unduly frightened. Large asteroids crashing into the glass windows would scare thousands of people at once, and the panic could cause problems, so the craft scanned, and Marta and Hozai kept watch.

The Star Craft was heading to a new world, and what seemed like a long journey at the time would soon be at the back of people's minds as they began their new life. Sierra passed a lot of her time by thinking about what life would be like on her new planet. She imagined spending time with her parents in their new home as the sun started to drop in the sky. She imagined running back in to their home as the sun set and having a hot chocolate made by her mother while the three of them spoke about their day. She imagined seeing her friends on a regular basis and laughing along with them about something stupid that they had heard earlier that day. She imagined the Cowboy Church being recreated somewhere on their new planet and the people all coming together to eat and drink as one. She imagined a future where she could go wherever her dreams took her and be whoever she wanted. She imagined following in the footsteps of her dad and being a preacher.

As they all walked down the recreated urban streetscapes inside the Star Craft, people were singing in groups. They passed one group that was singing a song that Simon, Sierra, and her mom recognized. Sierra stopped and said, "Mommy, Daddy, we know that song." They all stopped and smiled as they recognized the singers. The singers were country Western celebrities. They all had their instruments and were standing together, singing as they had done on Earth at major venues their entire careers. The song was an untitled hymn, "Come to Jesus."

Weak and wounded sinner
Lost and left to die
O, raise your head, for love is passing by
Come to Jesus
Come to Jesus
Come to Jesus and live!

Now your burden's lifted
And carried far away
And precious blood has washed away the stain, so
Sing to Jesus
Sing to Jesus
Sing to Jesus and live!

And like a newborn baby
Don't be afraid to crawl
And remember when you walk
Sometimes we fall, so
Fall on Jesus
Fall on Jesus
Fall on Jesus and live!

Sometimes the way is lonely
And steep and filled with pain
So if your sky is dark and pours the rain, then
Cry to Jesus
Cry to Jesus
Cry to Jesus and live!

O, and when the love spills over
And music fills the night
And when you can't contain your joy inside, then
Dance for Jesus
Dance for Jesus
Dance for Jesus and live!

And with your final heartbeat
Kiss the world good-bye
Then go in peace, and laugh on glory's side, and
Fly to Jesus
Fly to Jesus
Fly to Jesus and live!
Fly to Jesus
Fly to Jesus
Fly to Jesus and live!

As Sierra walked along the corridor, she was imagining all of these things and more. She pictured the trees, the rivers, the mountains that she hoped would be on the new planet. She imagined spending time with those that made her happy. At this point, Sierra realized that what she dreamt of was all the wonderful things that were present on Earth when she was back there without all the horrors of the Earth that were there too. She felt that leaving behind the nonbelievers and defeating the demonic President would mean that the new planet would have a great chance of being all that she had imagined. As long as she had the people around her that she loved, then Sierra knew she would be happy. As she walked and thought, Sierra was already surrounded by the people that made her feel safe and happy. Directly in front of her were her mother and father. They were behind two other men. One was Daniel, still full of glee for his new leg, and Daniel was talking to Jesus. The five of them were heading to a room around the next corner to talk with the religious leaders that were on board the Star Craft. They turned the corner and entered the room.

For some of the religious leaders, this was the first time they had seen Jesus. The fact that they were in his presence was enough for many to shed a tear of joy and happiness. The word that Jesus was coming to save people had arrived on Earth some time before, and now for certain people in the room, this was the final confirmation that it was all true.

As the room all stood as one for the arrival of Christ, he smiled and tried to look each one of them in the eye. It was a large room in Star Craft terms but was filled with the people that Jesus had chosen to lead the new world in their spiritual growth.

Jesus waited for Simon, Daniel, Sierra, and her mother to enter the room and find a seat before he began. Rather than the talks that Hozai and Marta were giving, this was more of a discussion. Jesus wanted to know what people felt in their heart. He became the facilitator rather than the teacher because he was surrounded by believers that wanted to do the right thing. That is why they were chosen. Jesus started by talking about what had happened. He wanted the people to know that there was no choice but to evacuate the Earth. He wanted people to know that he could not set foot on the Earth himself because it was ruled by the devil. The religious leaders spoke of the grip that the demonic President had on many people they encountered. Alcohol, drugs, and sex dictated the lives of many of the people that they had tried to reach. The religious leaders had never given up on anyone that they saw who needed help and were dad about those that had chosen to close their hearts and decide not to believe. Their fate was now millions of miles away.

But in many ways, the past was becoming more irrelevant by the day. The future was where the focus needed to lie. Jesus listened intently to the people speak. He had great faith in the people of the Earth and had watched as the believers fought temptation and kept the devil at bay for many of their followers. These people had endured a lot of hard work on Earth to keep their flock safe and on the right path. The temptations in the new world would be fewer, and the influence of the demonic President was removed. Jesus had faith that the new world would be a paradise.

The discussion moved on to the future. Jesus was keen to explain what will happen as part of God's will. He wanted the religious leaders to know what would happen from here on and how they were at the forefront of making sure the new Earth was peaceful and respectful. The discussion was pleasing for Jesus. He could see that the moral strength of the people he had gathered would be the guiding light in the new world. He would be there to guide them and make sure that the right path was followed. Jesus sat back for a while and listened to the people speak. The fact that they were positive and giving in their nature brought a smile to his face. After a while of taking all of this in, he stood up again. The discussion continued.

As the discussion went on, Sierra looked up. It was at this point she had noticed that where they stood was under a massive domed glass roof. Sierra was holding Jesus's hand as he spoke to the other men and women. Sierra looked at Jesus and said, "I'm happy we are with you."

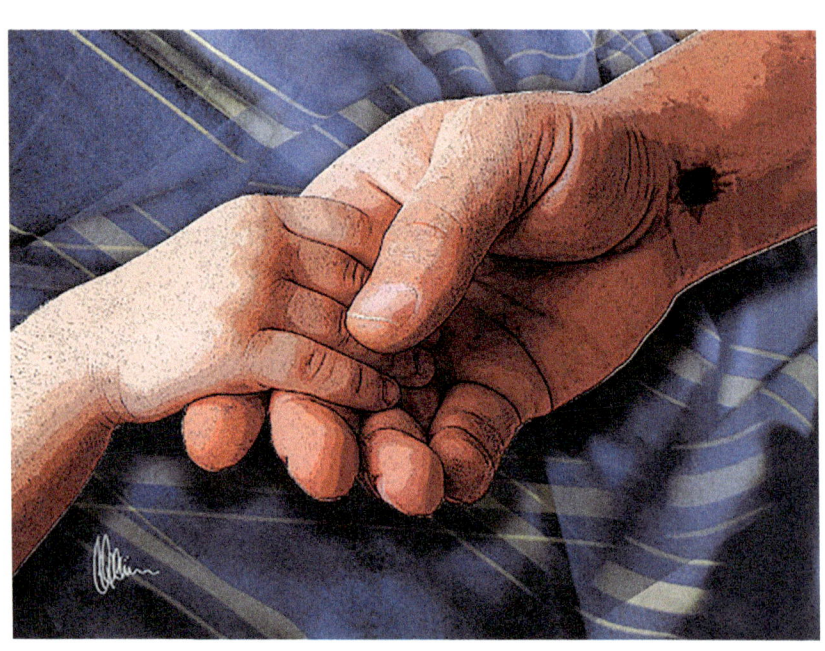

About the Author

Mr. Phillips is a native Texan born in Wichita Falls, Texas, in 1956. He grew up in North Texas in the Dallas/Fort Worth area. Mr. Phillips lives south of Dallas, Texas, on his ranch, Cherokee Ridge, where he writes, draws, designs, paints, and sculpts. His parents played a big role in his interests in the natural environment and education of his role as a steward of the land. His heritage is Native American (Cherokee and Choctaw), which also influenced his early appreciation of nature. This early education led Mr. Phillips to pursue a formal professional education in landscape architecture and design.

Mr. Phillips graduated from Texas A&M University in College Station, Texas, in 1979 with a BSLA and a master's degree (MLA) from UTA 2012 and began his PhD in Urban Planning in 2013. After working as a registered landscape architect for nine years, Mr. Phillips took a sabbatical leave for six months in 1988 and traveled throughout Europe. His studies took him through the streets, gardens, and plazas of London, Paris, Venice, Florence, Munich, Zurich, Berlin, Budapest, Brussels, Brugge, Amsterdam, and Vienna.

In 2005, Mr. Phillips became a registered member of the Texas Cherokee tribe known as Tsalagiyi Nvdagi. The Tribal UGU (principal chief) bestowed his tribal name, Standing Bear, upon him. Mr. Phillips' early family education about being a good steward of the land has now come full circle.

CPSIA information can be obtained
at www.ICGtesting.com
Printed in the USA
BVOW11s0140200118
505609BV00008B/49/P